EARLY PRAISE FOR THE ETERNAL SECRET

MARY ROMASANTA CRAFTS A SUSPENSEFUL AND THOUGHT-PROVOKING TALE THAT DIVES DEEP INTO THE MYSTERIES OF LIFE AND DEATH.

THE CONCEPT AND PLOT IS FASCINATING. THE AUTHOR EXPLAINS THE NEAR DEATH EXPERIENCE CONCEPTS SUFFICIENTLY AND WITH KNOWLEDGE, BUT NOT SO TECHNICAL THAT THE READER ISN'T ABLE TO FOLLOW ALONG.

THE NOVEL'S STRENGTH LIES IN ITS SPECULATIVE EXPLORATION OF NEAR-DEATH EXPERIENCES AND THE POTENTIAL TO CONTROL THE AFTERLIFE, KEEPING READERS ON THE EDGE OF THEIR SEATS.

I LOVE THE DIGGING INTO NEAR DEATH EXPERIENCES AND HOW EVERYTHING CONNECTED IN THIS SUSPENSEFUL STORY.

VERY PLEASED WITH THE BOOK. IT'S NOT ONLY EASY TO READ BUT ALSO VERY EXCITING.

WELL PACED AND IT SUCKS YOU IN PRETTY MUCH STRAIGHT AWAY.

I RECOMMEND THE ETERNAL SECRET TO ANYONE INTERESTED IN A SUSPENSEFUL MYSTERY NOVEL WITH SPECULATIVE ELEMENTS.

–NetGalley Reviewers

BY MARY ROMASANTA

Avīci Sagga
The Eternal Secret
Infestation

THE
ETERNAL
SECRET

THE ETERNAL SECRET

A NOVEL

MARY ROMASANTA

Sagga Publishing House LLC

SAGGA BOOKS, OCTOBER 2024

Copyright © 2024 by Mary Romasanta

LIBRARY OF CONGRESS CONTROL NUMBER: 2024906642

Premium Mass-Market Hardback ISBN: 979-8-9886746-4-1

Premium Mass-Market Paperback ISBN: 979-8-9886746-3-4

eBook ISBN: 979-8-9886746-5-8

All rights reserved.

No portion of this book may be reproduced, distributed, or transmitted in any form or by any means, including photocopying, recording, or other electronic or mechanical methods, without the prior written permission of the publisher, except as permitted by U.S. copyright law.

Published in the United States by Sagga Publishing House LLC, Texas.

This book is a work of fiction. Names, characters, businesses, organizations, places, events, and incidents either are the product of the author's imagination or used fictitiously. Any resemblance to actual persons, living or dead, events, or locales is entirely coincidental.

Cover design by Damonza.com

Visit the author's website at www.maryromasanta.com

Printed in the United States of America

For Sabrina.

Preface

Is it true? As a fiction writer, I get asked this question often. So, before diving into *The Eternal Secret*, I think it's important to address it.

My writing process starts with a foundation of real events—often those reported by credible news sources—blended with stories of personal interest and my own experiences. From there, I weave in creative fiction that aligns with the imagery playing out in my mind. While I can't guarantee this will apply to all my future novels, as I wrap up my third book, *Infestation*, I can confidently say this has been my approach so far.

So, what's the truth behind this novel? Various studies have shown that even after the human body is declared clinically dead, brain activity—specifically the kind associated with deep concentration—can still occur. Near-death experiences (NDEs) have also been the focus of numerous studies, revealing a common pattern of events during the period when a resuscitated person is clinically dead. Additionally, many animals possess an inherent ability called homing, allowing them to navigate toward specific locations through unfamiliar terrain. I won't delve into these truths in detail here, but you'll find them woven into the fabric of the story. Or, you can explore these phenomena on your own.

Writing this novel has been an absolute thrill and joy. I'm deeply grateful to my husband and children for their unwavering support, and to my editor and partner in crime, Alejandra Gonzalez, for her exceptional work, remarkable attention to detail, and cherished friendship. A special thank you to award-winning director and filmmaker Lisa France, whose incredible support and encouragement continue to inspire me.

I hope you enjoy the book, and I look forward to sharing the next one with you!

Mary Romasanta

THE
ETERNAL
SECRET

Chapter 1

AN EXPLOSIVE THUD SHATTERED the silence of the room, sending a jolt through everyone present. Heads whipped toward the window as the piercing wail of a siren grew louder, drawing closer. The hospital security guard instinctively reached for his gun, his eyes darting around the lobby, scanning for any sign of danger. Some watched in tense anticipation as paramedics rushed out of the ambulance parked outside, their movements a blur of urgency. Others remained transfixed by the ghostly imprint on the window—a scattering of feathers, the only trace of a bird's tragic, abrupt end.

"Looks like a code blue," Edward muttered, his eyes tracking the paramedics as they moved with the urgency that marked the thin line between life and death. "We'll have to continue this later." He stepped back, realizing he was standing directly in the path of the rushing medical team as they pushed the stretcher through the hospital corridors.

"Prasad?" he called out, expecting a response. But there was none.

Edward turned, finding Dr. Prasad Vedurmudi staring blankly at the window, his mind seemingly adrift, oblivious to the chaos surrounding them.

"Dr. Prasad Vedurmudi," Edward repeated, this time louder, his voice tinged with concern as the paramedics closed in on them.

"OUT OF THE WAY—COMING THROUGH!" one of the paramedics bellowed, their urgency slicing through the air.

Without a second thought, Edward grabbed Prasad by the lab coat, yanking him back just in time to avoid the barreling stretcher and the powerful momentum behind it. The two men stumbled slightly, Edward's heart racing from the near miss, while Prasad finally blinked, snapping back to reality.

Prasad's body jolted. "I'm sorry about that," he said. "Thank you."

"What's the matter with you?" Edward asked. "You seem distracted."

"Oh, no—I'm fine."

"I even called you by your full name—I figured that would get your attention."

"For the love of God, you sound just like my wife," he replied, walking alongside Edward.

"Yes, well, I just saved your ass again."

"Again?" he said with a look of puzzlement.

"I saved you the first time by accepting your request to partner with you in this study," Edward said, smiling inwardly.

"Good God, it was a stretcher, not a bullet train," Prasad said, shaking his head. "As for the study—get over yourself, man," he scoffed.

Edward swiped his badge at the emergency room corridor and pushed the door open. They walked inside and watched from a distance as the trauma team transferred the patient, a male with thick and wavy white hair, from the stretcher to a hospital bed.

"No heartbeat!" the ER nurse shouted.

"That's their cue," Prasad whispered, crossing his arms and watching intensely as a young man in green scrubs approached the top of the bedside.

Using a flexible ruler, the man measured the patient's head and marked various points on his scalp and forehead. He stepped back as a young woman stepped forward and scrubbed the marked areas with a creamy substance before placing electrodes over them.

"That's Vincent and Erica—they've made significant progress since we started," Prasad said. "It used to take them three times as long to place the electrodes."

Struggling to see the patient, Edward squinted tightly. His attention turned to the EEG machine. "He's flatlined," he said.

A sense of urgency filled the air.

The ER doctor positioned himself over the patient's motionless body. With a firm grip and focused gaze, he pressed his hands forcefully against the patient's chest. The sound of the patient's ribs cracking echoed through the room, amplifying the gravity of the situation.

"I see something," Edward said, looking at the EEG machine. He watched as the flat line on the machine transformed into spikes. "He must be on the other side," Prasad replied. "Hopefully he lives to tell you about it." He turned his gaze to the brain activity displayed on the EEG machine. "By the looks of it, he's thinking hard."

"Speaking of which—what were you thinking about back there? The dead pigeon?"

"I'll talk to you about it later," Prasad replied.

"Fine, but if you're considering a study on the near-death experiences of fowl, I'm not interested," he said, folding his arms. He turned his attention back to the activity in the ER. Beads of sweat formed around the doctor's forehead as he maintained a steady rhythm of compressions on the patient.

"We've got nothing!" the nurse shouted, reaching for a defibrillator.

"Not yet!" the doctor blurted; a look of determination washed over his face. "Respirator mask!"

The nurse carefully placed a clear silicone mask over the patient's mouth and nose, the attached air balloon-like mechanism inflating and deflating in a steady rhythm as she squeezed it, matching the cadence of the doctor's compressions. The doctor's eyes locked onto the defibrillator, his voice firm. "Now!" he commanded.

A tense silence fell over the room as the nurse picked up the defibrillator paddles, stepping forward with deliberate precision. Her fingers hovered over the shock button on the control panel, her gaze unwavering on the patient's chest. She pressed down, and the room held its breath.

The patient's body jolted violently, arching upward as if an invisible force was yanking him from the bed by his chest. Edward's eyes widened in astonishment. *It's him*, he thought, a subtle gasp escaping his lips.

The ER remained deathly quiet, the trauma team collectively holding their breath, searching for any sign of life.

Then, a single beep pierced the silence.

Another beep followed.

And then another.

"He's back," the doctor announced, his face breaking into an irrepressible smile. "Great job, everyone!"

Prasad turned to Edward, a grin forming on his face. "Looks like you're getting that interview after all," he said, patting Edward on the back.

Chapter 2

"I AM PRESENTING YOU with a finding that could revolutionize our understanding of life and death, yet you're telling me you don't approve?" Prasad's voice echoed through the room, thick with disbelief and simmering frustration. Standing before the University of Chicago Institutional Review Board, he struggled to reconcile their resistance with the monumental implications of his proposed afterlife study. He had anticipated a straightforward process, confident that the sheer magnitude of his research would speak for itself. The potential was so profound, so far-reaching, that he never imagined he would need to defend the very foundation of his work.

It wasn't just the study itself that warranted approval; it was the fact that the proposal came from him—a tenured professor with a sterling reputation. He had always been a figure of authority and respect within the academic community, someone whose ideas were met with enthusiasm rather than skepticism. Yet here he was, blindsided by their reluctance, unprepared for the unexpected challenge of justifying a study that, in his mind, transcended the ordinary limits of scientific inquiry. The weight of their doubt pressed down on him, forcing him to confront the reality that even the most groundbreaking ideas could be met with resistance when they ventured into uncharted territory.

A heavy silence settled over the room, thick and oppressive, as the board members exchanged glances, their raised eyebrows and incredulous stares speaking louder than words. The tension was palpable, hanging in the air like a storm on the brink of breaking. Prasad's gaze swept across the table, his frustration mounting with every second of silence. He could feel the collective dissatisfaction radiating from the board, a wall of resistance that seemed insurmountable.

"Explain," Prasad demanded, his voice slicing through the quiet as he looked each member in the eye. His eyes eventually locked onto Mr. Crenshaw, who sat near the center of the table, impeccably dressed in a dark blue business suit, his expression one of weary exasperation. "Mr. Crenshaw, John," Prasad urged, his tone tinged with desperation, "please help me understand your stance on this matter."

Mr. Crenshaw glanced around the room, his gaze briefly meeting the others' before settling back on Prasad. His sigh was almost imperceptible, but it carried the weight of his frustration. "Oh, come on now—read the room," he said, his tone clipped and final. "We've exhausted this topic and have other matters to discuss." He paused, allowing his words to hang in the air like a final verdict. "We've been over this—we can't fund it."

"Then don't fund it. Approve it without funding," Prasad shot back, his voice trembling as desperation seeped into his words.

Mr. Crenshaw's gaze hardened, his cool demeanor unshaken. "We're running a business," he replied, his tone as cold as ice. "Even if your theory proves true, and you can repair the TPO junction, no medical insurer in the world would cover the cost of a non-life-saving procedure."

"Screw the insurance companies!" Prasad roared, his fist slamming onto the table with such force that the glassware rattled and clattered. The sharp sound reverberated through the room, a piercing echo of his escalating frustration. "We are a nationally acclaimed research institution with an ethical obligation to contribute to the greater good, for Christ's sake!" His voice thundered through the silence that followed, but the outburst only seemed to widen the chasm between him and the board members. Realizing he had crossed a line, Prasad turned away from the table, squeezing his eyes shut as he took a deep, steadying breath. *Get it together, man,* he admonished himself, willing his emotions to settle before he faced them again.

When he spoke again, his voice was noticeably calmer, the tone measured and deliberate, each word chosen with care. "Advances in basic physiology have almost always led to breakthroughs in medicine," he continued, allowing his words to carry the weight of conviction rather than anger. His eyes swept across the room before landing on the only woman present, her composed and regal figure standing out amid the tension. Dressed in a sleek red tailored pantsuit, she sat with an air of quiet authority, her diamond earrings catching the light as she listened, seemingly unfazed by the turmoil that had just unfolded. Her posture exuded a confidence that radiated power and control, and Prasad clung to it like a lifeline, hoping to appeal to her reason and sense of purpose.

In that moment, she became his anchor, the one person in the room he believed might still be open to the potential of his research. He locked onto her gaze, hoping to connect on a level beyond the bureaucratic barriers that had been erected. This was his chance to regain control of the situation, to shift the conversation back to the extraordinary possibilities his study could unlock, and he wasn't going to waste it.

"Director General?" he whispered, his voice softening as he locked eyes with her. "Surely you, of all people, must believe this is a cause worth pursuing." His plea hung in the air, the last vestige of hope in a room that seemed determined to crush it.

"Dr. Vedurmudi, let me remind you of where you are," she began, her voice unwavering, each word infused with the weight of authority. "This is an Institutional Review Board meeting, not the Global Assembly of Religious Leaders. Here, you shall refer to me as Reverend Dr. Kay Welton."

Her words hung in the air like a gauntlet thrown down, the room thick with the tension of unspoken power dynamics. The other board members shifted in their seats, the gravity of her command settling heavily upon them all.

"Do I make myself clear?" she added, her gaze sharp and unyielding as she leaned forward, palms pressing into the conference table, a gesture that conveyed both dominance and an invitation to challenge her if he dared.

Prasad sighed audibly, the sound a blend of frustration, exhaustion, and reluctant acceptance. The fight in him wavered, but his resolve to push for what he believed in remained. "Yes, Reverend Dr. Welton," he conceded, the formality of her title a bitter pill he forced himself to swallow. "But surely you can provide your professional expertise on the matter and convince these men that they are making the worst decision of their lives." His words, though tempered, carried a plea that cut through the tension, a desperate appeal to the one person in the room who held the duality of spiritual insight and scientific rigor. He knew he was treading a fine line, but he also knew that if anyone could sway the board, it was her.

"Yes, well, in my professional experience, it's too risky," she replied, shaking her head slightly. "And you are well aware that this board is responsible for ensuring risks to subjects are minimized."

"Too risky? Too risky for a subject that's already knocking at death's door? What do we have to lose?" Prasad's voice rose again, his desperation breaking through.

"Besides, there is no way to prove your theory on this... What are you calling it? Project Afterlife," she scoffed. "It's a waste of time and resources."

"Allow me to prove it, then!" Prasad fired back, his brows furrowing, jaw clenched with determination. "I knew I would face opposition going into this meeting, but if there was one person I thought I could count on to support the basis and potential benefits of the study, it was you." He shook his head, pacing the length of the room like a caged animal.

"I will no longer entertain your questions. I firmly stand by my decision," she said, her tone final.

Prasad turned to the three other board members who had remained silent, desperation seeping into his voice. "Gentlemen? Will you please help me talk some sense into these two?"

The silence was deafening.

"Dr. Valencia?" Prasad prompted, his voice tinged with hope.

Dr. Valencia hesitated, then spoke. "I'm sorry. It sounds fascinating, but there is a reason this board does not consist solely of scientists, and it's clear to me that Mr. Crenshaw and Reverend Dr. Welton feel quite strongly about not moving forward with this." He paused. "Their consult weighs heavily in my consideration, as it should."

Prasad stepped back, his face contorted with disbelief. "Un-fucking-believable."

"Excuse me?" Reverend Dr. Welton snapped, her brow furrowing in anger. "What did you just say?" Her voice was cold, cutting through the room like a knife.

With a flurry of motion, Prasad gathered his documents from the conference table, his face flushed with fury, and stormed toward the door. But he stopped just before exiting.

"You know, you have a RESPONSIBILITY to ensure that risks to subjects are reasonable in relation to expected benefits," he said, his voice raised, still facing away from them.

An unsettling silence settled over the room as his words hung in the air.

Taking a deep breath, Prasad turned back to face the board members one last time. "I challenge ANY of you—dare you, really—to come up with a benefit greater than the opportunity of resting in eternal peace."

Chapter 3

IT WAS A CHANCE ENCOUNTER, or perhaps something more—she had long since stopped believing in coincidences. It had been over a year since she last saw him, yet the moment her eyes caught sight of him across the bustling hospital lobby, her heart skipped a beat. *Surely, my eyes are deceiving me*, she thought, narrowing her gaze as if to sharpen the image, to confirm what her mind could hardly believe.

She tilted her head, focusing on the familiar figure—the thick, wavy brown hair now streaked with more gray than she remembered, the way he moved with that same purposeful stride. He seemed lost in thought, his attention wholly absorbed by the notebook in his hand, oblivious to the world around him. The sight stirred a mix of emotions within her, memories flooding back with a vividness that made her chest tighten. He looks busy, she mused, considering for a moment whether she should let him pass by unnoticed.

But the urge to reconnect, to break through the barrier of time that had separated them, was too strong to resist. As if drawn by an invisible thread, she took a step forward, her heartbeat quickening with each passing second, until she found herself calling out his name, her voice soft yet filled with an undeniable longing.

"Dr. Clark!" she called out, raising her hand high, her voice echoing across the lobby.

He turned, surprise flashing across his face as he squinted through his wire-framed glasses. "Emma?" he asked, his voice tinged with disbelief. "Is that you?"

She jogged over to him, a smile playing on her lips, though it didn't quite reach her eyes. "How are you?" she asked, extending her hand.

He took it firmly, his grip reassuring. "I can't complain," he replied, a hint of warmth in his tone. "I'm actually here to meet Prasad. We've teamed up on a fascinating study."

"Prasad?" she echoed, her brow furrowing as she searched her memory. "Do I know him?"

"Oh, yes, of course—you remember Dr. Vedurmudi," he said, his face lighting up with recognition. "He performed the memory procedure on you last year."

Her expression shifted as the memory resurfaced. "Oh, yes—of course! I didn't recognize the first name," she said, nodding. "So what's this fascinating study about? I assume it involves lab rats?" she added, wrinkling her nose in mock disgust.

"No lab rats this time," he replied, shaking his head with a small smile. "The study is about—" He paused, his gaze sharpening as he took in her appearance more closely. "But hold on—why are you here? Is everything OK?"

She drew in a deep breath, the weight of unspoken thoughts pressing down on her. "As OK as it can be," she shrugged, her voice laced with resignation.

"The last time we talked, you mentioned that the nightmares had stopped. Is that still the case?" he asked, concern creeping into his tone.

"Mostly," she said softly, glancing away for a moment before meeting his eyes again. "But there's this one recurring dream...I'm not even sure I'd call it a nightmare—maybe just a dream."

"Oh?" His curiosity piqued, he tilted his head slightly. "What's it about?"

She hesitated, the words catching in her throat before she finally spoke. "It's about that night...With Brianna."

More than a year had passed since Emma's lifelong best friend Brianna died, but not a day went by that she didn't think of her—multiple times, every single day. Brianna lived on in her dreams too, not every night, but enough for Emma to believe, wholeheartedly, that her friend's spirit lingered, even if not in the physical sense. In the early months after Brianna's passing, the dreams had been frequent. She'd talked to Dr. Clark about them, and he reassured her that it was normal—nothing to be concerned about. He explained that what she was experiencing were known as visitation dreams, a phenomenon widely studied in psychology, not uncommon following the death of a loved one.

As time passed, the dreams became less frequent, but they never stopped altogether. Brianna continued to appear in Emma's dreams, always in ways that were quintessentially Brianna—just as she had been in life. On Emma's birthday, for instance, she dreamed she heard the doorbell ring, even though she wasn't expecting anyone. When she opened the door, there stood Brianna, smiling her wide, toothy smile.

"Surprise!" Brianna announced, stepping inside with a cake in one hand and balloons in the other.

"What are you doing here?" Emma asked, her expression a mix of puzzlement and joy.

"Em, since when have I ever missed your birthday?" Brianna replied, feigning incredulity.

Emma stood there, stunned into silence, her mouth slightly ajar in disbelief.

"I'll save you the trouble," Brianna added with a grin. "Never—the answer is never. And I'm not about to start now!"

Then there was the dream Emma had the night of her promotion. Once again, the doorbell rang, and once again, she wasn't expecting anyone. But when she opened the door, there was Brianna, holding a bottle of white wine in one hand and a teal gift bag in the other.

"Congratulations, Em!" Brianna exclaimed, wrapping her in a warm embrace.

"Oh my God, Brie—you didn't have to get me anything," Emma said, though her heart swelled with gratitude.

Brianna handed her the gift bag. "It's like I always said—"

"Never trust a man that can dance?" Emma interrupted, laughing.

"Yes," Brianna replied with a chuckle. "But that's not what I mean…" Emma reached into the bag and pulled out a pair of Tiffany's wine glasses, their elegance catching the light.

"You deserve the best," Brianna said softly. "And that goes for everything in your life, including glassware."

Emma had spent countless hours analyzing her dreams, searching for patterns, for meaning. She noticed that Brianna's appearances always coincided with times of celebration—the moments when Brianna would have been there, had she still been alive. And then there was the doorbell. Outside of her parents, Brianna had been the only person Emma trusted with a key to her home, and she never hesitated to let herself in, especially when a surprise was involved. *I guess there's a reason they call them 'visitation' dreams*, she thought.

But there was another kind of dream—one that wasn't about celebration. "I dream about what I could have done differently...that night," Emma said, her voice barely above a whisper, the weight of her sadness betraying her calm facade.

"Emma, we've been through this. You can't blame yourself," Dr. Clark said, his hand resting reassuringly on her shoulder.

"I never said I was blaming myself," she replied, her tone defensive. "I said I dream of what I could have done differently."

He tilted his head, his expression one of concern and curiosity. "Like what?"

"For instance, if only I knew Brianna owned a gun... If I had known where she hid it, maybe I could have done something."

"You did do something," he insisted, his voice gentle but firm.

"I know, I just mean—maybe I could have saved her," she said, her voice cracking.

"I see," he replied, his tone tinged with pity. "How about you schedule an appointment with my office? We can discuss this further."

She took a step back, crossing her arms, and his hand slipped from her shoulder. "I'm fine," she said, her eyes locking onto his, daring him to challenge her. She suspected he didn't believe her. Dr. Clark had always had a way of reading her, of seeing things about her that she couldn't see herself. From the first day she met him at his office at the University of Chicago, he had shown her that he was intuitive in a way that bordered on the uncanny. But she had stopped him now to distract herself from her thoughts, not to delve into the state of her mental health.

"I can assure you, Dr. Clark, I'm not who I was when I was your patient—not even close," she said, her tone firm, almost defiant. "One recurring dream, under the circumstances, is no big deal."

He stared at her silently, as though waiting for her to say more, to let down her guard.

But she didn't.

Discussing the real reason she was there—her father's condition and how his health had declined over the past year—was both the last thing she wanted to do and the only thing she could think about. To talk about it would give it life, make it real. She didn't want to tell him that some weeks, she spent more time at the hospital with her father than she did at her PR firm. She didn't want to acknowledge that her father, once a powerful protector in her eyes, was aging rapidly, growing frailer by the day. And she most definitely did not want to talk about the guilt gnawing at her—the irrational guilt that upset her just to think about, stemming from the time she lost with him when she went off to college so many years ago.

"Anyway, you were saying? About the study?" she said, tapping her toes nervously.

"It's about near-death experiences," he replied, a hint of reluctance in his voice. "NDEs."

"That's really interesting!" she exclaimed, latching onto the change in topic with enthusiasm. He could have said the study was about the intricacies of statistical analysis and research methodology, and she would have responded with the same level of excitement. *Anything to change the subject,* she thought. "Tell me more," she urged.

"I'm leading a global team of researchers interviewing patients who reported having an NDE," he explained. "It turns out people experience the same pattern of events during NDEs, regardless of culture or religious beliefs."

That really does sound interesting, she thought. "And Dr. Vedurmudi? What's a neurosurgeon's role in a study like this?"

"He's leading the team responsible for analyzing brain activity in the subjects."

Her brow furrowed as a spark of recognition flared within her. "My dad mentioned this! It's the global study on patients who crossed over and came back," she said, a tinge of excitement in her voice.

"That's the one," he confirmed, glancing at his wristwatch.

"My dad sent me an article about how the brain sort of reactivates after a person is clinically dead."

"Yes, it's been getting a lot of press—apparently, there are a lot of people interested in what happens in the afterlife," he said, his words suddenly spilling out in a rapid torrent.

"Am I keeping you from something?" she asked, noticing his sudden shift in demeanor.

"No... I mean, yes. I'm sorry... It's just, I have somewhere I need to be."

"Actually, I have somewhere I need to be, too," she said, taking a step back. "I have some therapy I need to get to."

"Oh? Who are you seeing?" he asked, his brow furrowing. "Maybe I know them."

"No," she replied, shaking her head with a slight smile. "I'm sure you don't."

"How can you be sure?" he pressed.

"Uh—it's a different type of therapy," she scoffed, her smile widening as she turned to leave.

Chapter 4

THE PATIENTS EDWARD AND HIS TEAM were interviewing as part of the NDE study were a select group. The criteria were stringent: the patients had to have been successfully resuscitated—a rare outcome, occurring in only ten percent of resuscitative efforts. They also needed to have reported experiencing a near-death experience to a medical professional, and, crucially, they had to be deemed healthy enough to be interviewed weeks after their ordeal. For this reason, interviews were never conducted in the patient's room during their recovery.

But this case was different.

Edward knocked on the hospital room door, his knuckles tapping lightly against the cold wood. "Hello," he called out, cracking the door open just enough to peer inside. "May I come in?"

"Who is it?" a deep, raspy male voice responded from within.

"It's Edward."

"Edward who?"

"Dr. Edward Clark," he said, stepping into the room fully. As his eyes settled on the man before him, a look of disbelief crossed his face. The man's aged, wrinkled features resembled a well-worn book, each line telling a story of a life well-lived. Yet, the bushy head of wavy white hair seemed to defy the passage of time.

The man squinted at him, recognition slowly dawning. "Well, I'll be damned," he muttered. "What are you doing here?"

"I came to check in on you," Edward replied, still trying to reconcile the sight before him with the memory of just hours ago. "I was told they just brought you in here."

"Yeah—they had me in the ICU. What a waste of time," his father grumbled. "But I'm fine, anyway. Get back to work."

Edward tilted his head, gazing at his father as though he were witnessing a modern miracle. Only hours ago, he had stood helplessly by as his father flatlined in the emergency room. Now, here he was, sitting upright on the hospital bed, alert and full of his usual fire. Edward inhaled deeply, struggling to contain the wave of emotions crashing over him. "I almost lost you, Dad."

"Oh, you're being dramatic," his father scoffed, brushing off the concern.

Edward folded his arms, his gaze steady and unyielding, a silent demand for honesty.

A tense silence settled between them.

His father, never one to back down, folded his arms in return, matching Edward's glare with a defiant one of his own.

The silence stretched on, each second heavy with unspoken words.

Anytime now, Edward thought.

"OK, fine, I was almost gone!" his father finally exclaimed, throwing his arms up in surrender. "But it wasn't my time."

It wasn't my time? The phrase struck Edward as odd, especially coming from his father. His mother had been a devout Catholic, faithfully bringing Edward to church every Sunday. But his father—he had never been a man of faith. He didn't believe in religion, in God, or in anything beyond the tangible world. A noble father and a devoted husband, yes, but not a believer. For as long as Edward could remember, his father had always dismissed the idea of an afterlife, comparing humans to ants—insignificant creatures in a vast, uncaring universe. *Here one minute, gone the next. Lights out. End of story.* That was his father's mantra.

"What do you mean, it wasn't your time?" Edward asked, his brow furrowed in confusion.

"That's what they told me, anyway. Who am I to argue?"

Who am I to argue? Edward stared at his father, the man who had always been so certain, so unshakable in his beliefs. "Dad, who told you it wasn't your time?"

His father crossed his arms tighter, his expression stubborn. "Dad?" Edward pressed.

"OK, fine!" His father inhaled deeply, as if preparing himself. "Ma and Pa told me."

Edward's eyes widened in shock. His grandparents had been dead for years. "Dad, tell me what you saw."

"I saw you in the emergency room," his father said, rolling his eyes as if recounting something mundane.

"Go on," Edward urged.

"I saw everything. I had a 360-degree view of the entire room. Then I got zipped away, and I saw a light."

"Zipped away?" Edward echoed, incredulous.

"That's what I said, didn't I?"

"What did the light look like?" Edward asked, leaning in closer, his heart pounding.

"It was brighter than anything I've ever seen, but it wasn't blinding. Then I started walking toward the light, but not exactly by choice."

"What do you mean, not by choice?"

"I don't know... It was like I was on autopilot. I was moving, but I wasn't the one controlling my movement. Anyway, through the light, I saw Ma and Pa."

He paused, his eyes darting around the room as if searching for something to anchor him in the present.

"They looked younger than they did when I last saw them," he continued, his voice softening, his eyes welling with tears. "A lot younger—not sure exactly how I even recognized them, but I felt it in my soul."

Your soul? Edward's mind raced. "Your soul?" he repeated, his voice barely above a whisper.

"That's what I said, didn't I? What are you, a parrot?" his father snapped, though the usual bite in his words was absent.

By now, Edward had heard hundreds of testimonies about experiences in the afterlife as part of his research. But hearing it from his father—a lifelong atheist who had staunchly denied any existence beyond death—touched him in a way nothing else ever had. He held his breath, his eyes wide and unblinking, desperate to hear more.

"When Pa died, I was devastated. He was only 62, you know," his father said, his voice growing distant as he slipped into memory.

"I remember," Edward replied softly. "I was sad, too."

"Ma took it better than me. They were married 45 years, and she took it better than me—and I was a grown man," his father continued, shaking his head in disbelief. "I remember breaking down on her one day, and she comforted me like I was still a little boy. I looked at her and said, 'Ma, how are you so strong?' She said it was because she knew being away from Pa was only temporary, and she had things to tend to here in the meantime." He scoffed, shaking his head. "Boy, oh boy, I thought she had gone loony."

"And now?" Edward asked, his voice gentle, almost afraid of the answer.

His father let out an exasperated sigh. "You want me to spell it out for you?" he asked, glaring at Edward with a mix of frustration and reluctance.

"No," Edward replied, a small, knowing smile tugging at his lips. "I'm just glad you're OK. I'll check on you later," he said, turning to leave the room.

"Edward!" his father called out, his voice unexpectedly urgent.

"Yes, Dad?" Edward replied, turning back to him.

"There's one more thing."

"What is it?" Edward asked, noticing a flicker of hesitation in his father's eyes, as if he was wrestling with the decision to reveal what he knew. "What is it, Dad?" Edward repeated, stepping closer to his father's bedside.

"Now, if I tell you this, promise you won't get all sappy on me," his father warned, his tone gruff but laced with vulnerability.

"OK. I promise," Edward said, his heart pounding in his chest.

"While I was up there... I saw... your mother."

Edward froze, his heart sinking like a stone into his stomach. His father's lips curled up in a faint, almost imperceptible smile.

"She had a message for you," his father continued, his voice tinged with a mix of nostalgia and bewilderment. "She said to tell you, 'Mind the potato chip,' whatever the hell that's supposed to mean."

Chapter 5

WHEN PRASAD ASKED EDWARD to co-lead the Near-Death Experience (NDE) study, Edward didn't immediately say yes. Instead, he spent considerable time mulling over the request, weighing the implications and potential biases that might cloud his judgment. He wasn't under any obligation to accept, and the thought of aligning himself with a field he had long regarded as pseudoscience made him hesitant. Edward had always been skeptical of afterlife claims, especially those presented by NDE researchers, which he often dismissed as lacking the rigor needed to produce clear and testable hypotheses. In his years as a clinical professor of psychiatry, only one event had ever defied scientific explanation—a memory that still unsettled him whenever it surfaced.

Edward's skepticism was deeply ingrained, shaped by his upbringing in a stable, loving household where his parents held starkly different worldviews. The differences ranged from the trivial—his father's love for chocolate versus his mother's preference for vanilla, or his father's aversion to spice contrasted with his mother's love for fiery flavors—to the profound. His father was an unwavering skeptic, rooted in the tangible and observable, while his mother was a devout Catholic, who ensured Edward attended church every Sunday and completed all the Catholic sacraments—Baptism, First Communion, Confirmation—whether he wanted to or not.

Edward inherited his mother's love for spicy food but took after his father in matters of belief. He found solace in science, in the things that could be seen, touched, and measured, dismissing the mysteries that lay beyond as unfounded. His world was one of evidence and rationality, leaving little room for the unexplainable.

Yet, after much contemplation, Edward ultimately agreed to co-lead the study for two reasons: curiosity and friendship.

Edward believed that curiosity could thrive even in a skeptic's heart. Despite his doubts, he couldn't ignore the lingering intrigue sparked by the paranormal event he had witnessed years ago—an event that had planted a seed of wonder, urging him to explore what else might be possible. Additionally, he recognized in himself a stubbornness and skepticism that mirrored his father's. This study represented more than just a professional challenge; it was an opportunity for personal growth, a chance to confront and perhaps even expand his understanding of the world. And then there was Prasad, whose friendship and trust mattered enough to make Edward reconsider his stance, leading him to embark on a journey he never thought he'd take.

He valued his friendship with Prasad, a bond built on trust and mutual respect. Their collaboration had always been marked by synergy, with each enhancing the other's performance. Prasad was one of the few colleagues Edward genuinely enjoyed working with. Unlike many university professors with their pompous accolades and smug achievements, Prasad was uninterested in fame and accolades. Edward had coined a term for those colleagues—*pompulent*—a cheeky fusion of "pompous" and "opulent." Prasad, however, was different. He was a professional with high standards and academic integrity, driven by a thirst for knowledge. Although they didn't always agree, they always listened to each other's perspectives and maintained unwavering respect for one another.

It was this respect that made Prasad undeterred when Edward admitted he leaned toward scientific explanations for NDE phenomena. Edward argued that damage to the bilateral occipital cortex from the dying brain could explain the visual features of NDEs, like seeing tunnels or bright lights.

But the morning changed everything.

"Maybe there's something to this afterlife stuff after all," Edward said, his voice subdued as he spoke on the phone.

There was a pause on the other end. "I'm sorry, who am I speaking with?" Prasad asked, his tone half-joking. "You sound like Dr. Edward Clark, but you don't *sound* like Dr. Edward Clark."

Edward scoffed. "Seriously—what changed?"

Edward exhaled audibly, the weight of the morning's events pressing on him. "The patient who was resuscitated in the ER this morning—"

"What about him?"

"He's my father."

"WHAT?!" Prasad's shout rang through the phone, causing Edward to jerk it away from his ear, wincing at the volume.

He slowly brought the phone back to his ear. "Why didn't you tell me?" Prasad asked, his voice now tinged with concern.

"I don't know—I suppose I was still processing the whole thing."

"How is he?"

"He's doing well. He had an NDE," Edward said, anticipating Prasad's reaction. He moved the phone away from his ear once more.

"WHAT?!" Prasad shouted again, the reaction as loud as expected.

Edward returned the phone to his ear. "He gave me a message from my mother."

There was a pause. "What was it?"

"'Mind the potato chip.'"

Prasad was silent for a moment, clearly trying to make sense of it. "What's that supposed to mean?"

"'Potato chip' was a nickname my mother had for my father," Edward explained. "I'm pretty sure he didn't even know she called him that."

"How could he not?"

"It was a secret between my mom and me. She'd call him 'sweet potato' when he was in a good mood and 'potato chip' when he was in a salty one," Edward said, a small smile tugging at the corners of his mouth. "It was her way of warning me when to tread lightly."

Prasad's voice softened. "I'm glad you're finally opening up to the possibilities," he said. "Brace yourself, my friend, because this is just the beginning."

A furrow formed between Edward's brows. "What do you mean, 'just the beginning'?"

But Prasad was in a hurry. "Listen, I need to run. I'll stop by your office later."

"OK, I'll see you—" Edward started to say, but there was a click, and the line went dead.

Edward slowly put down the phone, Prasad's words echoing in his mind. *This is just the beginning?* he thought, unease creeping into his chest. *What's that supposed to mean?*

Chapter 6

THE SOUND OF HER CRIMSON PRADA STILETTOS reverberated through the hallway, each deliberate step echoing like a war drum in the stillness. With every thunderous footfall, the floor seemed to tremble beneath her, quaking in anticipation of the storm she was about to unleash. Her eyes locked onto the nameplate on the office door—Dr. Prasad Vedurmudi. She inhaled deeply, fury coursing through her veins, and with a swift, forceful motion, she flung the door open, utterly indifferent to whatever—or whoever—might be on the other side.

"That better be the last time you disrespect me like that!" Reverend Kay stormed into the office, her fiery gaze fixed on Prasad.

"Pardon me?" Prasad responded, rising slowly from behind his desk, his calm demeanor a stark contrast to her seething rage.

"I have never, not once, voted against anything you've presented to the board. And the one time I do, you throw a fit—like a child!" she spat, her voice quivering with barely contained fury. "I will not allow you to speak to me—or to the board—like that."

"Oh, I see," Prasad said, leaning in slightly, his voice low and measured. "This isn't about the board... This is about you, isn't it?"

"Oh, please," she scoffed, rolling her eyes, her frustration bubbling to the surface.

Prasad stepped out from behind his desk, his eyes locked onto hers as he closed the distance between them. "You walk around like you're so important, grand and all," he said, his gaze sweeping over her with a mixture of disdain and challenge. "But behind the fancy pantsuit and pumps, it's all ego, and you know it."

"*I'm all ego*? Seems you're the one who's letting your ego run the show," she shot back, crossing her arms defensively. "You assume the board will rubber-stamp anything you present, no questions asked," she added, her words laced with accusation.

She paused, her eyes narrowing as she took in the man before her.

"And why wouldn't you?" she continued, her voice dripping with sarcasm. "You've always gotten your way."

"That's because I have only ever presented the board with things that truly matter," Prasad replied, his tone unwavering, his conviction unshaken.

"You think what you presented to the board really matters?" she scoffed, the disbelief evident in her voice. "Did you honestly think I would side with such a preposterous proposal?"

Not only did he expect Reverend Kay to side with him, but he also believed her opinion, her esteemed reputation as a religious leader, and her influential relationships with the other board members would be enough to sway them to approve his proposal. He was well aware that there was no sound business rationale for pursuing the study. Mr. Crenshaw was right—no insurance company on earth would even consider covering a procedure that had no tangible effect on quality of life. That's why Prasad knew the board's approval hinged entirely on her support.

"Is it so foolish to think that someone in your position would be in favor of helping people transition to the next dimension?" he asked, his tone a mix of frustration and disbelief. "To keep them from being stranded, their spirits wandering aimlessly in this dimension, if we could help it?" His eyes widened as a sudden realization dawned on him, a slow smile tugging at the corners of his lips. "That's it!" he exclaimed. "This is all about you, isn't it?"

"What are you talking about?" she scoffed, her eyes narrowing with suspicion.

"This is about self-preservation," he continued, his voice tinged with accusation. "Job security."

She crossed her arms, her expression hardening. "In the highest form—I suppose it is," she replied coldly. "Because if you think I'm going to allow you to walk around thinking you, pitiful, pitiful little you, can just swoop in and repair 'a mistake' made by Almighty God himself—you are dead wrong."

"You're being a bit dramatic, don't you think?" he retorted smugly. "Besides, I wouldn't call it 'repairing a mistake'—more like 'closing a gap,'" he added with a nonchalant shrug.

A look of shock and horror washed over her face, the emotion so intense it seemed to ripple through the air between them. Her fists clenched involuntarily, her knuckles turning ghostly white as the blood drained from her hands, while her face flushed a deep, fiery shade of red. Her eyes bulged, wide and unblinking, as unrestrained fury built within her. In an explosive burst of pent-up rage, she slammed her hand against the desk, the impact sending papers and documents flying in a chaotic whirlwind, scattering across the room like fallen leaves in a storm.

"I'm sorry, I'm sorry," Prasad stammered, his voice trembling as he realized too late the gravity of his words. He brought his palms together, pressing them under his chin in a gesture of contrition, as if pleading for some semblance of forgiveness. "Please, I didn't mean to imply that God, the Creator—anyone's Creator—made a mistake."

He paused, letting the tension simmer in the charged silence between them. "But what if us closing this gap is part of His plan?"

Her fists tightened even further, the tendons in her hands standing out like taut wires. When she spoke, her voice was a low, dangerous growl. "So what, you think you're the next Savior? The Chosen One?"

"No, I am not God," he replied, his gaze steady and unyielding as he locked eyes with her. "But neither are you."

She scoffed, her eyes narrowing into slits of contempt. "Do you honestly think you're the first person to come up with this idea? Have you ever considered that maybe there's a reason no one has ever pursued it?" Her words dripped with disdain, each one a sharp, cutting challenge.

They stood locked in a tense silence, the air between them thick with animosity, as if the very room had shrunk around them, pressing their wills against each other in a battle of dominance. Finally, she broke the silence with a muttered remark, her voice laced with venom. "Your poor wife."

His posture straightened, his eyes flashing with sudden, fierce indignation. "Excuse me? What did you say about my wife?"

"She's a saint," she replied, her tone dripping with sarcasm. "I mean, she must be... To put up with you and your load of crap every day."

He crossed his arms over his chest, his voice tight with controlled anger. "Well, you're not wrong. She is a saint."

She rolled her eyes and spun on her heel, her footsteps echoing loudly against the floor as she stormed toward the door. "I'm done here, Bruno," she muttered under her breath, the words barely audible as she reached for the handle.

"What was that?" he called after her, cupping a hand to his ear in mock confusion. But she ignored him, pulling the door open and stepping out with a final, decisive slam.

"Thanks for dropping by!" he shouted after her, his voice dripping with sarcasm, each word a taunt. "Nice talk!"

The door creaked open once more, and Prasad braced himself, his annoyance bubbling just beneath the surface. Ugh, now what?

"Oh, and I was wrong before," Reverend Kay said, pushing the door open wider, her expression hardening with disdain and a bitter finality.

"What about?" he asked, his eyes narrowing, suspicion lacing his tone.

"I do believe God made one mistake—and I'm looking at it."

Chapter 7

ALONE AND IN THE QUIET of his office, Edward leaned back in his chair, the worn leather creaking softly beneath him as he settled in. The room was dimly lit, with only the soft glow of his computer screen casting shadows across his face. He exhaled deeply, the weight of the day slipping away as he listened to the familiar cadence of his voice playing through the speakers. "Please start by providing your name, age, country of origin, and religion," his recorded voice prompted, echoing gently in the stillness.

"OK. My name is Nancy Thomas. I just turned fifty-eight. I was born and raised here in the US—in the south."

She paused.

"But you probably already knew that."

"No, that's not shown anywhere in your file," Edward replied. She giggled. "I mean, because of my accent, sugar plum."

"Oh—I see," he replied.

"Anyway, where was I? Oh yes... My religion—I've been a Southern Baptist all my life."

"What makes you think you had a near-death experience?" She scoffed. "Well... First, I was clinically dead."

"Right, of course. What exactly did you experience?"

"Well... I was at work one moment, and in the hospital the next. I was told I had suffered from cardiac arrest," she said. "At the hospital, I had to be resuscitated. I floated out of my body and watched the doctor try to resuscitate me. I saw them remove my hearing aid. And I could see and hear everything that was happening so clearly."

"You could hear clearly? Without your hearing aid?"

"That's the strangest part! Well, maybe not the strangest part," she scoffed. "I've been using a hearing aid since I could remember. My momma told me I fell off the back of a pickup truck and busted an eardrum."

She paused.

"At least I think that's what she told me. Anyway, I could hear everything," she said. "I even saw a nurse wearing pink scrubs drop my hearing aid on the floor and then pick it up."

"There is a note in your file that says there were six people in the room when you were being resuscitated. Only one wore pink scrubs," he said. "That nurse in the pink scrubs confirmed your account of what happened."

"Well, of course she did. I saw her clear as day," she replied. "I even heard the hearing aid hit the floor."

"You heard the hearing aid hit the floor?"

"I certainly did," she replied. "I could hear a pin drop."

"What happened next?" he asked.

"The next thing I know, I'm zipping through the sky."

"Zipping?"

"I mean floating... Flying, I guess, but fast. Very fast."

"Were you afraid?"

"Not the least bit!" she declared. "Which is also strange because I hate flying—I've been afraid of heights ever since I can remember."

She paused.

"I wonder if me falling off the back of the pickup truck has anything to do with that."

She paused again.

"Hmm... I never put that together until just now," she said. "Anyway, I wasn't afraid. I was at peace. On my way up, I'm thinking of my life and the choices I made, then I see a bright light. And I see my sister."

"Your sister? Is she living?"

"She died ten years ago in a car accident," she replied. "She was so beat up from the accident, we couldn't even give her an open casket. But she was there, welcoming me in, and she looked absolutely beautiful. And she sort of ushered me toward the light."

"Do you recall how you felt at that moment?"

"Oh, yes... I felt so much love and peace. I just knew I was home," she said.

"What was she ushering you toward?"

"Jesus, of course."

"You could see Him?"

"Well, no, but I could feel Him. I was stepping toward Him— suddenly, my sister reached for my hand and told me I had to go back. I remember telling her I didn't want to go back."

She paused.

"Anyway, that was it. Next thing I know, I woke up in my hospital bed."

He tapped on the phone screen and wrote in his notebook:

Out-of-body experience—check.

Heightened senses—check.

Transported to another dimension—check. Welcomed by deceased loved ones—check. Bright light—check.

Feelings of peace and love—check.

He gazed at his notes and tilted his head to the side. "By the looks of it, heaven has perfected their onboarding process." He tapped on his phone screen again.

"Please start by providing your name, age, country of origin, and religion," Edward's voice played through the phone.

"My name is Oliver Allen. I am twenty-eight, originally from Australia, but I moved to the US recently to live with my girlfriend."

"And your religion?"

"Oh, that's right. Sorry. I don't have one. Atheist I guess. Maybe not so much after my experience," he said. "I guess you could say it's being determined at the moment."

"Have you ever practiced any religion?"

"No," he replied. "My mum raised me to be a good person. To be kind, to treat people with love and respect. The golden rule, you know? But we never practiced religion."

"What makes you believe you had a near-death experience?"

"Well, I was riding my motorbike to work, and as I'm crossing the intersection, a people-mover headed in the opposite direction decides it's going to take a left turn and comes straight at me."

"A *people-mover*?"

"Oh, right. That's what we call vans back home," he said. "Anyway, it hit me. You'd think I would be furious, but I wasn't. And I see this man jump out of the people-mover, I mean van, to come to my aid. And I see a woman in the van that hit me on her mobile, calling for help. I hear and see that same woman consoling her crying little ones in the van, two boys and a baby girl. Then it occurs to me I've left my body."

"Your file shows there was a family of five in the vehicle that collided with you. Including three children—two males and one female."

"Yes, just like I told you."

"The van—was it near the location of your body?"

"Not even close," he replied. "I must have skidded 50 meters from where the van struck me. Yet I could hear the conversation going on inside the van, even though the doors and windows were closed."

"What happened next?"

"That was the last thing I saw—my body lying unconscious on the road—before I rocketed through what I can only describe as a tunnel," he said. "And when I got to where I was going, I saw my mum."

"Your mother? Is she deceased?"

"She died last year," he said, his eyes welling up with tears. "That's why I moved here. There was nothing left for me back home."

"Do you remember anything else?"

"Yes, I saw a bright, warm light," he said. "Mum took my hand and guided me toward it. I didn't know what to make of it—I mean, I suppose I knew I was dead, but it didn't bother me in the slightest. I just felt so much love coming from its presence."

He paused.

"Then mum stopped," he said, sniffling. "I tried to get her to keep going, but she wouldn't. Instead, she leaned in and gave me the most wonderful hug. Then she looked me in the eye and said I would be OK and that I had to come back."

There was a knock on the door. Edward tapped on his keyboard, paused the recording and cleared his throat. "Just a moment!"

Chapter 8

"WHAT'S SO IMPORTANT THAT you insisted we discuss it in person?" Edward asked, standing at the threshold of his office with a skeptical glare fixed on Prasad. The unusual request had piqued his curiosity, but it also set off alarm bells. He and Prasad were in frequent contact, often exchanging ideas and updates through quick texts, casual chats, or the occasional phone call. Prasad, who was typically at ease with these modern forms of communication, seemed out of character with his insistence on a face-to-face meeting. Edward's eyes narrowed as he scanned Prasad's expression, searching for any hint of what might have driven him to step out of his comfort zone.

"Nice to see you, too," Prasad replied, his tone light but laced with underlying urgency. "May I come in? Or would you prefer to have this discussion right here at the door?"

Edward remained unblinking, his expression unmoved. "You've got my attention. What's going on?" he pressed, intrigued by the unspoken urgency that lingered in the air between them.

"For Christ's sake, get out of the way," Prasad muttered, pushing past Edward and stepping into the office. His eyes immediately zeroed in on Edward's cluttered desk, piled high with notebooks and file folders. "How do you manage to get any work done around here?" he asked, shaking his head in disbelief.

"I'm just playing back interviews," Edward replied with a dismissive wave. "It's hardly work."

"You know we've assigned people for that."

"I know, but I enjoy getting into the weeds now and then," Edward said with a shrug. "Besides, I find it relaxing."

Prasad gave him a pointed look, his eyes narrowing slightly. "I take it you've farmed out the twenty-three percent?" he asked, his tone carrying a weight that made the question feel almost like an accusation. He was referring to the percentage of patients in their Near-Death Experience (NDE) study who had reported terrifying encounters—visions of plummeting into the earth's core, being mercilessly tormented by malevolent beings, or other nightmarish horrors that defied rational explanation.

Edward's thoughts immediately flashed to a particular interview from the study. The memory of the woman's harrowing account was still vivid in his mind. She had described seeing a towering set of rusty gates, which she was convinced were the gates of hell. The air around her had been thick with the sounds of guttural moans, agonized cries, and wails that seemed to resonate from the very depths of despair. Worse still, she spoke of a foul stench that seemed to linger on her, clinging even after she had returned to the waking world.

A shiver ran down Edward's spine, and his body tensed involuntarily as the unease of that memory crept back in. He forced himself to maintain composure, though his voice tightened as he replied, "Yes, we've assigned people to handle that."

He tried to sound dismissive, but the unease in his tone betrayed him. Prasad's question had touched a nerve, bringing back the unsettling reality of those darker aspects of the study that Edward preferred to keep at arm's length.

Edward watched as Prasad made a beeline for the couch, lying down and propping his feet on the armrest. "Make yourself at home," Edward remarked dryly.

Prasad exhaled audibly, his brow furrowing.

"Is there something you'd like to get off your chest?" Edward asked, taking a seat behind his desk and raising an eyebrow at his friend.

Prasad turned to him, his expression conflicted. "What do you mean?" he asked, sitting up as if an invisible force had pulled him upright.

Edward studied him for a moment, then spoke, his tone measured. "You seem a little... on edge."

"Oh," Prasad said, lying back down, trying to mask his unease. "It's the NDE study."

"What about it?"

"We've established a clear pattern of events—seems like it's hardly worth spending more time on it."

"You want to withdraw from the study?" Edward asked, furrowing his brow in surprise.

"No, not exactly," Prasad replied, his voice tinged with frustration. "But what if we could take the study further? What if, instead of only observing what happens as the spirit enters the afterlife, we could *affect* it?" His words hung in the air, heavy with implication.

"Go on," Edward said, his skepticism deepening as he narrowed his eyes at Prasad. "I'm listening."

"You and I have spent our entire careers focusing on improving the quality of our patients' lives. How many years do they have? Eighty-something, ninety-something if they're lucky?" Prasad's gaze drifted to the ceiling as he spoke. "But what if we could improve the quality of their afterlives—for eternity?"

"There's just no way," Edward replied, his voice laced with disbelief. *Is Prasad losing it?* he wondered silently.

"'Impossible'?" Prasad echoed, his eyes snapping back to Edward as he sat up abruptly. "Like it was 'impossible' to restart the human heart until Dr. Claude Beck proved otherwise in 1947 with the electric defibrillator?"

Fair point, Edward thought, tilting his head as he reconsidered Prasad's assertion.

"Edward, we're better than this!" Prasad insisted, rising from the couch with renewed energy. "We're smarter than this! We've spent our whole lives solving modern medicine's most complex problems, and now we're just going to coast through the rest of our careers? Our lives?"

Edward crossed his arms, watching Prasad pace the length of the office. He didn't need convincing that there was nothing groundbreaking about their current study. Sure, it was the most extensive and comprehensive study on near-death experiences in history, offering a unique perspective by comparing

NDEs across a cross-cultural context, but it ultimately just confirmed what smaller studies had already reported—that everyone experiences the same pattern of events in their journey to the afterlife, and that any variability is likely due to cultural interpretation, religious beliefs, and personal experiences.

"Enlighten me," Edward said, his curiosity piqued despite himself. "How can we possibly affect the afterlife?"

Prasad stopped pacing and turned to him, his expression intense. "Remember when you asked what I was thinking about before? At the hospital?"

"When you were staring out the window, lost in thought?"

"Right," Prasad replied. "But I wasn't lost in thought—I was *thinking*."

"OK."

"Did you hear about the birds that died after flying into the McCormick Place Lakeside Center?" Prasad asked, his tone shifting to one of urgency.

"Of course," Edward replied, recalling the news that had made national headlines. The building, made almost entirely of glass, had left its lights on overnight, causing thousands of migrating birds to collide with it. "How is it relevant?"

"The birds collided with the building while doing what they were hard-wired to do—migrate south for the winter," Prasad explained. "They didn't consciously decide to fly south; they were simply following their instincts, doing what comes naturally."

"Hard-wired. Understood."

"What if I told you that the human brain is wired the same way? But instead of being wired to fly north and south, it's wired to ascend or descend to the next dimension?"

Edward couldn't help but let out a small snort, quickly stifled by placing a hand over his mouth. "You're suggesting the human brain has a built-in homing device for the afterlife?"

"BINGO!" Prasad shouted, slapping his hands together with a resounding clap.

Edward was inclined to challenge him, as any great mind would. But on the surface, Prasad's theory wasn't entirely outlandish. Birds, bees, salmon, rats, cats, bats, and dolphins all had an inherent ability to navigate back home, even after traveling long distances over unfamiliar terrain. And then there was his father's claim, still fresh in his mind—he had said he was on autopilot, moving but not in control.

"Let's assume you're right," Edward said, taking a deep breath as he reluctantly entertained the idea. "Let's assume that somewhere in the vast, largely uncharted network of the brain, there's a homing device responsible for transporting the spirit to the next dimension." The very words felt foreign, even absurd, as they left his mouth. "So what? How can we possibly affect the afterlife?"

"Wonderful—now we're getting somewhere," Prasad replied, his eyes gleaming with excitement. "We know that when a patient's heart stops, brain activity flatlines."

Edward nodded, his skepticism still intact. "Agreed."

"Then we've observed that brain activity starts up again—we see beta waves—the brain is in an active, alert state, the same kind of activity we see during cognitive tasks that require concentration," Prasad continued, his passion evident in every word.

Edward nodded again, though more slowly this time. "Yes."

"And in each case, the same part of the brain is activated—let's assume this is where the homing device is located."

"OK," Edward said, his voice flat, his eyes dull with doubt.

"What do you think would happen if that part of the brain—the location of the homing device, so to speak—were inactive when the body dies?"

"You want me to guess?"

"I want you to hypothesize."

Edward drummed his fingers on his desk, searching for a suitable analogy. "If a red-bellied newt lost its ability to smell, it would lose its ability to navigate through the rugged California terrain."

"The red-bellied newt?" Prasad asked, furrowing his brow. "What's a *red-bellied newt*?"

"It's an amphibian."

"OK, sure, let's go with that," Prasad said, shaking his head in exasperation. "But you get my point."

"It's an interesting hypothesis, but it still doesn't explain how you think we can affect the afterlife," Edward said, glancing at the clock on the wall. "It's late—I need to finish up here and head home to my family."

"I can repair it!" Prasad blurted out, the words spilling from him in a rush.

"What?"

"I believe I can repair it."

"Because repairing it will enable the spirit to go to the next dimension," Edward said, crossing his arms and narrowing his gaze.

"Exactly."

"Have you presented this to the Institutional Review Board?" Edward asked, reaching for his coat.

"Yes, but they didn't approve it," Prasad admitted, his tone deflated.

"Why not?" Edward asked, his curiosity piqued again.

"I don't know, but it doesn't matter—this is too important. I'm doing it anyway," Prasad said, his determination unyielding. "I want you to partner with me on this—as a side project, so to speak. The NDE study is practically running itself."

Something isn't adding up, Edward thought, his instincts on high alert. As seasoned medical professionals and tenured clinical professors, both he and Prasad had successfully influenced the committee before. Given the wealth of information collected from the NDE study, resources could easily be reallocated to support this new direction without requiring additional funding.

"What are you not telling me?" Edward asked, his gaze sharpening as he scrutinized Prasad.

"Edward, I'm convinced that I'm on the brink of a revelation that will change the world forever," Prasad declared, his voice trembling with fervor.

A stifled scoff escaped through Edward's clenched teeth. He pressed his lips together, desperately trying to suppress the urge to laugh.

Prasad glared at him, incredulous. "What?" he demanded.

"I have to go—let's pick this back up tomorrow," Edward said, stepping toward the door. "Just a word of advice—if you want my help, you'll need to do way better than that."

Chapter 9

PRASAD'S OFFICE BUZZED WITH a ceaseless whirlwind of activity. The walls, a vibrant tapestry of brain images and color-coded sticky notes, formed a mosaic of interconnected ideas—each one meticulously placed, leading toward the next potential breakthrough. The room hummed with the energy of countless late nights and early mornings, a testament to Prasad's relentless pursuit of knowledge.

He had arrived on campus before dawn, the dark stillness outside contrasting sharply with the vibrant chaos within his office. The entire morning had been spent refining his presentation, every detail scrutinized in preparation for his meeting with Edward. The IRB's rejection of his afterlife study still stung, their dismissal of it as mere speculation gnawing at him. But Prasad was far from deterred. His determination to push forward burned brighter with each passing hour. He knew that convincing Edward to join him was crucial; while he was ready to forge ahead alone, he deeply valued Edward's insight and friendship. Having him by his side would not only lend credibility to the research but would also make the journey far less solitary.

The sound of footsteps echoed down the hall, growing louder as they approached his door. "Edward, you're here early," Prasad called out, turning toward the entrance.

Prasad shot him an incredulous look, though a faint smile tugged at the corners of his lips—a subtle acknowledgment of the camaraderie that had long defined their friendship. "Comments like that make me wonder why I keep you around," he teased.

"My guess—misery loves company," Edward quipped, a mischievous glint in his eyes. "Besides, whatever you have to show me must be worth coming in early for."

"Oh, it is, my friend—and I'm using that term loosely, of course," Prasad replied, his tone sparring with the same intellectual agility that had fueled their countless debates over the years. "Have a seat."

Edward settled into a chair in front of Prasad's desk. "So, what's this about?" he asked, his curiosity piqued.

"Let me begin by setting the stage," Prasad replied, his tone shifting from playful banter to one of serious intent.

"Alright," Edward nodded, leaning back slightly.

"We've already established that the human brain continues to function long after the heart stops, as evidenced by spikes in EEG activity, correct?"

"Correct," Edward affirmed.

"It is during these spikes in activity, we believe, that the spirit begins its transition—either ascending or descending, depending on its destination," Prasad explained, moving toward a large video screen mounted on the wall. "In other words, the afterlife experience is beginning."

"Right," Edward agreed, his gaze following Prasad.

"On the left, we have brain images of resuscitated patients who reported an NDE," Prasad said, pointing to the screen where a series of colorful brain scans were displayed. "On the right, images of resuscitated patients who did not report an NDE."

"Okay," Edward said, nodding as he studied the screen.

"Can you spot the difference between the two groups?" Prasad asked, his voice measured, his eyes narrowing as he watched Edward's reaction.

Edward's gaze swept across the images displayed on the screen, moving methodically from left to right. His expression shifted to one of intense focus, the lines on his forehead deepening as he tried to discern the subtle variations. "Not from here," he murmured, his curiosity piqued. He pushed himself up from his seat, stepping closer to the screen. With each step, his skepticism mingled with a growing curiosity. He leaned in, his eyes scanning the details with meticulous care.

"There's a difference?" he asked, his voice laced with both intrigue and doubt, as if he were on the brink of uncovering something significant yet elusive.

"Yes—look closely," Prasad urged, a note of excitement creeping into his voice.

Edward leaned in, his nose nearly touching the screen. Both sets of images showed bright hues of yellow, red, green, and blue in various parts of the brain. "I don't see a difference," he admitted.

"Here," Prasad said, gesturing to another, larger screen on the wall. With a few swift taps on his keyboard, he pulled up two more images side by side. "The image on the left, NDE. The image on the right, no NDE."

"They still look the same to me," Edward said, squinting at the screen.

"I'm going to magnify the images by five hundred percent," Prasad announced, clicking on the magnifying glass icon.

Edward scrutinized the enlarged images, his eyes narrowing as he focused. Suddenly, his expression shifted. "I see it!" he exclaimed, pointing to a brightly lit area on the left image. "In the area between the temporal, parietal, and occipital lobes—the TPO junction—there's activity on the left, but none on the right."

He stepped back, a puzzled look crossing his face. "Why is that?"

"Based on my research, the patients who did not report an NDE suffered from significant brain injury," Prasad explained. "These same patients showed no activity in the TPO junction before they were resuscitated."

He picked up a dry-erase marker and uncapped it with a deliberate motion. "To put it simply..." he began, writing on the board:

INACTIVE TPO JUNCTION = NO NDE

"In all cases?" Edward asked, his tone tinged with disbelief.

Prasad minimized the images on the screen and tapped on a folder labeled *No NDEs*. "Here, take a look at these," he said.

Edward swiped through the images, examining each one carefully. "None of these show activity in the TPO junction," he observed.

"I reviewed each patient's file," Prasad continued. "They all suffered from some type of brain trauma—car accidents, aneurysms, brain cancer, even gunshot wounds to the head."

Prasad tapped on another folder labeled *NDEs*. "Now look at these."

Edward flipped through the images, his brow furrowing. "They all show activity in the TPO junction," he said.

"And none of these patients suffered brain trauma," Prasad added, pointing to the screen. "They died from heart attacks, lung failure, breast cancer—you get the idea."

"But no brain injury," Edward confirmed.

"Exactly," Prasad said, writing on the board:

ACTIVE TPO JUNCTION = NDE

"I believe that without an active, functioning TPO junction, the spirit is unable to navigate to the next dimension," Prasad declared, his voice steady with conviction.

"Which would explain why none of the patients with an inactive TPO junction reported having an NDE," Edward mused, piecing the information together.

"Precisely."

Edward's curiosity deepened. "What do you think happens to them?"

Prasad's expression grew somber as he exhaled audibly. "Without the ability to navigate to the next dimension, I believe their spirits are left to roam aimlessly in this one for eternity," he said, turning back to the board. He wrote alongside his previous notes:

INACTIVE TPO JUNCTION = NO NDE = D1
ACTIVE TPO JUNCTION = NDE = Dx-D1
WHERE: D1 = THIS DIMENSION, Dx = ALL DIMENSIONS

"If I'm right, and if I can find a way to repair the TPO junction prior to death, just imagine the countless souls we could guide to the next dimension—how many families could be reunited," Prasad said, his voice swelling with a fervor that bordered on zeal. "It would be a service to humanity that surpasses anything anyone has ever accomplished before."

Prasad's eyes remained fixed on Edward, who stood in a contemplative silence, a perplexed expression flickering across his face. It was a look that blended confusion with incredulity, as if he were wrestling with the challenge of reconciling Prasad's grand vision with the rigid boundaries of reason and science. The weight of Prasad's words hung in the air between them, charged with implications that seemed to stretch the limits of logic Edward had always clung to so dearly.

"I understand this is a lot to process," Prasad continued, his tone softening as he stepped closer, trying to bridge the widening gap between them. "But I need your help, Edward. I can't do this alone."

Chapter 10

IT'S STILL NOT ADDING UP, Edward thought, his eyes narrowing as he fixed his gaze on Prasad, his look sharp and unwavering. The hypothesis was undoubtedly intriguing, with implications that could shake the very foundations of their field and draw unprecedented attention to the already prestigious university. Yet, the IRB's refusal to approve it gnawed at him, a loose thread in an otherwise compelling narrative.

He leaned forward, his voice measured but carrying an undercurrent of skepticism. "I'm willing to set aside my reservations and give you the benefit of the doubt," he began, each word deliberate, "but I need to understand why the IRB didn't approve your study."

The question hung in the air between them, heavy and charged, as Edward's mind raced through the possibilities. He knew the stakes were high, and he wasn't one to be swayed by speculation alone. The IRB's decision was a red flag that demanded an explanation, something concrete that could bridge the gap between the theory and the institution's refusal to approve it.

"They said there was no value in it; claimed it was too risky," Prasad replied, shifting uncomfortably in his seat.

"Too risky for who?" Edward pressed, his skepticism deepening.

"It wasn't entirely clear to me," Prasad shrugged, a trace of frustration flickering across his face. "The scientists were on board, but the other two members voted against it, and now I'm officially on Reverend Welton's shit list."

He paused, crossing his arms, his expression hardening into a subtle scowl. "She really is something else with that holier-than-thou facade, wouldn't you agree? She's so, so—"

"Pompulent?" Edward interjected.

"Come again?" Prasad asked, raising an eyebrow.

"Pompulent—it's the bastard child of King Pompous and Queen Opulent."

"That's not a word," Prasad replied, shaking his head with a bemused smile.

"It is, as far as I'm concerned," Edward said, a hint of amusement tugging at his lips. "Anyway, I've had enough of the IRB's bullshit. I'm doing this with or without their approval."

Edward's brow furrowed in a mix of confusion and concern as he tried to process Prasad's determination. Moving forward without IRB approval would be a professional suicide. *This must really mean something to him,* Edward thought, his mind racing to understand the gravity of the situation. "Why would you do this?" he asked, his voice tinged with uncertainty. "You know you can't use any data collected from an unapproved study."

"It doesn't matter," Prasad replied, his tone resolute.

"Of course it matters," Edward shot back, incredulous.

"Like I said, this is too important. I wasn't placed on this earth to satisfy the IRB. And neither were you," Prasad said, his words ringing with unwavering conviction.

"That's interesting and all, but I'm going to need more than that," Edward said, his voice steady but probing.

As a psychiatrist, Edward had honed the skill of reading people—of seeing through their masks to the truths they kept hidden. His gift for getting a good read on people, for understanding their fears, motivations, strengths, and weaknesses, had set him apart from his colleagues, and Prasad knew it. Normally, Edward kept this skill understated, letting his patients' behavior, language, and demeanor reveal their true selves over time. But Prasad's behavior was far from typical, and Edward knew it required closer scrutiny.

Leaning in toward Prasad, his gaze sharpened, Edward asked, "May I?"

"By all means," Prasad replied, holding his posture steady. "I have nothing to hide."

Edward leaned in further, his body mirroring his intense focus. His eyes scanned Prasad with meticulous attention, moving from left to right, up and down, as if he were deciphering a complex puzzle.

His gaze finally landed on a delicate gold necklace adorning Prasad's neck. The pendant, an intricately designed goddess, dangled gracefully, catching the light and drawing Edward's attention like a magnet. "Is that new?" Edward asked, pointing to the necklace.

Prasad glanced down, bringing his chin to his chest. "Oh, this?" he replied, gripping the pendant gently. "No, far from it—it's been in the family a very long time."

Edward's mind lingered on the pendant for a moment before returning to the matter at hand. There was just one more criterion to assess—his overall gut feeling. *Something's not right,* he thought, the weight of his uncertainty settling heavily on his shoulders. *Why would he risk everything over this?*

He leaned back in his chair. "OK, I'm done," he said, his voice measured.

"Well?" Prasad prompted, a note of tension underlying his words. "What do you think?"

Edward exhaled slowly, crossing his arms tightly against his chest. "You want my help, right?"

"Indeed, I do," Prasad nodded, his expression earnest.

"Then you need to explain your real motivation for doing this—no bullshit," Edward replied, his tone firm, eyes locked onto Prasad's. "Look, nothing about my read on you is raising any flags—except for my gut feeling," he continued. "So, if you want my help, you'll have to open up and tell me why you're willing to lose your job over this—there's no way around it."

He watched as Prasad considered his request, the silence in the room thickening as the weight of the question settled between them. Finally, Prasad nodded, the resolve in his expression softening. "OK," he said quietly. "OK."

"I'm all ears," Edward said, leaning back in his chair, his posture signaling readiness. "Are you familiar with spontaneous past life memories?"

"Of course I am—it's a widely studied phenomenon in parapsychology," Edward replied, his brow furrowing slightly. "Not my area of expertise, but I'm versed on the subject."

"So then, I take it you're familiar with the research on the reincarnation of Neelima Takkella?" Prasad asked, his tone careful.

Edward nodded slowly. "I'm familiar—it's a fascinating case study," he said, his mind sifting through the details he knew well. He recalled the story of a four year old girl named Prashanthi Karthik, born in the small village of Guntur in India in 1974. The girl had remained silent until the age of four when she suddenly claimed to be the reincarnation of a woman named Neelima Takkella—a woman who had died in a nearby town a year before Prashanthi's birth. Remarkably, Prashanthi spoke in a dialect different from that of her village and possessed the vocabulary of an adult woman. At first, her parents dismissed her claims, but Prashanthi persisted, recounting vivid memories of Neelima's life and even describing the details of the cesarean section that had taken Neelima's life just days after giving birth. Despite their initial skepticism, her parents eventually relented and took Prashanthi to the town where Neelima had lived, where she led them directly to her former husband's home, describing landmarks along the way with uncanny accuracy.

"Prashanthi knew details of Neelima's life with her husband that only Neelima and her husband could have known," Prasad said, his voice steady as he recounted the story.

Edward nodded again, remembering the more specific details of the case. He recalled how Prashanthi had recognized Neelima's brother-in-law, accurately identifying him despite his attempt to deceive her by pretending to be Ravi, Neelima's husband. Once inside the house, Prashanthi had led her parents to a hidden cache of money, precisely where she claimed to have left it in her past life as Neelima—an astonishing one hundred seventy-two rupees buried under the floorboards in a storage closet.

"I'm aware," Edward said. "Among many of the examples cited, it's said that Prashanthi asked Ravi if he kept the promise he made to Neelima on her deathbed—to never remarry."

"He remarried two years after Neelima's death," Prasad said, his voice tinged with the weight of old wounds.

Edward studied Prasad intently. "The case has been researched extensively—again, very fascinating, but where are you going with this?"

"Getting there," Prasad replied, a hint of hesitation in his voice. "The attention and research on Prashanthi continued throughout her life. Considering herself a widow, Prashanthi never married, in accordance with Hindu custom. But no one ever talks about what became of Neelima's husband, Ravi..."

He paused, his words trailing off as he gathered the strength to continue.

"My brother."

Edward's eyes widened, his breath catching in his throat as the revelation settled in. He blinked, trying to process the information. He and Prasad had shared countless conversations, countless moments of laughter and camaraderie over the years, and yet this was a part of Prasad's life he had never known.

"Ravi? You named your son after him," Edward said, his voice barely above a whisper, the realization dawning on him.

The light in Prasad's eyes dimmed, and lines of sorrow etched themselves deeply into his face. The grief that had long haunted him was now laid bare, an open wound that had never fully healed.

"I'm sorry for your loss," Edward said softly, his words sincere as he read the pain in Prasad's expression. "What happened to him?"

"When Neelima came back, it shook Ravi to his core. He never fully recovered from losing her. And he couldn't live knowing that Neelima knew he broke his promise to her," Prasad said, his voice breaking under the weight of his emotions. "It was more than my poor brother could handle—so he took his life in hopes of reuniting with Neelima in the afterlife."

Edward watched as Prasad's gaze grew distant, his eyes clouded with the memories of a past that still haunted him. The pain in his voice, the sorrow etched into his features, revealed the depth of his loss. And in that moment, Edward understood. Prasad's motives, the source of his passion, and his relentless pursuit of the afterlife study—it all made sense now.

Chapter 11

NEELIMA MYSTERIOUSLY RESURFACED through Prashanthi in 1981, when Prasad was just ten years old. Like most, he met the news with skepticism. He had no memory of Neelima—no reason to believe or disbelieve Prashanthi's claims. But when the seven-year-old Prashanthi, with a seriousness beyond her years, mentioned that she used to change his diapers and then described, with uncanny accuracy, the exact shape and location of his birthmark—a heart-shaped port wine stain on his upper thigh—Prasad's doubts began to crumble. The detail was too intimate, too precise, to be a mere coincidence. The seed of belief, once dormant, began to take root, leaving Prasad to grapple with the unsettling possibility that the past he thought was lost had found its way back through the eyes of a child.

"Having her back was nice at first," Prasad said, his voice tinged with nostalgia and a bittersweet smile. As a child, he found it thrilling, reveling in the newfound attention that came with being connected to Neelima. He eagerly shared the story with his classmates, embracing the popularity that followed. The unique and mysterious circumstances of Neelima's return through Prashanthi captivated the nation's attention, and soon, the tale spread throughout India like wildfire. The intrigue grew so immense that even the Prime Minister took notice, visiting their family and launching a commission to investigate Prashanthi's claim.

But the initial excitement of fame quickly soured. The weight of public scrutiny began to take its toll, and the once-innocent thrill was replaced by a heavy sense of dread. The story that had once brought Prashanthi into the spotlight turned darker when tragedy struck—Ravi, unable to bear the complexities and pressures that came with the situation, took his own life. A mother lost her son, a wife lost her husband, children lost their father, and Prashanthi was left to shoulder an unbearable burden of guilt.

The fame that had once brought her into the limelight now cast her into the shadows. For forty years, she lived in solitude, haunted by her regrets and the ghost of a life that might have been. The vibrant girl who had once captivated the nation faded into obscurity, her life marked by a tragedy too profound to overcome. And then, as mysteriously as Neelima had reappeared, Prashanthi's own life came to an untimely and unexplained end, leaving behind questions that would never be answered and a legacy steeped in sorrow.

"If Neelima had not come back, Ravi would never have cut his life short," Prasad said, his voice heavy with grief. "He had so much to live for."

"I'm so sorry," Edward responded softly.

"After my brother died, Prashanthi opened up about what she experienced in the afterlife. She described it much like the testimonies we've collected—about going to a heavenly realm," Prasad continued. "But there was one key difference."

"What was that?" Edward asked, leaning in, intrigued.

"Prashanthi said that she—Neelima—was determined, insistent even, on returning to Earth at all costs to reunite with Ravi," Prasad explained. "There were no feelings of peace like the others described—it was pure turmoil."

"Turmoil?" Edward repeated, his brow furrowing. "How so?"

"She said she pleaded to come back, to be reincarnated, so she could reunite with Ravi and her newborn son... And so she was. But she lived her entire life alone, regretting her selfishness," Prasad said, his voice tinged with sorrow.

"Let me get this straight," Edward said slowly, processing the revelation. "She believed she willed herself into being reincarnated?"

"She was certain she influenced it, at the very least," Prasad replied. "And when the commission got wind of her claim, they were outraged."

"What did they say?"

"They ultimately concluded that the evidence surrounding Prashanthi's reincarnation claim was insufficient," Prasad said, a hint of bitterness creeping into his voice. "My mother always believed it was a cover-up."

"Why would they do that?" Edward asked, his tone skeptical.

"I suspect for the same reason Reverend Kay voted against my proposal," Prasad shrugged. "To suppress the truth. To quash the idea that someone can influence what happens to them in the afterlife."

He paused, letting his words sink in.

"Did you know that never in history has a reincarnation claim been officially verified?" Prasad asked.

"No, I didn't," Edward admitted, the gravity of the statement hanging in the air.

"There's no other explanation for how Prashanthi knew what she knew, recognized the people she recognized, if she wasn't the reincarnation of Neelima's spirit. When the commission dismissed the claim, we wanted answers. It's why I pursued neuroscience," Prasad said. "I wanted the truth. And now, I believe I'm closer than ever to understanding the workings of the afterlife."

Edward exhaled deeply, weighing Prasad's words. "I get it. When someone loses a loved one under tragic circumstances, it's natural to want answers," he said. "But do you really believe Reverend Kay voted against your proposal as part of some cover-up?"

"Considering how she stormed into my office after the IRB meeting, I'm afraid so," Prasad replied, his tone somber. "She must believe I'm on to something she's trying to hide."

The room grew tense as silence filled the space, the only sound the faint ticking of the clock on the wall. Edward's skeptical gaze remained fixed on Prasad, his mind wrestling with the implications of what he'd just heard. Prasad could sense Edward was willing to hear more, but he could almost see the doubt gnawing at his thoughts, urging him to dismiss what sounded like the beginnings of a conspiracy theory.

"Let me show you something," Prasad said, breaking the silence. He stepped up to the video monitor mounted on the wall. "What stands out to you?" he asked, pointing to a brain scan displayed on the screen.

Edward's eyes moved across the image, taking in the details. He pointed to a vividly lit area in the scan. "There's activity in the TPO junction, but it's much higher than any of the other images I've seen," he said, his voice tinged with surprise. "A much, much higher level of activity—it's not even in the same ballpark," he added, staring at the bright red and yellow areas at the back of the brain.

"That's right," Prasad confirmed. "Does anything else stand out?"

Edward leaned in closer, scrutinizing the image. "Was this image taken when the patient was deceased?" he asked, his brow furrowing further.

"Forty-one minutes after the heart stopped," Prasad replied.

Edward pointed to a bright yellow cluster near the front of the brain scan. "If that's the case, I wouldn't expect to see any activity in the prefrontal cortex."

"It's unusual, to say the least," Prasad agreed.

Edward turned to him, his expression a mix of curiosity and concern. "What does this mean?" he asked.

"I've presented you with two scenarios so far—one where there's no activity in the TPO junction, and one where there is," Prasad said, stepping toward the whiteboard. "But I assert there's a third scenario—one where there's hyperactivity in the TPO junction. The area is overstimulated, as I believe was the case with Neelima in her final moments."

Prasad picked up a dry-erase marker and wrote on the board:

$$ACTIVE\ TPO\ JUNCTION = NO\ NDE = D1$$
$$INACTIVE\ TPO\ JUNCTION = NDE = Dx\text{-}D1$$
$$HYPER\text{-}ACTIVE\ TPO\ JUNCTION = NDE = Dx$$
$$WHERE\ D1 = THIS\ DIMENSION,\ Dx = ALL\ DIMENSIONS$$

He stepped back, watching as Edward processed the information. As the realization sank in, Edward's gaze became distant, his mind racing to comprehend the implications. "Holy crap," he muttered, staring at the board in astonishment.

"What do you think?" Prasad asked, his tone almost cautious.

"I think... Reverend Kay should be the least of your worries if this gets out," Edward replied, his voice barely concealing the magnitude of the revelation.

Chapter 12

UNBLINKING AND INTENSE, Edward's intense gaze locked onto the whiteboard as if he could decipher the secrets of the universe within the lines and diagrams before him. His brow furrowed deeper, each wrinkle on his forehead a testament to the mental effort he was expending to challenge the validity of Prasad's theory. On the surface, the logic appeared sound, but nagging doubts lingered, urging him to probe further.

"The hyper-aroused TPO junction triggers activity in the prefrontal cortex—that's why the image shows activity in both parts of the brain," Edward said, his voice filled with growing intrigue as he examined the brain scan more closely.

Prasad nodded in agreement, a faint, knowing smile playing at the corners of his mouth, as if he anticipated Edward's next realization.

Edward's eyes widened slightly as the pieces began to fall into place. "Which means when the TPO junction—the homing device—and the prefrontal cortex—the part of the brain responsible for decision-making—are both active in the afterlife, the spirit retains its decision-making abilities," he continued, his voice tinged with astonishment at the implications.

"Exactly. It's a mind hack in the most literal sense," Prasad replied, his excitement evident. "It's what I believe gave Neelima the ability to return, to be reincarnated. I think both the TPO junction and prefrontal cortex were active, allowing her decision-making ability to remain functional even in the afterlife."

Decision-making in the afterlife? It's unheard of, Edward thought, grappling with the enormity of the concept. "But what causes the TPO junction to become hyperactive, and why haven't we encountered this before?"

"I'll address the second part of your question first... Because it's uncommon, and frankly, we haven't been looking for it."

"Fair enough, but what about the first part?" Edward pressed.

"In stressful situations, beta waves become faster and more intense, indicating heightened mental activity and increased vigilance," Prasad explained, his tone measured.

"Yes, that's well-known."

"It's also well-known that prolonged or excessive beta wave activity can lead to restlessness, over-thinking, and difficulty relaxing or sleeping."

Edward nodded, his curiosity piqued. "Go on."

"Now imagine you're in Neelima's situation. After years of trying, she finally becomes pregnant. She's over the moon, happily married," Prasad continued, his voice growing somber. "Then, after giving birth, she's told she has only days to live. Imagine the level of beta wave activity she must have generated, starting from the moment she received that devastating news, continuing through the hours after she died, while her brain was still functioning."

He paused, letting the gravity of the situation sink in.

"This is what I believe caused Neelima's TPO junction to become hyperactive."

Edward winced at the thought of the young mother and the mental anguish she must have endured until the very end. "It's a heartbreaking and fascinating theory, but do you have any data to support your assertion?"

"I just told you the case was rare," Prasad responded, his voice tinged with frustration. "The data will come from the study!"

Edward's eyes widened. "Alright! But if you want my help, let me think this through," he said, his tone calming the tension.

"You're right—I'm sorry," Prasad replied, taking a deep breath and forcing a smile. "Take your time."

Edward began pacing the length of the room, his mind racing through the possibilities. *When a specific area of the brain becomes active during a thought process, that activity can propagate to other areas of the brain through neural pathways, allowing for the transfer of information between different regions.*

Communication from the TPO junction could easily modulate prefrontal cortex activity and influence cognitive processes within that region. He stopped abruptly and turned to Prasad.

"Ready when you are," Prasad said, looking impatient.

Edward resumed pacing. *The brain is highly interconnected, operating through complex networks,* he thought. *It also makes sense, at least in theory, that a person who dies suddenly—say, from an accident or heart attack—wouldn't be lucid enough to build up a hyperactive level of activity in the TPO junction prior to death, particularly if they failed to regain consciousness beforehand. But someone who dies from a terminal illness—from cancer or some other prolonged condition, even old age—might have time to process their impending death.*

He stopped in his tracks, a spark of brilliance lighting up his eyes. "Let me step in here," Edward said, walking to the whiteboard. "If we think of the brain as a computer, we have to assume there's a maximum amount of processing associated with particular cognitive functions, or areas of the brain, at any given time," he said. "Pass me the dry-erase marker."

Prasad handed him the marker and stepped back, curious.

"What is the frequency range of a beta brainwave?" Edward asked.

"Approximately 12 to 30 Hz, cycles per second," Prasad replied.

Edward wrote on the board:

$$\beta \; Frequency = 12 - 30 \, Hz$$

"In theory, a high level of brain activity in a person with a prolonged illness could be processed over time—six months, for example. But a lucid person processing the same level of activity over a shorter period—six days, for instance—could cause the brain to go into overdrive."

He paused, examining the writing on the board.

"So, in theory, if we can pinpoint the frequency and duration required to send the TPO junction into a state of hyperactivity at the time of death..." He wrote on the board:

Hyper-Active TPO Junction = β Frequency/Time

"And if we can manipulate brain activity to match the level required to send it into a hyperactive state at the time of death..." His eyes widened as the weight of the realization settled in. "We could give the spirit the ability to decide where to navigate in the afterlife."

"Sounds like I've managed to pique your interest," Prasad said, a smile breaking across his face.

"The idea of free will in the afterlife? The possibility of controlling one's own eternal destiny? The chance to scientifically test reincarnation claims?" Edward said, his voice filled with awe. "I couldn't hide my interest if I tried."

"There's a lot to explore," Prasad replied. "But first things first—it's just you and me for now, and this theory hinges on the three points I've outlined," he said, pointing at the whiteboard:

$$\textbf{INACTIVE TPO JUNCTION} \rightarrow \textbf{NO NDE} = D_1$$
$$\textbf{ACTIVE TPO JUNCTION} \rightarrow \textbf{NDE} = D_x - D_1$$
$$\textbf{HYPER-ACTIVE TPO JUNCTION} \rightarrow \textbf{NDE} = D_x$$
$$\textbf{WHERE } D_1 = \textbf{THIS DIMENSION and } D_x = \textbf{ALL OTHERS}$$

Edward's excitement dimmed as he dropped his head. "How do you expect me to study spirits in another dimension?" he asked, the challenge weighing on him.

"I don't," Prasad replied, much to Edward's relief.

"I expect you to study spirits in this dimension."

"How? There's no way," Edward said, skepticism creeping into his voice.

"Perhaps not definitively, but what makes this any different from the NDE study?" Prasad countered.

He has a point, Edward thought, shaking his head. "What do you want me to do?"

"I need you to conduct interviews while I work on a solution for activating the TPO junction," Prasad replied, his eyes gleaming with hope.

"Interviews with who?" Edward asked, his curiosity tinged with caution.

Prasad picked up a thin yellow manila folder from his desk and handed it to Edward.

"What's this?"

"It's a starting point—the contact information for the families of local patients who died with no activity in the TPO junction," Prasad explained. "I want you to interview the families to see if they've experienced any paranormal activity since their loved one's death."

"You want me to do what?" Edward asked, crossing his arms, incredulous.

"I'd like you to interview the families—"

"No, I heard you," Edward interrupted. "But why? What insight could that possibly—"

He stopped mid-sentence, his eyes darting around as he pieced together the implications.

"Do you want to answer your question, or should I?" Prasad asked, a knowing smile on his face.

"You're looking for testimony that supports your theory that the spirits of patients who had no activity in the TPO junction are still here, in this dimension."

"BINGO!" Prasad exclaimed, clapping his hands together in a resounding slap. "This will get us closer to proving that the TPO junction is the key to the afterlife."

"Alright, I'm in," Edward said, tucking the folder under his arm. "Especially if it gets you to stop with the clapping."

"Not a chance," Prasad replied with a grin. Edward shook his head, heading toward the door.

"Wait!" Prasad called after him.

Edward turned, eyebrow raised. "Yes?"

"What's your plan for conducting these interviews? You know, given that we don't have IRB approval?"

"You've got enough to think about," Edward replied. "Work on a solution for activating the TPO junction and leave the interviews to me."

Chapter 13

He stood outside the quaint red brick home, the Chicago cold biting at his cheeks as he mulled over how to conduct the interview—if it could even be called that. The wind, sharp and unforgiving, seemed to cut through his coat, chilling him to the bone as his thoughts swirled like the snowflakes drifting aimlessly around him. Each flake, a fragment of a plan, dissolved as quickly as it formed, leaving him with a sense of unease.

He had anticipated more time—time to think, to plan, to rehearse how he would carefully weave Prasad's probing questions into the comforting guise of grief counseling. But Mrs. Jones had agreed to see him immediately, catching him off guard and leaving him with little more than his instincts to guide him. Now, as he approached the door, the weight of anticipation settled over him like a heavy, invisible coat, pressing down on his shoulders, making each step feel deliberate and measured.

The red bricks of the house, dusted with a light layer of snow, stood in stark contrast to the gray sky above. The house itself was unassuming, yet as he reached for the doorbell, it felt as though he were about to cross a threshold into something far more significant than the modest exterior suggested. The door, dark wood with a brass knocker that had seen better days, loomed in front of him, a silent gatekeeper to the unknown.

His finger hovered over the button for just a moment before he pressed it, the soft chime of the bell echoing inside. *Too late to turn back now,* he thought, steeling himself for whatever awaited on the other side.

The door creaked open.

"May I help you?" A woman with curly silver hair stood in the doorway, her expression one of cautious curiosity.

"Hello, Mrs. Jones? I'm Dr. Clark," he said, his voice slightly muffled through the screen door.

"Come in, Dr. Clark," she replied, her voice quivering as she pushed the door open wider.

"Thank you for seeing me," he said, stepping inside, notebook in hand. As he crossed the threshold, he was greeted by a wave of musty air that seemed to hang in the atmosphere like a heavy curtain. The scent was familiar—he had encountered it in homes like this before, where time seemed to have stopped, leaving behind the distinct odor of age. He knew it wasn't just about getting old; the human body undergoes changes at every stage of life, each with its own scent. *But no one ever complains about the smell of a newborn baby*, he thought wryly.

"Take a seat wherever you'd like," Mrs. Jones offered, gesturing to the living room.

He stepped further in, the old wooden floors creaking beneath his feet, and lowered himself onto a worn-out couch covered in crackling plastic. "Thank you," he said as he sat, the couch groaning under his weight.

"I didn't know the hospital offered house visits," Mrs. Jones said, settling into a chair across from him.

"Yes, well, grieving is a difficult process. We want to ensure you're managing as well as you can under the circumstances," Edward replied, choosing his words carefully.

"Can I get you some water?" she offered, her hands fluttering nervously in her lap.

"No, I'm fine. Thank you," he replied, offering a gentle smile. "Please, sit—tell me how you're doing."

She lowered herself into a chair across from him, her movements slow and deliberate. "I'm fine," she said, her voice soft but steady.

Edward gazed at her through the dust particles floating in the dim light that filtered through the old curtains. "Are you getting out of the house and engaging in your normal activities and hobbies?"

Mrs. Jones tilted her head slightly, her eyes narrowing as she considered his question. "Funny you ask about getting out of the house."

"Oh?" he said, raising his brows, intrigued by the unexpected response. It was a standard question, but something in her tone suggested there was more beneath the surface.

"It's strange, but I don't feel like he's gone."

"That's quite normal," Edward replied, leaning forward slightly. "When we form strong emotional bonds with someone, their presence can remain alive in our hearts and minds."

"I know, but that isn't what I mean." She paused, taking a sip of water. "After being married so long—fifty-two years this November—I developed a sense of knowing when he wasn't home," she explained, her voice tinged with nostalgia.

"Please, elaborate," Edward encouraged.

"You know, he'd run to the corner store, go out and fetch the mail, work out back in the shed... He didn't always announce when he was leaving or going outside; he didn't need to. I could just sense when he wasn't in the house," she said, her eyes flicking around the room as if expecting to catch a glimpse of him. "The house just felt—"

"Empty?" Edward offered, his voice gentle.

"Exactly," she replied, nodding slowly. "Empty."

"I've been married for almost twenty years," Edward said, trying to connect with her on a personal level. "I think I know what you mean."

"But I never get that sense anymore—that sense that he isn't in the house," she said, her voice growing quieter. "Not that I lost it... It's just I feel like he never left, like he's always here... With me."

Edward hesitated, unsure how to proceed. "I know it's hard, but the first step in processing grief is accepting the reality of loss," he said, his words feeling inadequate.

"Reality of the loss? I've accepted the reality of the loss," she said, shaking her head firmly. "My husband had terminal brain cancer; he suffered for a very long time, and he lived much, much longer than doctors ever expected. He was ready to pass, and I was ready to let him go."

"But have you really?" Edward asked, his brow furrowing in concern. "Have you really accepted the reality of the loss, I mean?"

"The doctors and medical staff prepared us, and we had a long time—more time than we imagined—to process, make peace with it, make arrangements and whatnot," she said, her voice steady but tinged with lingering sorrow. "He was in so much pain. Every day he lived only prolonged his suffering."

Edward looked into her eyes, trying to read the emotions hidden there. She spoke as if she had accepted her husband's death, but the pain in her eyes suggested otherwise.

"It's been six months since he passed, is that right?" he asked, flipping through his notebook for confirmation.

There was silence. He looked up to find Mrs. Jones staring off into the distance, lost in thought.

"Mrs. Jones?" he prompted gently.

She jolted slightly, as if suddenly remembering she wasn't alone. "I'm sorry. What was the question?"

Edward set his notebook aside and leaned back in his seat, trying a different approach. "What's on your mind, Mrs. Jones?"

"Do you think it's possible that my husband's spirit is still here?" she asked, her voice tinged with both curiosity and hesitation.

Edward's eyes widened slightly. Thoroughly unprepared for the question, he cleared his throat. "Well, finding an enduring connection with your loved one while embarking on a new life is an important part of the grieving process," he said, attempting to steer the conversation back to familiar ground.

"You know that's not what I mean," she said, her tone growing firmer. "What I mean is, do you think it's possible that his spirit is still here? In the house?"

Edward shifted uncomfortably in his seat, the plastic covering clinging to his skin like a barrier between him and the worn cushions beneath. "I don't know," he admitted, clearly out of his comfort zone. "That's not exactly my field of expertise."

She gazed at him with squinted eyes, as if measuring his response. "May I show you something, Dr. Clark?" she asked.

"Yes, of course," he replied, curious about what she was about to reveal.

Mrs. Jones turned to a small wooden cabinet beside the couch and opened the top drawer. "This will just take a moment," she said, rummaging through the contents. "Here it is! Look here. Tell me what you see," she said, handing him a photograph.

Edward examined the color photo, which depicted a younger Mr. and Mrs. Jones, likely in their early forties, standing with two children.

"It looks like a family vacation photo," he said, raising his brow. "Interesting setting."

She chuckled softly. "Growing up, my children loved Halloween almost as much as they loved Christmas."

"Are they yours?" Edward asked.

"Yes, they were twelve and fourteen back then," she replied, her voice tinged with fondness. "We visited Boston on vacation, and our boys convinced us to take them on one of those guided cemetery tours."

"I'm not sure I would have agreed to that," Edward said, a faint smile tugging at his lips.

"The kids showed us a brochure they picked up at our hotel—in the photos, the tour guides were all dressed up in old-timey costumes. My husband and I didn't believe in ghosts, spirits, whatever you want to call them, but it looked like it could be fun, so we figured, why not?"

"That's nice," he said, handing the photo back to her.

"Wait!" she exclaimed. "Take a closer look."

Oh, I get it, Edward thought. *She must be trying to tell me she captured a photo of a ghost. He brought the photo closer to his face.* "I'll be honest, Mrs. Jones, I don't know what I'm look—"

He froze.

His eyes darted across the photo, quickly noticing the anomalies he had overlooked before. Two glowing green figures with child-like silhouettes hovered in the background over Mrs. Jones's shoulder. He blinked, doubting what he was seeing. *Probably just a lighting issue*, he thought, but the more he stared, the more he noticed—orbs of different sizes surrounding the family, some white, some yellow, all emitting a warm, ethereal glow.

He handed the photo back to Mrs. Jones, his mind grappling with the image that defied logical explanation.

"Did you spot the unusual fellow that smiled for the camera?" she asked, her voice a mix of curiosity and anticipation.

"The unusual fellow?" Edward repeated, his brow furrowing in confusion. "Are you referring to Mr. Jones?"

"No, of course not," she said, shaking her head. "Go ahead—have another look."

With a sigh, Edward brought the photo back to his face.

His heart skipped a beat. There, in the moonlit background, was a ghostly figure—a fog-like presence with the distinct shape of a man. The apparition floated, ethereal and unsettling, with a thin frame and shoulder-length swirly hair that seemed to dance in an unseen breeze. The figure's features were clearly defined, with hollow eyes that appeared to peer into his very soul, their depths filled with an eerie emptiness. The figure's gaunt cheeks hinted at a life drained of vitality, and yet it stood among the living, perfectly positioned between the Joneses' children, exuding a chilling self-awareness that seemed to acknowledge its own demise. Most unsettling of all was the haunting smile stretched across its lips, too wide, too knowing—a visceral reminder of the fragile boundary between life and death.

Edward placed the photo on the coffee table, his hands trembling slightly as he retreated into his seat. An unexplainable heaviness settled upon him, bridging the gap between disbelief and a newfound sense of uncertainty.

"You saw him, didn't you?" Mrs. Jones asked softly.

Edward nodded slowly, his mind reeling.

"Would you like some water, Dr. Clark?" she asked again, her voice gentle but concerned.

"No, thank you," Edward replied, clearing his throat, his voice betraying his unease.

"Are you sure?" she pressed, her concern deepening.

"Yes—why do you ask?" he inquired, his voice tinged with confusion.

"Because—"

She hesitated, searching for the right words.

"Well, there's really no other way to put this, now is there? You look like you've just seen a ghost."

Chapter 14

THE GLOBAL ASSEMBLY OF RELIGIOUS Leaders operates as a specialized subset of the United League of Nations, with the mission to promote spiritual values, peace, and harmony worldwide. This influential organization meets monthly and is composed of respected religious and spiritual leaders from member states, representing both traditional religions and indigenous traditions. An emergency meeting was convened at the urgent request of the United States Director General, Reverend Kay Welton.

Amidst the vast emptiness of the video conference room, Reverend Welton sat alone, her fingers drumming impatiently on the table as she awaited the start of the meeting. *Let's get on with this already,* she thought, her gaze fixed on the large blue video screen mounted on the ceiling above the center of the table. The screen flickered to life, transforming into a portal to a world of remote connections. The faces of over thirty religious leaders, representing Buddhist, Christian, Hindu, Jain, Jewish, Muslim, Orthodox, Sikh, and various indigenous traditions—men and women adorned in diverse cultural attire—appeared on the screen.

A man, adorned in a majestic headdress that exuded authority and reverence, stood from his seat. "The meeting is called to order," he announced in a deep, commanding voice. "Thank you all for attending on such short notice. We have just one order of business today. Director General Reverend Welton, the floor is yours."

"Thank you, Chief President Grand," she replied, her tone steady. "I come before you today with a matter that concerns all religions and indigenous traditions," she began, her voice firm. "As you know, I am a member of the University of Chicago's Institutional Review Board. My job is to review research studies to ensure they comply with applicable regulations, meet ethical standards, follow institutional policies, and protect research participants," she explained, her eyes scanning the faces displayed on the screen.

The assembly members nodded in acknowledgment.

"It is not my usual practice to bring IRB matters before this Assembly, but I feel it is my God-given duty to make you aware of this issue," she continued, her voice taking on a grave tone.

With a swift click of her mouse, she shared her screen, revealing an image for all to see—a headshot of a bushy-haired man with a medium-dark complexion, wearing black-framed glasses. "While conducting an international study on near-death experiences, renowned Clinical Professor and Neuroscientist Dr. Prasad Vedurmudi, shown here, believes he has stumbled upon a discovery that could crack the very foundation on which all religions are based."

"And what is that?" Chief President Grand asked, his brow furrowing.

Speaking deliberately, emphasizing each word, she said, "That man can play God."

A hush fell over the virtual room, an unsettling silence that hung in the air. "Go on," Chief President Grand urged.

"He asserts that a specific part of the brain, the TPO junction, is the precise location of what he describes as the human equivalent of a homing device," she explained. "He also claims that the synaptic connections within the TPO junction are responsible for transporting spirits to the next dimension."

She paused, letting the gravity of her words settle in the room. As she scanned the assembly's faces, she saw a mixture of intrigue and growing discomfort reflected back at her—furrowed brows, crossed arms, and silent stares.

"He claims that if the TPO junction is not functional, the spirit cannot move to the next dimension. He also believes he can repair the TPO junction, enabling spirits to transition," she continued.

A wave of disbelief rippled through the assembly. The Jewish Rabbi was the first to break the silence. "That's preposterous—the man sounds like a lunatic."

"Be that as it may," Reverend Welton replied, her voice steady, "I have worked with him for years. He wouldn't have brought this to the board for approval if he didn't believe he could do it." She leaned forward, her tone becoming more urgent. "We must assume he can do it." The word *must* hung heavily in the air, each syllable deliberately stretched to emphasize its importance.

"Did the board approve the proposal?" Chief President Grand asked, his voice measured.

"No. But I could see it in his eyes—he is personally invested in this. I highly suspect he will proceed with the study, with or without the IRB's approval. In fact, I'm certain of it," she said, her gaze fixed on the image of Dr. Prasad Vedurmudi still displayed on the screen.

The atmosphere in the room grew tenser, the weight of the issue pressing down on the assembly. Discontent spread like a dark cloud, shadowing the faces of the gathered leaders.

"I have so many concerns with this, I don't know where to begin," the Lutheran Archbishop said, his voice edged with anxiety. "Man stepping in for the Creator?"

"More like man stepping in to fix the Creator's mistake," the Senior Monk countered.

"*The creator makes no mistakes!*" the Archbishop thundered, slamming his hands down on the table, the force of the impact reverberating through the room and causing Reverend Welton to flinch even from across the globe.

"That is precisely my point," the Senior Monk replied, his tone unruffled.

"The consequences could be disastrous," the Chief Rabbi interjected.

"If this gets out, what's to prevent hell-bound souls from flooding the earth?"

Murmurs of dissent and exasperated sighs filled the virtual gathering, a cacophony of unease and frustration.

"The Creator did not intend for man to wield that kind of control," the Cardinal stated firmly.

"But if we handle this responsibly, we could save souls bound for heaven that would otherwise be stranded on earth," the Elder suggested, his voice filled with quiet conviction.

"No, absolutely not. It's not in the Creator's plan," the Archbishop retorted.

"And who are you to claim you know the Creator's plan?" the Elder shot back, his brow furrowing with challenge.

"This man is meddling with forces he cannot begin to understand, let alone control!" the Archbishop responded, his fury palpable. "It would be catastrophic for us all!"

"That's ENOUGH!" Chief President Grand's voice boomed, silencing the discord. "Let us remember, we were assembled to safeguard against such catastrophes." He took a deep breath, his tone calming. "But as it stands, we will put this to a vote, as our bylaws dictate."

Reverend Welton cleared her throat. "Before we proceed with the vote, I believe it is necessary to disclose one more piece of information," she said, her voice steady but weighted with the significance of what she was about to reveal.

A hush fell over the room, the sound of anticipation mingling with the faint hum of the video connections.

"QUIET," Chief President Grand commanded.

Silence fell immediately.

"You may continue, Director General Reverend Welton."

She inhaled deeply, bracing herself. "Dr. Prasad Vedurmudi is the brother-in-law of Neelima Takkella," she announced, her gaze piercing through the video camera.

Gasps filled the virtual room, and shock washed over the faces on the screen like a tidal wave.

"You need not say more," Chief President Grand said, his voice heavy with the weight of old memories. "I recall the reincarnation claim of Prashanthi Karthik and the controversy it created for our predecessors."

He paused, letting the memory linger in the air.

"I believe everyone here remembers," he added, his eyes scanning the assembly.

The members nodded in agreement, their nervous glances bouncing from one face to another.

"Let's proceed with the vote," Chief President Grand said. "All in favor of ensuring Dr. Prasad Vedurmudi's study never sees the light of day—say 'Aye.'"

Reverend Welton allowed herself a small, inward smile as she watched hand after hand rise. In a resounding chorus, the assembly members emphatically declared, "Aye."

Chief President Grand gave a firm nod. "Then it's unanimous,he declared, his voice deepening with resolve. "*Deploy Armonon!*"

Chapter 15

EXCEPT FOR THE PHOTO he had just seen—if it even counts—Edward had never seen a ghost. He'd never believed in them, either. Usually, he would be inclined to dismiss the photo Mrs. Jones had shown him as a trick of light or a figment of imagination, but that was before he experienced paranormal activity himself. It was a demonic encounter—an experience that had shattered his skepticism and taught him about the subtle and not-so-subtle differences in supernatural phenomena. It was an experience that had opened his mind to the unsettling possibility that spirits of all kinds might walk among us. Now, standing by the elevator, his gaze was locked on his notes from the interview with Mrs. Jones, his thoughts tangled in the eerie implications of what he had just witnessed.

The elevator dinged.

He looked up to see a familiar face. "Emma? What, do you live here now?" Edward asked, his tone a mix of surprise and concern.

"Practically," she replied with a weary smile. "Well, I used to. Today is move-out day. My mother just took my father home. I'm just picking up some things."

"Is he OK?" Edward asked, his brow furrowing in concern.

"I'd rather not get into it," she replied, shaking her head, her voice tinged with fatigue.

"I understand," he said softly, sensing the weight of her unspoken emotions.

"Well, I guess I'll see you around," Emma said, stepping toward the elevator door, eager to leave the hospital behind.

"Emma, wait."

She turned to him, her expression curious but guarded. "Yes, Dr. Clark?"

He exhaled deeply, as if trying to gather the right words. "No need to call me Dr. Clark. You can call me Edward."

She smiled, a genuine warmth in her eyes. "OK, what is it, Edward?"

"Can we talk?" he asked, gesturing toward a set of chairs around the corner in the hospital lobby.

"Sure," she said, following him to the lobby. She stopped abruptly. "As long as it's not about my father."

He shook his head. "It's not. I don't think."

They took a seat, the sterile white walls of the hospital lobby a stark contrast to the conversation that was about to unfold. Emma placed her purse on the side table between them, her fingers absently tracing the edge of it.

"This might be a long shot," Edward began, his voice cautious, "but I was wondering... Do you believe in, or rather, have you ever seen a spirit with your own eyes?" He lowered his head slightly, still maintaining eye contact with her, his question hanging in the air between them.

"You know I have," she replied without hesitation, her eyes steady and serious.

"Yes, of course," he said, mentally kicking himself for not thinking it through. "I should clarify—have you ever seen a spirit outside of a physical body?"

"Yes," she answered simply, her voice calm and matter-of-fact. "I've seen several—too many to count, actually."

Edward's eyes widened in surprise. "Why didn't this come up in any of our sessions?" he asked, his tone a mix of curiosity and disbelief.

She gave him a knowing look, a slight smirk tugging at the corner of her lips.

"It wasn't pertinent," he said, answering his own question. He paused, gathering his thoughts. "Can you tell me about what you experienced? Now? If you have time, that is?"

"Sure, I have some time," she said, leaning back in her chair, as if ready to unburden herself.

Edward opened his notebook, his pen poised to capture every detail. "You never leave home without that thing, do you?" she teased, glancing at her purse, where a bound daily planner peeked out.

He chuckled, glancing at her purse. "I could say the same of you."

She smiled softly. "I guess we all have our thing, don't we?"

He cleared his throat, trying to steer the conversation back on track. "Yes, well, I must admit, when I asked you if you've seen a spirit, I thought there was at least a chance you'd say yes, given what I know about you," he said, his voice thoughtful. "But I never expected you to say you have seen several spirits."

He paused, searching her face for any sign of doubt. "How is that? I mean, I've never seen even one," he said, his brow furrowing in disbelief. "Were you raised near a cemetery?"

She smiled again, this time more wistfully. "Sort of," she replied. "When I was young, we stayed at my aunt's house while my father was trying to get the family's finances in order."

Edward recalled how Emma had once mentioned her family's financial struggles when she was growing up, with most of their resources going toward keeping her father's church running. "I see," he said, nodding for her to continue.

"My aunt's house was right behind a small flower shop she owned and ran. My mom used to help around the shop in exchange for free rent, and I had no choice but to tag along."

"You saw the spirits at the flower shop?" Edward asked, his curiosity piqued.

"I wasn't finished," she said, her tone patient. "The flower shop was just down the street from a funeral home. It's a great location for a flower shop, really. My aunt got a lot of business from funeral orders. I would often go on flower delivery runs with my mother."

"To the funeral home?" he asked, scribbling furiously, trying to keep up with the rapid flow of information.

"Yes, we'd deliver casket sprays and coronas."

"Coronas?"

"Yes, oh right... that's what my dad called them in Spanish." Her eyes darted from left to right as though searching for the right words. "Standing sprays!" she exclaimed. "They're called standing sprays. Anyway, we'd deliver the standing sprays to the funeral home's office, but they made us deliver the casket sprays to the viewing rooms, where we had to place them over the coffins." She inhaled deeply, the memory clearly weighing on her. "I don't miss those days. I really don't."

"That's where you saw the spirits? At the funeral home?" Edward asked, leaning in, his pen still racing across the page.

"Yes, among other places," she replied. "I saw my first one when I was young—maybe five years old. I still remember what he looked like." Her eyes squinted, and she looked away as though the memory brought back fear or pain.

"If it's too difficult, we can stop talking about it," Edward offered gently.

"No, it's fine. It's not so bad. I mean, except for that one experience, especially given the circumstances."

"The circumstances?" he prompted, sensing a deeper story.

Her eyes widened, and she gulped audibly. "Anyway, I told my parents about it and tried to move on. They figured that would be the end of it. But then I saw more of them."

Edward leaned in closer, his curiosity intensifying. "You saw spirits every time you went to the funeral home?"

"Not every time," she clarified, shaking her head. "Did your mother see them, too?"

"No, never," she replied, her voice steady. "My father did occasionally, but not like me." Her eyes grew wide, her voice dropping to a whisper. "Nothing like me."

"Why do you think that is?" Edward asked, his voice soft but insistent.

"My father told me the Holy Spirit gives gifts, talents, I suppose, to believers for use as a service in the body of Christ," she explained. "He said I have the gift of discerning spirits, and he mentioned that the reason for my gift would one day reveal itself."

She paused, searching his face for any sign of judgment. "I know, that must sound really dramatic, but that's what he told me." Her brows furrowed as if lost in a deep trance of concentration, her gaze distant. "All these years later, and I still haven't figured out why."

"You said you didn't see a spirit every time you visited the funeral home. Why do you think that is?" Edward asked, his voice careful, as if walking on fragile ground.

"I've asked myself the same question. There were countless times when I saw nothing. So when I was old enough, I started investigating the spirits and how they died."

Edward imagined a young, determined Emma with her daily planner, pencils, and magnifying glass, playing detective in the funeral home like a character from a mystery novel. He couldn't help but smile.

"What's so funny?" Emma asked, noticing his expression.

"Sorry—I was just thinking how interesting it would have been to see this investigative side of you come out at such a young age."

"It was easy," she replied, her voice lightening a bit. "When my mother and I returned to the flower shop from the delivery, I would pull up the customer's receipt and search the internet for the name of the deceased."

That makes more sense, Edward thought, nodding. "Did you identify any patterns?"

"Yes, at least I think I did. It seemed like the spirits I saw normally died under tragic circumstances," she said, her voice growing more somber. "But I suppose some might say all causes of death are tragic."

"What kind of tragic circumstances?" Edward asked, his pen poised to capture every detail.

"Well, for example, one man died from a gunshot wound to the head. Then there was this one kid that fell into a quarry—a falling rock, a boulder, crushed his head."

Edward's pen scribbled furiously, trying to keep up with the rapid flow of information.

"Then there was the man I saw when I was five—"

He looked up, sensing the weight of the memory. "What happened to him?" he asked, his voice soft.

"He was found dead; his brain was missing, presumed to have been eaten."

Edward's eyes widened in shock. "You're kidding," he said instinctively.

"My parents told me he was killed as part of a satanic ritual."

Edward's pen froze, his gaze distant. He knew Emma well enough to know she wasn't joking about something like this. He remembered her telling him that she didn't have a normal childhood, but he never imagined it was like this. "I'm so sorry, Emma," he said, his voice filled with genuine sympathy.

"It's no big deal... It was the first spirit I ever saw, and it spooked me, that's all," she shrugged, trying to brush it off.

"Did you outgrow it? I mean, do you think you can still see spirits?" Edward asked, his curiosity piqued.

"I know I can," she replied confidently. "I mean, I hadn't in a long time. But since I've been spending so much time here, it's been inevitable."

Right—we're in a hospital, he thought, understanding dawning on him.

He sat silently, compartmentalizing his thoughts. It wasn't that he didn't believe her—he knew she was a woman of integrity, not one to exaggerate or seek attention. Certainly not one to volunteer information like this unless prompted. He had come to her with the questions, after all. *I could sure use her help with Prasad's study*, he thought, his mind racing with possibilities. He put down his pen. "Emma—"

"Oh crap," she interrupted, glancing at her phone. "Sorry, time got away from me. I have to get to..."

She paused, searching for the right words.

"... To... Therapy."

"I have to admit, I'm curious about your therapist. It certainly seems to be working for you," Edward said, his curiosity getting the better of him.

She stood up, preparing to leave. "You're welcome to check it out for yourself," she shrugged. "No appointment necessary."

What kind of therapist doesn't require an appointment? Edward thought, intrigued. "Really? You don't mind if I tag along?"

"Not at all," she replied with a smile. "We're adults. I know you're not a creep. I trust you."

He stood up, feeling a mix of curiosity and anticipation. "OK, then. Do you still have my number?" he asked.

"I do."

"Great—text me the address, and I'll meet you there."

Chapter 16

"THIS CAN'T BE RIGHT," Edward muttered, his voice tinged with confusion as he steered his car into the parking lot. The surroundings felt all wrong. Instead of the clinical sterility he expected from a doctor's office, he found himself in front of what looked like an unremarkable strip mall. The building before him seemed to house a single tenant, but there were no clear signs to indicate that it was the right place. His eyes scanned the area, searching for any hint of an office—an address, a nameplate, anything—but there was nothing.

He shifted the car into park, his fingers tapping anxiously on the steering wheel as his mind raced to make sense of the situation. The whole scene felt off, like a puzzle piece that didn't quite fit. Just as he reached for his phone to double-check the address, a sharp knock on his window startled him. His heart skipped a beat, and he quickly turned to see Emma standing outside, her face alight with a smile that seemed to chase away his doubts.

"You came!" she exclaimed, her voice bright with excitement as he opened the car door. The warmth in her tone contrasted sharply with the unease that had been gnawing at him moments before.

"I said I would," he replied, still somewhat bewildered by his surroundings.

"I know, but I thought you'd back out once you figured out where I was going," she teased, her eyes sparkling with amusement.

"You're probably right—except I just figured out where you were going," he admitted, glancing up at the sign:

MARIO'S GUN RANGE

Emma laughed, a light, carefree sound that contrasted sharply with the setting. "Apparently, a woman spending time in therapy is more socially accepted than a woman spending time at a gun range... It's different, I know. But it's really helped me deal with what happened with Brianna."

"You bought a gun to cope?" Edward asked, his eyebrows shooting up in disbelief. *That's not in any grief counseling textbook I've ever read*, he thought.

"No," Emma shook her head, her expression softening. "Mrs. Brown gave me Brianna's gun—she said she thought Brianna would want me to have it. Since then, I've made a ritual of coming here. It makes me feel like I'm still connected to Brianna somehow."

Edward considered her words, nodding slowly. "That actually makes a lot of sense." A brief, awkward silence hung between them.

"Well, I'll be going now," he said, turning to close the car door.

"Wait!" Emma said, placing her hand on the door to stop him. "I've gotten pretty good—do you want to come in for a bit?"

Edward hesitated, leaning back in his seat. He had never fired a gun before, let alone set foot in a gun range. But this might be an excellent opportunity to ask Emma the questions he didn't get to earlier. "Sure, why not?" he said, throwing his hands up in a gesture of surrender.

"Yay!" Emma squealed, her excitement palpable. "Let's go inside."

As they entered the building, Edward's eyes darted around, taking in the unfamiliar environment. The retail area was filled with guns, ammunition, and various related merchandise. The faint, distant sound of gunfire buzzed in the background, a constant reminder of where they were.

Emma approached the counter and placed a discreet black bag on it, unzipping it carefully. The store attendant, without a word, leaned over to inspect the bag's contents.

"What's he doing?" Edward asked, curious.

"He's checking to make sure the gun is unloaded and clear," Emma explained, her tone casual.

"Isn't that the same thing?" Edward asked, puzzled.

"No," she replied, shaking her head. "A gun can be unloaded but not clear—something could still be lodged in the chamber."

The attendant, his voice gruff and seasoned, looked up at Edward. "First time?"

"Yes," Edward admitted.

"You'll need to sign this waiver," the attendant said, slapping a sheet of paper onto the counter.

Edward reached for a pen.

"I need two IDs. I assume you need ear and eye protection?" the attendant continued.

"Yes," Edward replied, handing over his IDs.

The attendant placed a pair of earmuffs and safety glasses on the counter. "You're all set," he said.

"Follow me," Emma said, leading him toward a steel door with a sign over it:

EYE AND EAR PROTECTION REQUIRED BEYOND THIS POINT

"Put on your gear," Emma instructed, slipping the earmuffs over her ears. "Don't be alarmed when I open the door. You'll get used to the noise."

Edward did as she said, placing the earmuffs over his ears. As the door opened, a muffled echo of gunfire resonated through the corridor.

This isn't so bad... I expected it to be much louder, he thought, feeling a slight sense of relief as he followed her through the door and into the hallway.

Emma opened a second steel door, and the atmosphere changed instantly. The sharp crack of gunfire erupted like a thunderclap, each shot reverberating through the room with a force that made Edward involuntarily gasp. The sound was overwhelming, a brutal contrast to the relative quiet of the outside world. He cast a glance at Emma, who met his eyes and flashed him a confident thumbs-up. He forced a smile, the gesture more reflex than reassurance, as he tried to mask the unease bubbling up inside him.

She moved with the methodical precision of someone who had performed this task countless times. She approached the target stand with an air of calm authority, her actions smooth and deliberate. With a quick flick of her wrist, she tore off the bullet-riddled target, discarding it as though it were an insignificant piece of paper. The fresh target she smoothed out was treated with care, each wrinkle meticulously pressed away until the surface was perfectly flat.

Her composed exterior betrayed nothing of the intensity that must have been simmering beneath the surface. It was as if she had compartmentalized her emotions, sealing them away to focus solely on the task at hand. She turned to Edward, her eyes serious, and pointed to the bold red line that was marked on the floor—a clear boundary in a space where precision and safety were paramount. "Stay behind this line," she mouthed, her gaze locking onto his with an intensity that left no room for misinterpretation.

Edward nodded, his throat dry, and stepped back until his heels were firmly planted behind the line. His heart pounded in rhythm with the distant echo of gunfire, but he forced himself to remain composed, knowing that he was a guest in Emma's world, where control and discipline reigned supreme.

The gun range buzzed with a symphony of muffled shots and the acrid scent of gunpowder that clung to the air. Emma unzipped her bag with a steady hand, retrieving her weapon with the confidence. She loaded the magazine with practiced ease, each click resonating with purpose, and took her stance. In that moment, the weight of the gun seemed to anchor her, transforming her into someone who was more than just confident—she was a force to be reckoned with.

Edward watched, captivated, as Emma zeroed in on the target, her focus as sharp as the edge of a blade. The world around them seemed to dissolve into a haze, leaving only the thin barrier of air between Emma and the paper target. Everything else faded into the background—the distant echo of other shooters, the acrid scent of gunpowder, even the pounding of his own heart. It was as if time itself slowed, bending to the rhythm of her breath.

Her finger curled around the trigger, and with a measured exhale, she unleashed a rapid series of shots. Each one struck the target with uncanny precision, the paper punctured in a tight, methodical cluster that left no doubt about her expertise. Shot after shot, the holes formed a near-perfect circle, a testament to her unerring accuracy. The ease with which she handled the weapon, the fluidity of her movements, and the absolute control she exhibited—each element added to the surrealness of the moment.

Edward's jaw dropped, unable to hide his shock. The scene before him felt like something out of a dream, a distortion of reality that made him question what he was witnessing. Was this really happening? He blinked, half expecting to wake up, but the crisp scent of gunpowder and the muffled thud of spent casings hitting the floor grounded him in the present.

Brianna had passed away just over a year ago... Could that possibly be enough time for Emma to have built this level of expertise? The thought gnawed at him, unsettling his grasp on the situation. Her skill was not just impressive; it was extraordinary, almost unnaturally so. It defied the timeline he knew, the timeline that made sense. A growing sense of unease crept into his mind, mingling with awe as he struggled to reconcile the Emma he thought he knew with the sharpshooter standing before him.

A group of men, their bodies clad in tactical gear, stood behind the red line, their attention drawn to the display of expertise unfolding before them. Their expressions were stoic, yet their subtle nods of approval were impossible to miss. They exchanged glances, silently acknowledging the discipline and control Emma wielded over her weapon. There was no need for words—their respect was evident in the way they watched her, recognizing her as an equal, if not a superior, in the craft of marksmanship.

When Emma finished, she lowered the gun and turned to Edward with a radiant smile. The men behind them clapped and offered her words of praise, which she acknowledged with a modest wave before turning back to Edward.

"Can we talk outside?" Edward mouthed, pointing toward the exit.

She nodded, packing away her equipment with the same care she had shown upon arrival. He could hardly wait to get out of the noise and ask her the burning question that had been on his mind since they arrived—how did she become so skilled so quickly?

Once outside, Emma removed her earmuffs, a triumphant look on her face. "Not bad, huh?"

"That's an understatement," Edward replied, his voice filled with genuine astonishment. "You were like a seasoned FBI agent out there... or a spy—something out of the movies!"

Emma shrugged, her confidence unwavering. "Maybe I missed my calling."

"How often do you come here?" he asked, still trying to reconcile the Emma he knew with the sharpshooter he had just witnessed.

"Maybe twice a month."

He furrowed his brow. *Twice a month over the course of a year doesn't add up to that kind of skill and precision*, he thought, his analytical mind searching for answers. He remembered their conversation at the hospital, the one where she mentioned her recurring dreams about Brianna. "I recall you telling me you're having a recurring dream about that night with Brianna."

"That's right," she nodded, her expression growing more serious.

"You said that in your dreams, you think about what you would have done differently. Does that mean the recurring dream yields different outcomes?"

"It's a slight variation of the same dream, of what happened that night—except in my dreams, I know she owns a gun, and I know how to use it."

"How often do you have this dream?" Edward asked, his curiosity piqued.

"Frequently at first. Now, a few times a month." She paused, her gaze drifting as if recalling the details. "Recently, more—probably stress-induced with my father being in and out of the hospital."

"How much more?" he pressed, sensing there was more to this than she was letting on.

"Twice a week."

"Twice a week?" His eyes widened in surprise. "Since when?"

"I don't know—maybe six months ago. Anyway, it's no big deal. I don't even mind them," she said, shrugging as she dried her hands with a paper towel. "What's with the questions?"

Edward's phone chimed, breaking the moment. He reached into his pocket, considering how to respond to her question. Given what she had been through, she seemed to be doing remarkably well, and he feared that providing her with a scientific explanation for her newfound skill might reopen old wounds. "I was just curious," he said, glancing at his phone screen. "I have to get going... It's my wife—she's expecting me. But can you come by my office tomorrow?"

"What for?" Emma asked, her curiosity now piqued.

He exhaled audibly, realizing he was about to ask more of her than he had initially intended. "I don't normally do this, but I have a favor to ask."

Chapter 17

ARMONON PART I

ARMONON HAD KNOWN LOVE once, long ago. The memories of his mother, once sharp and clear, had grown increasingly hazy as the years slipped by—not entirely forgotten, but softened by time, like a light mist that blurred the edges of his past. His father, however, was nothing more than a shadow—a ghostly figure with no substance, no tangible presence in his mind. Whether his father had died before Armonon could walk or simply left, abandoning them without a word, it didn't matter. In Armonon's heart, he was as good as dead.

Armonon was just eight years old when his mother packed up their car for a trip to Rome and Vatican City, a journey that filled him with a deep sense of dread. He had always loathed long car rides; they made him sick to his stomach, a misery that lingered with him long after they arrived at their destination.

"Bitte, Mama, nicht," he pleaded in his small, trembling voice, his German tinged with a desperation that tugged at his mother's heart. "I don't want to go. You know long car rides make me sick."

His mother's eyes, warm and filled with an endless well of patience, met his with a tenderness that only deepened his reluctance. She knelt beside him, her hands gentle as they brushed a lock of hair from his forehead. "I've packed plenty of peppermints to help with your motion sickness," she reassured him, her voice as soft as a lullaby. "Just close your eyes during the ride, my love. It won't be so bad," she added, fastening his seatbelt with a soft, reassuring click. The scent of her lavender perfume enveloped him, a familiar comfort that made him feel safe, even if only for a fleeting moment.

As the car engine roared to life, Armonon glanced at his mother through the rearview mirror one more time, her profile illuminated by the soft morning light. Despite his dread, he knew that he would follow her anywhere—because she was his world, the only light in the shadowed corners of his young life.

It would be the first time Armonon missed a day of school. His life had always been governed by a meticulously crafted routine—school, homework, church, and chores—each one instilled in him by his mother and grandparents with the utmost care. It was unlike his mother to break that rhythm so abruptly, and yet, if she ever did, it would certainly be with him by her side. Despite understanding his mother's need for a change, he couldn't bring himself to support it. "We shouldn't go on such a long drive alone," he pouted, crossing his arms defiantly. "It's not safe."

Silence filled the car, thick and heavy.

He turned to his mother and saw her eyes welling with tears—a sight that struck him like a blow to the chest. His heart clenched painfully. It wasn't like his mother to show such raw emotion. She was love personified—light-hearted and whimsical, a beacon of joy in his life. She had always been the one to chase butterflies with him in sun-dappled meadows, their laughter mingling with the rustle of wings. They were drawn to the butterflies' delicate beauty and effortless grace, symbols of freedom and transformation. He had always seen her that way—free and majestic, a creature of light.

But now, as he watched the tears gather in her eyes, she seemed more fragile than he had ever known. The vibrant colors of the butterflies they once chased seemed distant, as if a shadow had fallen over their world. "What's the matter, Mama?" he asked softly, his voice trembling with concern, hoping to understand the pain that dimmed her radiant spirit.

"I miss your grandparents just as much as you do... maybe even more," she confessed, her voice quivering as she knelt beside him, her face close to his. "Do you think they would want Mama to stay home alone and sad, just waiting for you to come back from school, with nothing else to look forward to?" she asked, pressing her forehead gently against his, seeking solace in their closeness.

"Ni. They would never want you to be sad," Armonon admitted, though the words came out grudgingly, his small body tense with the weight of her sadness. "Not in a million years."

"That's what I believe, too," she replied, a tender smile breaking through her sorrow. "And you know how much it would mean to me to visit the Pontifical Sanctuary of the Holy Stairs—especially on a Friday in Lent."

He nodded, fully aware of how deeply this pilgrimage meant to her. She had spoken of it often, her voice tinged with the quiet desperation of someone searching for solace. His mother had convinced herself that her heart could be healed from the crushing weight of her grief if only she could climb the Holy Stairs. These twenty-eight steps, sacred and steeped in Christian tradition, were believed to be the very ones Jesus had ascended multiple times on the day of his condemnation in the Palace of Pontius Pilate.

In 326 A.D., the Holy Stairs were brought from Jerusalem to Rome by the praetorium of Pilate at the request of Empress Saint Helena, mother of Constantine. For centuries, they had been a destination for the devout, a place where faith met the tangible remnants of Christ's suffering. Every Friday during Lent, the faithful climbed the Holy Stairs on their knees, each step a prayerful journey meant to relive the passion of Christ. For his mother, this act of devotion was more than just a ritual; it was a profound hope, a belief that by reliving Christ's suffering, she could somehow mend the wounds of her own soul.

The promise of a plenary indulgence—a complete remission of the temporal punishment due for sins—only deepened her resolve to make the pilgrimage. It wasn't just about seeking forgiveness; it was about finding peace, about believing that in the act of climbing those steps, she might finally lay her grief to rest and find the healing she so desperately sought. The Holy Stairs represented a sacred intersection of faith and personal redemption, a place where she believed the weight of her sorrows might be lifted, if only for a moment.

"But I still don't think it's safe. You driving so far all alone."

"Armonon, sweetheart, I'm not alone. I have you. You will keep us both safe," she said, looking into his eyes with a steady, unwavering gaze. "You know, there's a reason I named you Armonon."

"There is?" he asked, furrowing his brow in curiosity.

"Yes."

"Well, what is it?"

"Your name—it stems from a German word that means warrior."

His eyes grew wide with wonder. "Really, Mama?"

"Yes—really!" she exclaimed, her voice lifting with enthusiasm. "And what do warriors do?"

"They fight! And protect!" With wide eyes and a playful grin, he straightened his posture, throwing punches into the air with all the vigor his small body could muster. With each punch, he imagined himself in an epic battle, his movements filled with energy and excitement.

"That's right," his mother replied, her heart swelling with pride. "Which means you will keep us both safe."

"Ja!" he declared, nodding enthusiastically. "I'll protect you, Mama." His voice resonated with a deep sense of duty and palpable pride, the weight of her words settling into his young heart.

Chapter 18

HE PACED THE ROOM with barely contained energy, each step resonating with the adrenaline still coursing through his veins from the previous day. His excitement was a palpable force, as if the very air around him vibrated with it. His eyes were wide, his movements quick and deliberate, reflecting the rush of emotions he struggled to articulate.

"I wish you could have been there to see it," he exclaimed, his voice brimming with awe. "I've never seen anything like it! It would take us hundreds, maybe thousands of hours of training to even come close to her level of expertise."

Prasad, seated calmly at the desk, raised an eyebrow, a flicker of skepticism in his gaze. "Are you certain her recurring dreams amplified her skill level?" he asked, his tone measured.

"Absolutely," Edward responded without hesitation, his conviction unwavering. "It's a tried and true visualization technique." He paused, gathering his thoughts, his mind racing. "You know, like the ones we use in our field to enhance performance in skill-based activities, create desired emotional states, and even achieve life goals. This technique is so effective that even sports psychologists rely on it to sharpen the abilities of elite athletes."

He continued, his words gaining momentum as his excitement bubbled over. "All the components are there. She's using her recurring dream to visualize herself firing the gun, achieving real-life outcomes just like she learned in dream training—except she doesn't even realize she's doing it. And don't forget, she's no average dreamer—she's capable of having multiple lucid dreams in a single night, every night!"

The room seemed to buzz with the intensity of his words, the implications of what he was describing hanging in the air between them. Prasad leaned back slightly, absorbing the information, while Edward stood before him, every fiber of his being alive with the thrill of discovery.

Prasad leaned back, absorbing the information. "That's incredible," he admitted, his voice laced with awe.

"Isn't it?" Edward's eyes sparkled with enthusiasm. "Combine her dreams with the real-life practice she's getting at the gun range, and the fact that it's all being experienced from her perspective—it's just amazing."

"Wow," Prasad replied, nodding slowly. "Wow, indeed."

"Is she aware that her recurring dreams have affected her skill level on the gun range?"

Edward shook his head, a knowing smile playing at his lips. "She's an incredibly smart woman, but I don't think she's put that part together—she has no reason to. When she was my patient, I told her the dream training would rewire her thoughts. Even for me, it took some time to piece together what was happening, and I'm supposed to be the expert."

Prasad's eyes narrowed thoughtfully. "Do you intend to tell her?"

Edward paused, his gaze turning inward as he considered the implications. "What good would it do?"

Prasad tilted his head, considering. "It's a fascinating finding, and technically, she's no longer your patient. You're not obligated to weigh the potential benefits and harms of disclosing the information."

He paused, choosing his next words carefully. "But information is a tricky thing. Regardless of the doctor-patient relationship, I believe we have a duty to use our personal judgment to determine if the benefits of sharing knowledge—whatever it may be—outweigh the potential consequences."

Edward furrowed his brow, deep in thought. "Right," he murmured, almost to himself. "Like I said, what good would it do?"

Before Prasad could respond, a soft knock echoed through the room, cutting through the tension like a knife. Edward and Prasad exchanged a quick glance, the unspoken question hanging in the air as they turned their attention to the door.

Chapter 19

EMMA PUSHED THE DOOR OPEN, her voice bright with a practiced casualness. As she stepped inside, her eyes immediately found the familiar blue microfiber couch—a worn but comforting presence, like an old friend waiting with open arms. Though it had been some time since she had last been in this room, the sight of the couch made her feel instantly at home, as if no time had passed at all.

"Hi, it's me," she said, her tone light as she crossed the threshold. Her gaze lingered on the couch for a moment before she turned her attention to the rest of the room. "So, what's this favor you wanted to see me about?" she asked, curiosity threading through her voice as she settled into the familiar surroundings.

"Thanks for coming," Edward said, gratitude evident in his tone. "I know you have a lot going on."

"No problem." Emma moved toward her old spot on the couch but stopped short when she noticed Prasad. "Oh, hi, Dr. Vedurmudi. I wasn't expecting you."

"Hello, Emma. Please, call me Prasad," he replied warmly. "I'm just here to listen."

"OK," she said, though her tone held a hint of uncertainty. She glanced between them before settling into the couch across from Prasad, placing her purse and phone neatly on the coffee table.

Edward leaned forward, his expression serious. "I mentioned that I was working with Prasad on a study."

"The one on near-death experiences," Emma said, nodding as she recalled their previous conversations.

Edward nodded in return. "Yes, but the scope has expanded since we last spoke."

"Oh? How so?" Her curiosity was piqued, the intensity in her gaze revealing her interest.

Prasad spoke up, his tone measured. "We've developed a hypothesis that if a certain part of the brain, the TPO junction, is not functional at the time of death, the spirit may remain in this dimension, among the living."

"Interesting," Emma murmured, her thoughts already racing through the implications.

"If we can prove that," Prasad continued, his voice gaining momentum, "we'll be one step closer to validating the next part of my hypothesis."

Emma raised an eyebrow, leaning slightly forward. "Which is?"

"That the TPO junction is key to unlocking other possibilities in the afterlife," Prasad explained.

"Other possibilities? Like what?" Emma's skepticism was evident, but so was her intrigue.

"Like the possibility that a person's brain activity—their thoughts—during the moments leading up to death could activate the prefrontal cortex, the decision-making part of the brain," Prasad said.

Emma's eyes widened as the realization dawned on her. "Are you saying it may be possible for a spirit to choose where it goes after death? To decide whether to ascend, descend, or even stay here?"

Edward turned to Prasad with a grin. "I told you she was smart."

"This is fucking huge!" Emma exclaimed, jumping to her feet, only to pause as the gravity of the situation sank in. "Wait—why are you telling me this?" she asked, suspicion creeping into her voice. "This seems like something you'd keep on a need-to-know basis."

"We need your help," Prasad said plainly.

Emma's gaze shifted between them, her mind working through the implications. "How could I possibly help?"

"We need evidence," Edward interjected, his tone serious.

"What kind of evidence?" Emma asked, her eyes narrowing as she tried to anticipate where this was going.

"Evidence that supports Prasad's theory—that the TPO junction is responsible for transporting the spirit," Edward explained.

Emma thought back to the hospital, remembering the unusual questions Edward had asked her about her experiences seeing spirits. Now it all made sense. "You want me to track down spirits—ghost hunt—to see if their TPO junction was functional when they died?" she asked incredulously.

Prasad nodded. "Something like that."

Emma crossed her arms, staring into the distance as she processed the request. "You aren't afraid of ghosts, are you?" Edward asked, attempting to lighten the mood.

Emma shot him an unimpressed look. "I know what you're doing, and I'm not going to justify that with an answer."

Prasad leaned forward slightly. "Have you ever seen the spirit of someone who died of natural causes? Perhaps a heart attack?"

Emma considered the question, recalling the spirits she had encountered over the years. Most of the ones she remembered clearly had suffered significant brain injuries—the victim of the satanic ritual, the man with the gunshot wound, the boy crushed by a boulder. "Not that I recall, but I suppose it's possible."

"Well, given your gift—" Edward began.

"Gift," Emma corrected him firmly.

Edward nodded. "Right. Given your gift, we were hoping you might assist us with some, uh, validation activities."

Emma's eyes darted around the room as she tried to gauge their seriousness. "Exactly what do you want me to do?" she asked, her voice cautious.

"Do you have a Proton Pack that I can use?" she added, half-joking.

Edward couldn't help but chuckle. "She's smart and funny," Prasad remarked, smiling.

Emma mimed a curtsy, her expression still guarded.

"We've identified patients whose TPO junction was inactive at the time of their death," Prasad explained.

Emma nodded slowly. "Okay."

"We need you to—" Edward began but was cut off.

"You need me to tell you if I can see the spirits of those patients, right?" Emma interjected, her tone firm.

Edward offered a small, tight-lipped smile. "Yes, and—"

"And you need me to confirm that I don't see the spirits of those with an active TPO junction," she continued, her gaze sharp.

Edward's smile widened slightly, impressed by how quickly she grasped the plan.

"And let me guess," she added, "you won't be telling me which is which."

"Exactly right," Edward confirmed.

"Sounds simple enough," Emma said, though her voice carried a hint of reluctance. "But how would this actually work? You don't expect me to crash funerals, do you?" she asked, her tone incredulous.

She turned to Edward, who averted his gaze, clearly uncomfortable with the implication.

"You're kidding," she scoffed, crossing her arms.

"I would accompany you," Edward offered, trying to sound reassuring. "If that helps."

Emma considered the offer, her mind flashing back to the funeral homes of her childhood—the cold, sterile air, the overwhelming scent of flowers. A shiver ran down her spine at the memory, a sense of dread she hadn't felt in years.

She glanced at Edward, who was watching her intently, a hopeful smile tugging at the corners of his mouth. He had helped her so much in the past; maybe this was her chance to repay him. "I suppose it's not like anyone would question us for being there," she said slowly, her voice tinged with reluctant enthusiasm. "At a funeral, there's really only one person who can dispute your reason for being there. And that person is dead."

"Does that mean you'll do it?" Prasad asked, his voice barely able to contain his excitement.

Before Emma could respond, her phone buzzed on the table, its vibrations cutting through the tension in the room. She picked it up and glanced at the screen. "Just a moment—I need to take this," she said, her tone suddenly serious. "It's my mother." She brought the phone to her ear. "Hello?" Her eyes widened, and a sharp gasp escaped her lips as whatever she heard on the other end hit her like a tidal wave. She turned to Edward, her face pale and filled with distress. "I have to go," she said urgently, still clutching the phone to her ear.

Chapter 20

ARMONON PART II

"TELL ME A STORY, MAMA," Armon said, his small voice struggling to cut through the drowsiness that clung to him in the back seat of the car as they embarked on the ten-hour drive from Munich to Vatican City.

"Hmmm," his mother mused, glancing at him through the rearview mirror. "How about the legend of the Farfalla Dorata?"

"Ni," he replied, shaking his head slightly.

She turned, her brow furrowed in playful annoyance. "And why not?"

"I've heard it before... Oma told me," he shrugged. Armonon knew all about the legend set in a small village nestled among the rolling hills of Italy, where people believed in the existence of a rare and mystical butterfly known as the Farfalla Dorata. Its wings were said to shimmer with golden hues, catching the sunlight as if crafted from the finest precious metal. The butterfly's appearance was so rare that few had ever seen it, and those who did were considered incredibly fortunate. The legend spoke of how the Farfalla Dorata would only reveal itself under special circumstances—often in times of great need or deep personal reflection.

"Oh, really?" she replied, a hint of surprise coloring her voice. "Did your grandmother tell you that seeing the Farfalla Dorata is considered a blessing?"

"Ja."

"And that it's believed the butterfly emerges from the heart of a flower, waiting for the perfect moment to take flight?"

"Ja. Heard it all."

"Oh... I guess you know all about *Isabella* then."

Armonon's interest piqued, and he straightened his posture. "Who?"

"The tale of Isabella and the Farfalla Dorata. She was about your age, actually."

"Tell me the tale, Mama," he urged, his earlier reluctance melting away.

She took a deep breath, preparing to share the story. "Isabella lived in a small village, and she was known far and wide for her kindness and generosity. But despite her good heart, her family had fallen on hard times. They struggled to make ends meet, and Isabella often found herself feeling hopeless about the future. One day, while walking through a meadow bathed in the golden light of late afternoon, she spotted the Farfalla Dorata fluttering above a field of wildflowers. Captivated by its ethereal beauty, she couldn't resist following the butterfly, which led her to a hidden glen she had never seen before."

She paused, momentarily checking the road ahead as the car curved around a bend.

"And then what happened, Mama?" Armonon asked, leaning forward, eager to hear more.

"In this secret place, Isabella discovered a crystal-clear spring, its waters sparkling in the sunlight. This spring would save her village from a devastating drought that had been threatening their crops. The appearance of the Farfalla Dorata not only brought Isabella personal joy but also provided the means to rescue her village," she said softly. "From that day forward, Isabella's life changed for the better, and she became a symbol of hope and renewal in her village."

Silence settled in the car.

"Armonon?"

"Ja?"

"You've heard that tale before, haven't you?"

"Ja," he replied, his voice softened by fatigue. "But it's much better when you tell it," he added, as the steady hum of the engine began to lull him into slumber.

Time blurred as the miles stretched on, and before he knew it, his mother's gentle voice woke him. "We're almost there, Armonon," she announced.

"Already?"

"Yes," she said with a smile. "I told you it wouldn't be—" Her words were abruptly cut off. Through the rearview mirror, Armonon saw his mother's eyes widen in terror like never before. She jerked the wheel hard to the left. His body jolted violently as the car trembled under the force, the screeching sound of metal colliding with metal piercing the air. Armonon instinctively closed his eyes as the world around him shattered—the sound of breaking glass, the deafening roar of impact as a waste collection truck barreled into them from behind with unstoppable force.

When he opened his eyes, he found his mother slumped over the steering wheel, her head bleeding as though a crown of thorns had been wrenched from it. Panic surged through him as he unbuckled his seatbelt and clawed his way to the front seat. Without saying a word, he gripped her hand tightly and locked eyes with her as she struggled to breathe. In that fleeting moment, their unspoken bond spoke volumes.

Chapter 21

EMMA SPRINTED TOWARD THE ER, her feet struggling to keep pace with the whirlwind of fear and worry that swirled in her mind. Her mother's voice, sharp and strained, had given no details—just a single, urgent command to come quickly. It left Emma with nothing but the worst scenarios playing out in her head. The world around her blurred as she dashed through the hospital's sliding doors, her breath coming in short, panicked gasps.

As she burst into the lobby, her frantic gaze immediately found her mother. She was sitting alone, arms tightly folded across her chest as if trying to hold herself together, her knees bouncing with a nervous energy that betrayed her outward composure. Tears welled in her mother's eyes, threatening to spill over at any moment.

"Mom!" Emma called out, her voice thick with desperation as she reached her mother's side. "Where's Dad? Why aren't you with him?"

"They told me to wait out here," her mother replied, her voice trembling with a mix of fear and sorrow.

"Tell me what happened."

"I was driving home, and your father was talking about how he was looking forward to finally being home," her mother began, her voice faltering. "Then, all of a sudden, he didn't sound like himself. His speech got slurred, and when I looked at him, the left side of his face was... droopy."

"A stroke?" Emma whispered, her heart plummeting.

Her mother nodded, her eyes filled with unshed tears. "Yes, angel."

Emma's world tilted as the blood drained from her face, leaving her trembling with dread. "Is he... is he gone?" she asked, her voice barely audible.

"No, angel. The doctors are working on him. We just need to wait here until they call us in." Her mother reached out, taking Emma's hand in hers, guiding her to sit. "Let's pray."

Emma watched as her mother bowed her head, her lips moving in a whispered, fervent prayer. The sight of her mother's desperate plea should have been comforting, but it only deepened the hollow ache in Emma's chest. She wanted to pray too, to find solace in faith, but the words wouldn't come. Her mind was a blur, incapable of forming coherent thoughts, let alone a prayer. The unsettling churn in her stomach grew with each passing second, a gnawing dread that told her this time might be different—this time, her father might not leave the hospital.

Her eyes drifted to the clock on the wall, its ticking unbearably loud in the oppressive silence. Each tick seemed to stretch time, dragging it into an agonizing slow motion that made every second feel like an eternity. Emma's breath hitched as she watched the second hand move, its relentless pace a cruel reminder of the uncertainty hanging over them. She clenched her fists, trying to suppress the wave of fear threatening to overwhelm her, but it was no use. The fear was there, lurking in the back of her mind, refusing to be ignored.

"Mrs. Perales?" A voice suddenly broke through the silence, pulling both women from their thoughts.

"Yes!" her mother exclaimed, leaping to her feet. "Is my father okay?" Emma asked, her voice trembling.

"My name is Dr. Paul Bower," the doctor said, his expression serious. "Please, follow me so I can explain Mr. Perales's condition in private."

"Yes, of course," her mother replied, her voice strained.

They followed the doctor, leaving the lobby behind and entering a small, sterile room across from the emergency entrance. The walls were adorned with detailed diagrams of human anatomy, the clinical setting adding to Emma's growing dread.

"Have a seat," Dr. Bower offered, pulling out two chairs in front of his desk.

Emma looked down at the chair, a deep breath shuddering through her. "I'd rather stand, if that's okay," she said, the idea of sitting still in this moment unbearable.

"As you wish," the doctor replied, taking his seat. He focused on Emma's mother, his gaze steady and professional. "Your husband suffered a massive stroke, likely aggravated by the heart surgery he was recovering from."

"Will he be okay?" her mother asked, her voice tight with hope.

Dr. Bower paused, his expression softening. "He's in what we call a persistent coma."

Emma's heart clenched. "Is he in a vegetative state?" she asked, her voice breaking.

"No," the doctor reassured her.

Oh, thank God, she thought, a small wave of relief washing over her.

"But the cerebral embolism has caused some damage," Dr. Bower continued.

"What kind of damage?" her mother asked, her voice trembling.

"The damage occurs when the brain doesn't receive enough blood supply," he explained, pointing to a large brain diagram on the wall. "The temporal lobe and surrounding areas suffered the brunt of it."

"Temporal lobe?" Emma's mind flashed back to the conversation she'd just had with Edward and Prasad. "What surrounding areas, exactly?" she pressed, her voice growing more urgent.

Dr. Bower blinked, momentarily taken aback by her question. "Do you work in the medical field?" he asked.

"No," Emma replied, her voice flat.

"Oh, okay," he said, recovering quickly. He turned the computer screen toward them. "Here—near the back of the brain," he said, pointing to the image.

Emma stared at the screen, her mind racing. "Is there activity in the TPO junction?" she asked, her voice almost a whisper.

Dr. Bower's eyebrows shot up in surprise. "No, it doesn't appear so," he said, after a brief pause.

Emma swallowed hard, fighting the storm of emotions brewing inside her. Her jaw clenched, and she could feel the weight of despair pressing down on her.

"Can you repair it?" her mother asked, a sliver of hope still in her voice.

Dr. Bower shook his head, the movement slow and deliberate. "Unfortunately, no. The brain has a certain amount of plasticity, which allows it to repair itself to some extent by forming new synaptic connections. But given the severity of the trauma, that's unlikely to happen here."

"So what are our options?" Emma asked, her voice hollow.

A heavy silence filled the room.

"It is with deep regret that I must tell you it is highly unlikely that Mr. Perales will regain consciousness," Dr. Bower said gently.

Emma felt the floor drop out from beneath her. "How long does he have?" her mother asked, her voice barely a whisper.

"It's difficult to say," Dr. Bower replied, his tone cautious. "I've seen patients in his condition pass on their own within days, others much longer without intervention."

As the doctor's words sank in, time seemed to grind to a halt. Emma turned to her mother, her own eyes filling with tears. The reality of the situation was almost too much to bear.

"I know this is distressing news," Dr. Bower said softly. "Our team is here for you as you navigate through the next steps."

Navigate next steps? The finality in his words hit Emma like a sledgehammer. "That can't be it," she whispered, shaking her head in denial. "There must be something you can do... some other option or, or, possibility."

"I'm afraid not," the doctor said, his voice heavy with sympathy.

Emma stood frozen, her mind refusing to accept what she was hearing.

"I'll give you two some time alone," Dr. Bower said, rising from his chair. He stepped out of the room, closing the door behind him with a soft click.

Memories of her father flooded Emma's mind—his laughter, his kindness, the way he had always been there for those in need. She remembered the time he had given his shoes to a homeless man, walking home barefoot without a second thought. How could God let this happen? The question echoed in her mind, relentless and unanswered.

She sank into the chair, her legs finally giving way beneath her. She turned to her mother and saw the single tear escape down her cheek. Her mother's face remained composed, but Emma could see the deep, aching pain she was trying so hard to hide.

Emma's gaze shifted to the brain diagram on the wall, her mind racing. *This can't be how his story ends*, she thought fiercely, her resolve hardening. *I won't let it.*

Chapter 22

EMMA FORCEFULLY PUNCHED HER PILLOW in frustration, letting out an exasperated sigh as she desperately tried to surrender to sleep. Rolling onto her side, she closed her eyes, willing herself to calm her restless mind, but the thoughts continued to race, stubborn and unyielding. "Ugh!" she groaned, feeling the familiar spiral of anxiety tightening around her chest. Her mind replayed a recent conversation in the break room, where she had confided in a colleague about her struggles with insomnia. She had blamed it on the relentless mind chatter that jumped from work stress to the ever-present worry about her father. Her colleague, an Army veteran, had suggested a sleep technique known as the Military Method.

She glanced at her phone. *1:04 AM. It's worth a shot*, she thought.

With a deep breath, Emma decided to give it a try. Although she preferred to sleep on her side, she turned onto her back as her colleague had instructed. She rested her arms at her sides, letting her shoulders drop, and closed her eyes. Slowly, she focused on each part of her face, consciously relaxing her eyelids, jaw, lips, and brow. *I think that's right*, she thought, struggling to keep her mind from wandering. She moved on to her chest, taking slow, deep breaths, allowing the tension to melt away. Then she concentrated on relaxing her lower body, starting from her hips and working her way down through her legs to her feet.

As her breathing slowed, she visualized herself leaning against the railing of a massive cruise ship, drifting in the vast, deep blue waters of the Pacific Ocean. The rhythmic crashing of the waves against the bow became a soothing lullaby, pulling her thoughts into a gentle drift.

He can't die like this.

It's not fair.

I have to do something.

Struggling to stay focused on the peace and calm of her visualization, she repeated the phrase her colleague had instructed her to use to combat intrusive thoughts.

Just don't think.

Just don't think.

Just don't think.

Gradually, her limbs grew heavy and relaxed, her breathing becoming steady and rhythmic. A welcome heaviness settled over her, as if gravity were gently pulling her down into the realm of dreams.

DING-DONG.

The sudden chime jolted her body in bed.

"Are you expecting anyone?" Emma asked, turning to Brianna.

"Em, listen to me," Brianna said, her eyes wide with alarm. "I need you to go into the pantry and wait there until I come back and tell you it's OK to come out."

"Why?" Emma asked, confusion and concern flooding her mind.

Brianna gripped Emma's hand tightly, trying to pull her toward the pantry. "I need you to go, now," she insisted, her voice firm and urgent.

Emma dug her heels into the floor, resisting Brianna's force. "Brie, why? What's going on?" she demanded, refusing to be pushed aside.

"I don't have time to explain right now, but I promise I'll explain later," Brianna said, her voice trembling as she tried to force Emma into the pantry.

Emma clutched onto the door frame, her grip unyielding. "I don't know who's out there, but if you plan on opening that door and want this person to leave, I should go with you," she said, her tone resolute.

Exhausted from struggling with Emma's resistance, Brianna finally relented, crossing her arms and tapping her toes anxiously on the floor.

"I'm not leaving you, Brie," Emma said, her expression unwavering, her determination clear.

Brianna let out a deep sigh. "OK, but just so you know, I have no intention of opening that door."

"Open up! Let me in!" a deep voice bellowed from the other side of the door, the sound resonating with menace.

They cautiously approached the living room, moving toward the front door. "Go away!" Brianna shouted through the intercom, her voice filled with both fear and anger.

"I just want to talk!" the voice yelled back, louder and more insistent.

"You are not welcome here!" Brianna roared, her voice trembling slightly but firm.

Emma watched as Brianna paced the length of the living room, her movements deliberate and rhythmic as she weighed her options.

"Brie, didn't you say you bought a gun?" Emma asked, her voice tinged with urgency.

Brianna's eyes widened as the weight of the situation settled on her. "Well, y-yes, but I've... I've never used it," she stammered, her voice trembling. "Besides, it's only for extreme emergencies."

Emma crossed her arms, her face set with determination. "I think this qualifies. We don't know what we're dealing with here, and I don't have a good feeling about this."

The pounding on the door grew louder, each strike sending a jolt through the silence of the night, as if the very walls were shuddering in fear.

"That doesn't sound like someone who's just stopping by to say hello. It's best to be prepared and have the gun on hand, just in case."

Brianna hesitated, shaking her head. "I don't know, Em..."

"LET ME IN!" The voice on the other side of the door bellowed, filled with a terrifying mix of aggression and menace.

"This is a quiet neighborhood. Someone is bound to call the cops! Please, leave!" Brianna shouted, her voice betraying her fear.

They both watched the intruder on the screen of Brianna's phone. He leaned into the doorbell camera, his face eerily close, and placed a finger over his lips. "Oh, you're right, I better get inside then," he whispered with a chilling hiss.

"Get your gun. Now!" Emma commanded, her tone leaving no room for argument.

Brianna bolted into the dining room, her hands trembling as she reached for the edge of a photo frame on the wall. The sound of mechanical whirring filled the room as she lifted the frame, revealing a hidden compartment. She reached deep into the wall, her fingers brushing against cold metal, and pulled out the gun, her hand shaking as she handed it to Emma.

Emma's eyes darted between Brianna and the phone, where the intruder was now picking up a large rock, preparing to force his way in. "He's got a huge rock—he's going to break the door down," Emma said, her voice tight with urgency. "BRIE, HURRY!"

Brianna stepped forward, pressing the gun into Emma's hand. "Here—it's already loaded," she said, her voice barely above a whisper. "Please don't fire it—just use it to scare him—OK?"

Emma's eyes narrowed as she gripped the gun. "I'll use it to scare him—but I can't promise I won't fire it."

"What? No!" Brianna exclaimed, her face pale. "What if you miss? Or worse, what if you kill him?"

Emma's gaze hardened. "I wish he were as concerned about us as you are about him," she said, her voice cold. "I will do whatever I need to do to protect you."

"ME?!" Brianna's voice broke with panic. "What about you?!"

Emma's voice softened, but her resolve did not waver. "To protect us, OK?"

Suddenly, the sound of shattering glass exploded through the house as the intruder smashed his way in.

"Problem solved," he sneered, flashing a sinister grin as he reached through the broken glass to unlock the door from the inside. The stench of alcohol and marijuana filled the room as he stumbled in, his eyes wild with malice.

Emma stepped forward, the gun steady in her hands, and aimed it directly at his head. "I don't want to hurt you, but I will not let you hurt us," she said, her voice firm. "Turn around and leave—now."

He took a step closer, his grin widening.

"Stop. This is your final warning," Emma said, her fingers tightening around the handle. The weight of the gun felt both foreign and natural in her grip. "Turn around and leave now, or I'm firing."

A twisted smile stretched across his face. "You would never—"

Emma moved with deadly precision, lowering her arm just enough to take aim. Without hesitation, she pulled the trigger.

A deafening blast filled the room, followed by an eerie silence. The intruder gasped, his eyes widening in shock as he raised his hand to reveal a gaping hole in his palm. Blood dripped steadily onto the floor, a crimson reminder of Emma's resolve.

"You're fu—"

"NOT. ANOTHER. WORD!" Emma commanded, her voice cutting through the air like a blade. Her eyes, filled with a steely intensity, bore into his, leaving no doubt that she would shoot again if necessary.

His chest heaved with labored breaths, anger and disbelief warring on his face. He turned to leave, but his blood-slicked shoes slipped on the floor, sending him crashing down. Emma watched, unblinking, as he struggled to push himself up, his movements slow and desperate. Time seemed to stretch, every second drawn out in painful detail.

"Hurry," she ordered, her voice cold.

With gritted teeth, he finally managed to stagger to his feet and stumble out the door. The sound of screeching tires and the acrid smell of burned rubber filled the night as he fled.

Emma lowered the gun, her hands shaking as the adrenaline began to wear off. She turned to Brianna, who stood frozen, her eyes wide and her face drained of color.

"I had to fire," Emma said, her voice barely above a whisper. "He left me with no choice."

Brianna's lips moved, but no sound came out. Her body trembled as she tried to process what had just happened.

"Take your time," Emma said softly, reaching out to rub Brianna's back. She waited, giving her friend the space to find her voice.

Finally, Brianna's words came out in a broken whisper. "How...how did you...do that?"

Chapter 23

"ANGEL, WILL YOU PLEASE drop by the house and pick up some socks for your father?" Josephine asked, her eyes lingering on her husband's feet as they peeked out from under the hospital covers. The stark white of the hospital-issued socks seemed to irritate her as much as they did him. "He says they're itchy," she added, speaking on his behalf, even though he couldn't express the discomfort himself.

It was a habit she had developed, a way to keep her sanity intact amidst the overwhelming silence. She imagined his voice, strong and clear, as if the request were coming directly from him, filling the void left by his quiet struggle. It was her way of maintaining a semblance of normalcy, of pretending, if only for a moment, that things were as they used to be.

"Sure," Emma replied, taking a deep breath. "But I want to sit for a minute first." She settled beside her mother, leaning her head against Josephine's shoulder, seeking comfort in the familiar gesture. Josephine felt the weight of Emma's head resting on her shoulder, a silent plea for solace. She responded instinctively, her fingers tracing gentle circles on Emma's back, a ritual from Emma's childhood that had always brought peace. *Angel, God knows if I could make your father better and take away all your worries, I would*, she thought, her eyes never leaving her husband's still form.

"Can I talk to you about something?" Emma asked softly. Josephine inhaled deeply, sensing the gravity in her daughter's voice.

"I haven't made any decisions yet," Josephine said, her gaze still locked on Emmanuel. "I'm praying, asking the Lord to guide me. Just taking it one day at a time for right now," she added, her voice tinged with the melancholy of the situation. "Like that title of your father's favorite song, *Un Día a La Vez*."

A faint smile tugged at her lips as she bowed her head. "I know how much he loves that song," she said, almost to herself. She lifted her head and looked at Emma, concern etching lines on her face. "Mom, I know you're dealing with a lot right now, but I really need to talk to you about something."

Josephine picked up on the anxiety in Emma's tone and turned to face her. "What is it, angel?" she asked, worry creeping into her voice.

"Remember Dr. Clark, the psychiatrist I told you about—the one I used to see?"

"Yes, of course, I remember," Josephine replied, her eyes widening slightly. "Oh dear God, are you having nightmares again?" she asked, her voice trembling with fear. "Please don't tell me you're having those nightmares again."

"No, no," Emma quickly reassured her, shaking her head.

"Oh, thank God," Josephine breathed, relief washing over her like a soothing wave. She had always believed that God never gives you more than you can handle, but the weight of her burdens had been pushing her faith to its limits. The memory of Emma's nightmares, the long nights when she was under a doctor's care, seeing her daughter so sick, thin, and frail—it had been a torment all its own. Josephine had felt her heart breaking a little more each day, torn between caring for Emmanuel and worrying over Emma. The thought that she might have to bear the weight of both of them at once was almost too much to contemplate.

"It's just that I ran into him, and he told me about this study he's working on."

"Oh? Well, that's nice, angel," Josephine said, trying to sound more at ease. "How is he doing?"

"He's fine," Emma replied, her thoughts already shifting back to the study. "Anyway, the study he's working on—it's about this theory they're trying to prove—they think a part of the brain works like a homing device that the spirit uses to find its way to... wherever it's going."

"Wherever it's going?" Josephine echoed, her brow furrowing in confusion.

"You know, up, down, and anywhere in between," Emma explained, trying to make the concept more palatable.

"Ha!" Josephine scoffed, her eyes narrowing. "You're joking, right?" But when Emma shook her head, Josephine's expression turned serious, searching Emma's face for any sign of jest. When she found none, her skepticism gave way to a deeper, more contemplative concern. "That's nonsense—there's only one thing the spirit needs to go home, and that's God."

"Yes, of course, but just hear me out," Emma said, rising from her seat and crouching down in front of her mother.

Josephine, startled by Emma's intensity, tried to dismiss the conversation. "What's this about, angel? Get up off the floor."

"Mom, just listen—hear me out," Emma insisted, gripping her mother's hand firmly, her eyes pleading for understanding.

Josephine watched as Emma's face grew more serious, her brows furrowed with a sense of purpose that made Josephine's heart ache. "God created all things, right?" Emma began.

"Yes, of course," Josephine answered, her voice quieter now.

"That includes the brain and how it works, agree?"

"Well... yes."

"So then, is it that far-fetched to believe that God created the brain with a built-in homing device so that the spirit can get to where it needs to go after death?" Emma's sincerity hung in the air, demanding her mother's attention.

Josephine turned her gaze to Emmanuel, struggling to reconcile Emma's logical reasoning with her deeply rooted beliefs. "I mean, he designed the heart to pump blood through our veins, the lungs to breathe, right?"

"When you put it that way," Josephine admitted with a shrug, "I suppose it doesn't sound so far-fetched." She expected to see a triumphant smile on Emma's face, but instead, she saw only worry and fear, etched deeply into her daughter's expression. "Angel, what's this about?" she asked gently. "I thought you'd be happy that you convinced me about this—what did you call it—homing device?"

Emma's gaze drifted to her father. "What if they're right? And what if the stroke damaged Dad's so-called homing device?"

"Angel, no," Josephine whispered, her voice trembling.

"But what if it's true?" Emma pressed, her eyes wide with the anxiety that gripped her heart. "Even if the chances are one in a million? What if the damage in Dad's brain causes his spirit to remain here? On earth? For eternity? You'd want to try to do something about it, right?"

Josephine stared at Emmanuel—the love of her life, the man she had shared over thirty years of laughter, tears, and quiet moments with. He was the man she had always believed she would see again in heaven, their souls reunited in eternal peace. But now, as she looked at his still form, the very idea of his spirit being stranded on earth, wandering lost and unable to find its way, was a grief too profound to bear. It gnawed at her heart, a fear so deep it threatened to unravel her faith, leaving her adrift in a sea of uncertainty.

"Wouldn't you want to do anything and everything in your power to give him a chance at reaching heaven?" Emma asked, her voice breaking with despair.

"Of course I'd want to do something," Josephine replied, her voice filled with determination. "I would do anything, everything, in my power to help."

"OK. That's all I needed to hear," Emma said, standing up and reaching for her coat.

"I don't understand," Josephine said, confusion clouding her features. "You heard what the doctor said—they can't repair the brain."

"No, the doctor said he can't repair it," Emma clarified.

Josephine stared at her daughter, trying to decipher the meaning behind her words. "Are you saying we should get a second opinion?"

"No, there's no time," Emma replied. "You heard what the doctor said—he could only have a matter of days."

"In that case, can you please help me understand what on earth you're getting at?" Josephine asked, her frustration seeping through.

"I don't have all the details yet," Emma admitted, stepping toward the door.

Josephine nodded slowly, a silent understanding passing between them. In that brief moment, Emma's eyes became a mirror of her mother's soul, reflecting the deep bond they shared.

"Be careful," Josephine said, her voice soft but firm. "Will you at least tell me where you're going?"

Emma nodded. "I'm going to see Dr. Clark—I think he can help."

Chapter 24

EMMA RUSHED DOWN THE STAIRS of the parking garage, her heart pounding in sync with the urgency driving her forward. Across the narrow street, the entrance to the Psychiatry and Behavioral Neuroscience building at the University of Chicago loomed ahead, its glass doors gleaming in the afternoon light like a beacon. She charged through them without hesitation, her eyes laser-focused on her destination. Each stride was propelled by a turbulent mix of determination and dread, the burn in her legs intensifying as she ascended the stairs to the third floor, her breath growing more labored with every step.

Normally the perpetual planner, Emma found herself in uncharted territory—this visit was entirely unplanned, and she had no idea how it would unfold. But she knew one thing: Dr. Clark held the key to something she needed, whatever that might be. If necessary, she was prepared to leverage the favor he had asked of her in return. It wasn't her usual way of operating, especially with someone like Dr. Clark, who had been there for her in the past. But desperate times called for desperate measures.

When she finally reached Dr. Clark's office, her pace faltered only briefly. She knocked on the door with a sense of urgency, her hand trembling slightly. Her voice, strained and breathless, echoed in the quiet hallway as she called out, "Dr. Clark, it's me—Emma!"

"Come in!" his voice answered from within.

Emma pushed the door open and stepped inside. Dr. Clark looked up from behind his desk, the soft glow of his phone screen casting a faint light on his face. "Again, you can call me Edward," he reminded her, setting his phone aside.

"Right," she replied, the habit still unfamiliar. "That's going to take some getting used to."

He offered a slight smile, though his eyes returned briefly to the screen. "Is this a bad time?" she asked, noting the distraction.

"Not at all—I was just watching something my wife sent me," he explained, waving the phone slightly. "Social media content."

"I see," she said, her tone flat, her thoughts elsewhere.

"Still not big on social media, huh?"

"Nope."

"Same here," he chuckled softly. "But I watch what she sends me anyway. It gives us something to talk about after a long day," he added with a casual shrug.

Emma gave a half-hearted nod, her arms swinging restlessly by her sides.

"You hurried off rather abruptly yesterday. I hope everything is OK."

"Could be better," she replied, lowering herself onto the couch opposite his desk.

"Oh? How so?" he inquired, his brow furrowing with concern.

"My father had a massive stroke yesterday," she said, her voice catching in her throat as she forced the words out.

His eyes widened with sympathy. "Emma, I'm so sorry."

"The doctor said it was a cerebral embolism," she continued, her composure faltering as tears welled up in her eyes. "He told us it happens sometimes... to people recovering from heart surgery. You know, the irony is, he was just released from the hospital. If it had happened while he was still checked in, they could have gotten to him sooner, maybe prevented the brain damage."

"What part of the brain was damaged?" Edward asked gently.

"The temporal lobe and surrounding areas," she answered, her voice barely above a whisper.

Edward sighed deeply, the weight of her words settling heavily between them. "Again, I'm so sorry, Emma."

She cleared her throat, trying to steady herself. "Anyway, that's why I'm here. I came to tell you I'll help you with your study, but I need your help in return."

He leaned forward, his chair creaking softly as he shifted his weight. "How can I help, Emma?"

"My father is in a coma. The doctor told us the odds are he won't come out of it." She paused, searching his face for any sign of hope. "You know my father is a pastor."

"Yes, I remember," Edward replied, his tone somber.

"So you must be able to imagine how devastating this must be for my mother and me, given what you told me about the study."

"I can't even begin to imagine," he said, shaking his head. "But Emma—it's only a theory. There's no substantial evidence—it's just a hypothesis."

"Do you think it's a coincidence that the day my father suffered from a massive stroke is the same day you ran into me and told me about this hypothesis? That we reconnected after all this time, and this theory of yours is what brings me into your office?" Emma's words tumbled out in a rush, her voice tinged with desperation.

Edward stared vacantly into the distance, his mind racing. "I didn't think so," Emma continued, her tone growing firmer. "I'm supposed to see him again one day—that was the plan. My mother and I are supposed to see him again. That's always been the plan!" she exclaimed, her voice rising with emotion.

"I understand, Emma," Edward whispered, his eyes reflecting the sadness he felt. "But there's nothing I can do."

Emma's disbelief was palpable as she remembered the lengths Edward had gone to for her in the past—the countless hours spent researching, dream training, consulting with colleagues—all to help her when she needed it most.

"If you had that kind of attitude when I came to you for help, I wouldn't be standing here today," she said, her voice unwavering, filled with conviction.

"I, I, I—" he stuttered, visibly shaken by her boldness. "I'm sorry. I just don't know what I could possibly do to help."

Her eyes narrowed, determination hardening her resolve. She crossed her arms, standing taller as she spoke. "Well then, maybe you're not thinking hard enough."

Edward could see the anguish etched into every line of Emma's face, the heaviness in her voice, and even the scent of grief in the shallow breaths she took. The overwhelming urge to help her welled up within him, but his rational mind insisted on understanding the full picture before he could act. "Emma, before we go any further, can I ask you something?" Edward said, his voice gentle but probing.

"What is it?" she replied, wiping away a tear with the back of her hand.

He hesitated for a moment, gathering his thoughts. "First, I want you to know that I can't even begin to understand the pain you're going through—so please believe me when I say I'm not trying to diminish your feelings in any way." He raised his hands as if to physically convey his sincerity. "But... could something else be going on here?"

Emma's brow furrowed in confusion. "What do you mean? What else do you want to know?"

He took a deep breath, preparing himself for the delicate subject he was about to broach. "It's just... I get the sense that maybe you're carrying some unresolved guilt, and that might be making this situation even harder for you."

Emma stiffened, her posture straightening defensively. "What makes you think I have unresolved guilt?" she asked, her voice tight.

Edward paused, recalling a conversation they had shared when she was his patient, something that had always lingered in his mind as a potential source of her stress—and maybe, her nightmares.

"Hold on a moment," he said, moving behind his desk. He opened the bottom drawer, rummaging through its contents until he found what he was looking for. "Here it is," he said, pulling out a black notebook. Flipping through its pages, he found the entry he sought. "You told me it was hard for you to leave home and go away to college."

Emma's eyes narrowed as she recalled the memories. "Yes," she said cautiously. "But I also told you that how my father felt didn't stop me from leaving. It didn't stop me from graduating, either."

Edward looked up from his notebook, his gaze steady. "And you know you did the right thing, don't you?"

"I know," she replied, but there was a hint of hesitation in her voice, a slight tremble as she rubbed her neck.

Edward caught the nuance and pressed further. "Then why does it seem like you don't believe yourself?"

Emma crossed her arms, leaning back on the couch with a sigh. "Okay, fine. I'm carrying some guilt—it's no big deal."

"Guilt about what?" he asked, his tone inviting her to unburden herself. "You feel guilty for going to college on a full scholarship and earning a degree?"

"Two degrees," she corrected him, holding up two fingers.

"What?"

"I earned two degrees," she repeated.

Edward gave her a look, clearly wanting to know more. "You picked up a second major? And you think that's no big deal?"

"I had some extra time my senior year, so I figured, why not? It was all paid for, after all," she shrugged, as if dismissing the significance.

Edward shook his head in disbelief. "You picked up a second Bachelor's degree at one of the best universities in the country on a full scholarship, and you think that's no big deal?"

She shrugged again, clearly uncomfortable with the attention.

"I knew it," he muttered under his breath.

"Knew what?" Emma asked, her curiosity piqued.

He moved closer, sitting on the edge of the coffee table in front of her. "Do you remember when I tried to get you to open up about your parents and your childhood?" he asked.

"I remember. I thought it was a waste of time," she replied, her voice tinged with impatience.

"I wasn't so sure," Edward said. "I did some research to see if your experiences with your father and your decision to leave for college had anything to do with your dreams."

"And it didn't," she cut in.

"No, it didn't," he conceded. "But that doesn't change the fact that you're harboring guilt. It's something we call 'breakaway guilt'—a term psychologists coined in 1989."

"What's that supposed to mean?" she asked, her brow furrowing.

"It refers to the psychological impact on first-generation college students who feel like they're abandoning their families by leaving for college," Edward explained. "It's like their success comes at the cost of leaving their loved ones behind. That guilt can even lead them to downplay their achievements—just like you're doing."

Emma sighed, clearly frustrated. "So what? Psychology has an explanation for everything, doesn't it? Can we move on now?"

Edward leaned back, studying her for a moment. "Listen, I know you shouldn't feel guilty about going to college, and I know you shouldn't see it as lost time. But I also know that this isn't just about you. It's about your father, and you wanting to fight for what you believe he deserves."

"But I just don't know what I can do to help him," Edward admitted, his voice tinged with helplessness.

"Convince the hospital to repair the TPO junction in my father's brain," Emma said, her tone desperate but resolute. "That's what you can do."

Edward's face softened with empathy, but his expression remained pained. "Emma, I wish I could help you—I really do. But what you're asking for... it's not something I have any control over. Even if I could—what you're asking for—it's never been done before."

"Edward, please! You have to try!" she pleaded, her voice cracking under the weight of her emotion. "Listen, I'll help with your study—starting today. I'll go to a funeral home. I saw one on my way here. I'll go right now. It's not far."

"Emma, please. Stop," Edward said, his heart breaking at the desperation in her voice. He reached out, placing a comforting hand over hers. "I'm so sorry, but if I could help, I would. You have to believe that."

Chapter 25

PRASAD NAVIGATED THE FAMILIAR PATH between the Psychiatry and Neuroscience building and the Center for Advanced Medicine at the University of Chicago with the ease of routine. He knew every detail of this path by heart—the soft hum of the ventilation system, the occasional hurried footsteps of students, and the confident stride of professors. It was all part of the daily symphony that played in his mind. But today, an unfamiliar noise disrupted the harmony.

He paused, straining to identify the sound. It was faint, almost imperceptible, yet it sent a ripple of unease through him. Instinctively, he reached for his watch, tapping the icon that controlled his hearing aid. With a quick swipe, he amplified the volume, bringing the sound into sharper focus. Footsteps. But these were different—too slow, too deliberate to belong to any student or professor.

Prasad glanced over his shoulder, expecting to see someone trailing behind him. But the walkway was empty, the only movement the gentle swaying of leaves in the breeze outside. His breath hitched, and a whisper of paranoia crept into his mind. Shaking off the feeling, he forced himself to move forward, his pace quickening as he made his way to Edward's office, trying to dismiss the lingering unease that clung to him.

"Knock, knock," Prasad said, opening the door and stepping inside. "I hope I'm not interrupting."

Edward looked up, the tension in his posture easing as if Prasad's arrival was a relief. "Not at all, come in," Edward said, gesturing to the chair beside Emma.

"I could use your help," he added, his voice carrying an undertone of concern as he nodded toward Emma.

Prasad turned to Emma, his usual lighthearted demeanor softening at the sight of her. Her face was a canvas of distress, her eyes dim and clouded with unspoken turmoil. "What's the matter, my dear Emma?" Prasad asked gently, taking a seat beside her.

"Hello, Dr. Vedurmudi," she murmured, her voice devoid of its usual warmth.

"You can call me Prasad," he said, his heart aching at her visible anguish. "Edward mentioned your gift, but I can see that using it has been hard on you. Don't worry, we'll find another way."

Emma shook her head, her lips pressed tightly together.

"That's not why she's upset," Edward interjected.

Prasad looked at him, confused. "Are you having nightmares again?" he asked Emma.

Edward answered for her. "That's not it, either."

Prasad frowned, his concern deepening. "Well, what is it, then?"

Edward turned to Emma, seeking her permission. "Is it okay if I tell him about your father?"

Emma nodded silently.

"Her father had a massive stroke yesterday," Edward explained. "He's in a coma, with severe damage to his temporal lobe and surrounding areas."

Prasad's hand went to his mouth, his eyes filling with sympathy. "Darling, I'm so sorry. I wish there were something we could do."

Emma's gaze locked onto his, and he saw a flicker of something he hadn't expected—hope.

Edward dropped his head, avoiding her eyes.

"What did I say?" Prasad asked, bewildered.

"There *is* something you can do," Emma said, her voice a whisper, but the intensity in her words was unmistakable.

"Anything—just tell me," Prasad responded, leaning in closer.

"You can repair my father's TPO junction," she said, the desperation in her voice cutting through the room.

Prasad's confusion deepened. "I don't understand," he said.

"Please, Prasad—you have to try," Emma implored, her grip tightening on his hand.

"Why are you asking me to do this?" Prasad asked, his voice tinged with bewilderment.

Edward answered, "She's concerned that without a functioning TPO junction, her father's spirit won't find its way to the next dimension."

"But we haven't proved that's the case," Prasad said, his brow furrowed.

Emma's grip on his hand tightened further, her gaze intense. "Without my help, you never will."

Prasad hesitated, the ethical dilemma weighing heavily on him. He wasn't one to be easily swayed by emotions or manipulation, but this was different. This was about a daughter fighting for her father's soul. He looked at her, his expression softening. "What exactly are you asking me to do, Emma?" he asked.

"You're a brilliant neurosurgeon—I'm asking you to do whatever it takes," she said, her voice firm and unwavering. "Even if it means doing it yourself."

Prasad, known for pushing the boundaries of medical science, had never faced a request quite like this. This was a different kind of challenge—a different kind of boundary. "I'm sorry, Emma, but it's never been done before," he said, shaking his head.

"When Edward first talked to me about you, he said you were one of the best neurosurgeons in the country," she pressed, her tone growing more desperate.

"Not the best," Edward added, trying to lighten the mood, but the attempt fell flat.

"There must be something you can do," Emma pleaded, her voice breaking.

"There's no solution for this," Prasad said, the words tasting bitter as he spoke them.

"No, I refuse to accept that for an answer—not from you," Emma said, standing to her feet, her voice rising with the force of her conviction. "Maybe from him," she gestured to Edward, "but not from you."

"Emma, I'm not the bad guy here," Edward interjected, his tone defensive. "I'm just being honest and realistic."

"Yes, well, apparently, we don't agree on what that means," Emma shot back. She turned to Prasad, her eyes pleading. "You can't just sit there with that genius brain of yours and declare defeat when you haven't even tried to find a solution. You have to think! Get creative if you have to, because doing nothing is not an option!"

Prasad felt the weight of her words and took a deep breath, trying to steady his thoughts. "Do you have a daughter, Prasad?" Emma asked, her voice softer now.

"A son... Ravi," he replied, the mention of his family bringing a shadow of sadness to his eyes. "He's in India with his mother."

"You miss them," she stated.

"Yes... very much," he admitted.

"Why are they away without you?" she asked.

"It's an extended trip," he explained. "My wife thought it would be good for Ravi to immerse himself in the culture."

"Okay, well, put them in my situation," she said, her voice trembling. "Imagine how you would feel, what lengths you would go to, if there was no chance of reuniting with them in the afterlife."

Prasad's heart clenched at the thought, visions of his wife and son flashing through his mind. "I couldn't bear it," he said, his voice thick with emotion.

He cleared his throat, trying to regain his composure. "Emma, let's say I do this. How would we even know if the procedure was successful?"

"Wait, wait, wait," Edward interjected, his voice tinged with disbelief. "Why are you even asking that question?"

"If he moves on, I won't be able to see his spirit," Emma explained, her voice firm. "Not for long, anyway."

Prasad paused, considering her words. "In Buddhism, when someone passes away, it is said that 49 nails are hammered into their body and soul, restraining it from moving," he mused, almost to himself.

"How is the spirit supposed to reach one of the seven Buddhist heavens if their soul is restrained?" Edward asked, his brow furrowed.

"Buddhists have seven heavens?" Emma asked, surprised.

"Memorial services are held every seven days for seven weeks," Prasad explained. "Each time, seven nails are removed to eventually free the soul."

Emma shook her head. "My father isn't Buddhist," she said, her voice firm but not unkind.

"None taken," Prasad replied. "And for the record, I'm not a Buddhist—just adding some perspective."

Prasad crossed his arms, lost in thought, his mind racing with possibilities. "Where was your father when he had the stroke?" he asked suddenly.

"Twenty minutes from the hospital," Emma answered, confused by the question.

Edward's glare intensified. "Why are you asking her these questions? Why are you giving her false hope?"

Prasad turned to Edward, his expression unreadable. "Edward, do you know me at all?" he asked quietly.

Edward sighed heavily. "Since I've known you, you've never failed at something you set out to do," he said, his voice laden with resignation. "But this... this is different. There's nothing we can do for Emma's father."

Prasad looked at Emma, her eyes still holding onto that last shred of hope, now dimming into something more akin to resignation. She was waiting for him to confirm the inevitable.

"Prasad, she should hear it from you. Tell her you can't repair the TPO junction," Edward urged.

Prasad stopped pacing; his mind made up. He looked directly at Emma. "I can't repair the TPO junction," he said, the words heavy with finality.

Edward exhaled a long sigh, the room settling into a somber quiet.

"But," Prasad continued, a faint smile playing on his lips, "you don't need to defy gravity to get to the moon."

Emma's eyes widened, a flicker of hope reigniting. "What do you mean?" she asked, her voice barely above a whisper.

Prasad's smile widened slightly. "It means, Emma, that there might be another way."

Chapter 26

EMMA WASN'T THE SAME WOMAN she had been when she was under Edward's care. The old Emma would have never dared to question her father's doctor, taking their words as gospel. She would have nodded politely, swallowed her doubts, and accepted "no" as a final answer from anyone who even remotely resembled an authority figure. She would have apologized for her feelings, if she even voiced them at all, and tiptoed around her concerns, offering apologies for the slightest hint of curiosity. The old Emma had a tendency to shrink herself, to mold her actions and thoughts to fit what she assumed were the expectations of others, even when those expectations were imagined.

But this Emma? Not anymore.

Her eyes, once clouded with uncertainty, now sparkled with a renewed sense of purpose. She leaned forward, every fiber of her being alive with anticipation. She was no longer content to be a passive participant in her own life, waiting for answers to be handed to her. "How do we get to the moon?" she asked, her voice brimming with determination. Every word she spoke carried the weight of someone who refused to be sidelined, who had found the courage to demand answers, to push beyond the boundaries others had set for her.

This was the authentic Emma—bold, unafraid, and hungry for knowledge. She was a woman who had reclaimed her voice and her agency, who was no longer willing to settle for anything less than the truth. The transformation was palpable, and as she faced the challenge before her, it was clear that this Emma was ready to take on whatever came next, with a fierce resolve that left no room for doubt.

Prasad smiled gently. "By being creative," he replied, moving toward the whiteboard. "Let me walk you through it."

Emma crossed her arms and leaned back in her seat, ready to follow his explanation.

"The brain has approximately 100 billion neurons," Prasad began, writing on the board as he spoke. "The average stroke patient loses about 1.9 million neurons each minute the stroke goes untreated."

He quickly jotted down a formula on the whiteboard:

$$(VI/VB) \times TB/TIME$$

"VI represents the infarct volume, while VB is the total volume of the brain region—excluding the ventricles, naturally. TB stands for the total number of elements, like neurons and synapses, in the brain region," Prasad explained.

"Oh boy," Edward muttered, shaking his head. "Prasad, can you please get to your point?"

Prasad capped the marker and turned back to Emma and Edward. "Emma's father was just twenty minutes away from the hospital when he had the stroke. Even if it took twice that time for him to receive treatment, there may still be enough there to—"

"To save his life?" Emma interrupted, her hands clasped tightly.

Prasad exhaled slowly. "To temporarily activate the TPO junction," he clarified.

Edward leaned in, skepticism evident in his gaze. "How?"

"By using DBS," Prasad replied.

"DBS?" Emma echoed, her brow furrowing.

"Deep Brain Stimulation," Prasad explained. "It's a neurosurgical procedure that involves delivering electrical current to very specific regions of the brain. It's already approved for treating conditions like tremors, epilepsy, and Parkinson's disease."

"But it takes years of research and clinical trials to apply it to conditions outside its approved use," Edward interjected, his voice tinged with doubt.

Prasad frowned, his tone growing firmer. "The procedure is already being studied for several other conditions," he countered, clearly annoyed by Edward's skepticism.

"How does the electrical current reach the brain?" Emma asked, trying to piece together the technicalities.

"Through targeted implants," Prasad explained. "I would implant stimulation leads into the brain. The current is delivered through wires connected to a small device, a neurostimulator, implanted under the skin."

"But the neurostimulator can't be programmed to deliver an electrical signal for weeks after implantation," Edward said, shaking his head.

"I can program it on the spot," Prasad shot back, stepping closer to Edward.

Edward stood, his concern evident. "It takes weeks, maybe months, to adjust the current properly."

"*I will make it work, damn it!*" Prasad suddenly erupted, his fist slamming onto Edward's desk with a force that sent papers fluttering to the floor.

A tense silence filled the room, the air thick with unresolved conflict.

Prasad quickly composed himself, turning to Emma with an apologetic expression. "I'm sorry, darling. That was uncalled for."

Emma, however, smiled. "No need to apologize—I like it," she said, surprising both men. "I like it a lot."

Prasad blinked, puzzled by her response. "Oh... Well, okay then."

Emma sensed his passion, not just in his words and actions, but in the intensity of his gaze. She recognized the fire that burned in him—a deep, almost desperate drive to push boundaries, to turn the impossible into reality. She had encountered people like him before: geniuses whose extraordinary potential was often stifled by the very systems meant to support them. He was the kind of person who could design a rocket and fly to the moon, if only the red tape, endless paperwork, and stifling bureaucracy didn't hold him back.

"So, what's the plan?" Emma asked, her voice tinged with renewed enthusiasm. She leaned forward, eager to be part of something groundbreaking. But as she turned to Edward, who remained seated behind his desk with his arms crossed, her excitement wavered slightly. His lack of visible enthusiasm was a sharp contrast to the fervor she felt from Prasad, and it tempered her excitement, if only for a moment. The air between them thickened with unspoken tension, but Emma refused to let it dampen her resolve. She needed to know what came next, and she wasn't about to let anyone's hesitation stop her.

"Don't worry about him," Prasad said reassuringly. "He'll come around."

"I'm sorry," Emma said, feeling a pang of guilt. "I didn't mean to pit you two against each other."

Edward sighed and stood up. "You have nothing to apologize for," he said. "Believe it or not, this is actually a good thing."

Emma looked between the two men, confused by the sudden shift in mood. "Is this some kind of oxymoron I've never heard of?"

"Yes," Prasad quipped. "I'm the oxy, and he's the moron."

Emma couldn't help but laugh, the tension in the room lifting with the joke.

Edward rolled his eyes but smiled as well. "Ignore him. We get heated in our disagreements—it's what we call creative conflict. It usually means we're on the verge of a breakthrough."

"You seriously have a name for everything, don't you?" Emma said with a look of disbelief.

"Alright, back to business," Prasad interjected, bringing the focus back. "It's a straightforward procedure, but there's no way I can get authorization—not for a study, not as an experiment."

He paused, considering the implications. "I'll have to do it at his home. Can you get your father there by the day after tomorrow? I need time to prepare."

Emma nodded eagerly. "Absolutely. They already have a hospital bed at home for his recovery after the heart surgery. I'll arrange the transport."

"Perfect," Prasad replied. "I'll need your mother's consent as well."

"No problem," Emma assured him. "Anything else?"

"That's all for now, darling," Prasad said with a reassuring smile. "In the meantime, it would be wonderful if you could start working on the study."

Emma, overcome with gratitude, wrapped her arms around Prasad in a tight embrace. "Thank you so much."

Prasad patted her back gently, his touch reassuring. "You're welcome, darling," he said with a warm smile.

Emma stepped back, feeling a wave of gratitude wash over her. But beneath that gratitude, a question burned within her, a question she tried to keep buried deep inside. She didn't want to appear ungrateful, especially not to someone who had just offered her a glimmer of hope in the midst of her despair. But the reality was that Prasad didn't know her the way Edward did, and that unfamiliarity gnawed at her. She couldn't stay quiet, not when this question threatened to consume her thoughts. She needed to understand, to know why this man, who barely knew her, was willing to take such a risk for her family.

"Prasad, I just have to ask," she began, her voice tinged with hesitation.

"Yes, darling, anything," he replied, his tone as open and inviting as ever.

She took a deep breath, her eyes searching his for any sign of what lay behind his actions. "Why do you care so much?"

Chapter 27

ARMONON PART III

UNABLE TO LOCATE ANY EXTENDED FAMILY, the authorities placed Armonon in an orphanage in Rome. At eight years old, he was what the orphanage staff called "borderline," meaning that with enough effort—batting of the eyes, giggles, and tender smiles—he could be a viable candidate for adoption. But unlike the other orphans, Armonon had no interest in finding a new mother. His mother had been perfect, irreplaceable—no one could ever take her place in his heart. *Not that anyone ever could,* he thought.

As he sat in the sterile examination room, Armonon tilted his head back, allowing the doctor to examine him. The man gently gripped Armonon's chin, angling it just right to get a clear view of his throat. The penlight flickered as the doctor used a tongue depressor to inspect him, searching for any signs of abnormalities. "That's a good boy—you're doing just fine," the doctor said, offering a reassuring smile. He then turned to the nun sitting quietly by Armonon's side.

"Sister, there is nothing medically wrong with him," the doctor said with certainty.

"Are you certain?" the nun asked, her tone laced with concern. "He was talking when he arrived. Perhaps he got bitten by a tick?"

The doctor stifled a sigh. "Sister, that's not quite how it works."

"Then what is it?" she pressed, her voice growing sharper. "I could almost swear he prayed The Lord's Prayer aloud at Sunday Mass," she continued, though her eyes flickered with doubt.

The doctor shot her a skeptical glance.

"I said almost, didn't I?"

"You heard him?" he asked, arching an eyebrow.

"Well, no, I didn't hear him; I couldn't, possibly! I was seated way across the chapel from him, but I saw his lips moving—that's something," she insisted, though her conviction wavered.

The doctor's gaze returned to Armonon, his forehead creased with concern. "He just lost his mother, yes?"

"Yes," the nun confirmed softly. "And his grandparents not long before that. He said his mother came here to be closer to God—to find peace from her grief," she added, her voice trailing off as the flicker of doubt in her eyes was replaced with a distant and melancholic gaze.

"Sounds like she was quite the devout Catholic," the doctor remarked.

"Yes, it does," the nun replied, her voice heavy with sorrow as she brought her fingers to her forehead, chest, and shoulders, forming the sign of the cross. "God rest her soul."

"And his father?" the doctor inquired.

"He knows none," she answered, her tone solemn.

"And you're certain he has no other family?"

She nodded. "He said he knew of no aunts or uncles. We even searched for his surname—Onus—and found no one."

The doctor stared off into the distance, his expression pained. "Armonon Onus," he murmured, as if tasting the weight of the name. "You poor, poor child," he muttered under his breath. He turned back to the nun. "The most likely explanation is a condition known as traumatic mutism."

"Traumatic mutism?" the nun echoed, her brows knitting together in confusion. "I've never heard of such a thing."

"Yes, well, severe trauma can cause a person to go mute," the doctor explained.

"As I mentioned, doctor—the boy was speaking when he arrived, and by then, the trauma had already occurred," she argued, shaking her head slightly. "He was actually quite chatty, if you ask me."

"That's a fair point," the doctor conceded, crossing his arms as he studied Armonon intently. "In that case, it's more likely that he's suffering from a condition known as trauma-induced selective mutism."

"Well, that's quite a mouthful," the nun replied, still puzzled. "How is that any different from what you explained before?"

"A person who suffers from trauma-induced selective mutism finds it impossible to speak to select people or in select situations," he elaborated. "You can think of it as an anxiety-induced coping mechanism."

"Do you mean he simply chose to stop speaking?" she asked, her eyes wide with disbelief.

"It's a bit more complicated than that, but in a sense, yes."

The nun turned her gaze back to Armonon, her eyes softening with sympathy. She gently placed her hand on his cheek, her touch warm and reassuring. "You'll talk when you're ready," she whispered.

Armonon's eyes drifted down to a pendant affixed to the nun's habit, its golden hues shimmering in stark contrast against the black fabric. He stared at it for a moment, then slowly lifted his hand to point at the pendant. With a voice barely above a whisper, he uttered a single word.

"*Farfalla.*"

Chapter 28

LOST IN HIS WORK, TIME ESCAPED HIM, as it frequently did when he was fully absorbed in his research. Prasad was lost in thought, his mind fully absorbed in the intricate details of the DBS procedure. The idea of using deep brain stimulation to temporarily activate the TPO region was tantalizing, yet fraught with complexity. He had spent hours meticulously planning, considering every angle, every possible outcome. Time had slipped away unnoticed, as it often did when he was deeply engaged in his work. A low rumble from his stomach finally pulled him from his reverie. He glanced at his watch—*11 PM*. A sigh escaped his lips as he pushed back from his desk, the weight of exhaustion settling into his bones.

As he shrugged into his heavy coat, a familiar wave of loneliness swept over him, settling deep in his chest. With Asha and Ravi away, the once comforting routine of coming home had become a hollow echo, an empty shell of what it used to be. The warmth and laughter that once filled his evenings were now replaced by silence and the hum of the microwave. His dinners—overpriced, frozen meals—had become a pitiful ritual, a poor substitute for the family he missed so much.

Bow-tie pasta with Prosciutto and Pesto, he thought bitterly. *Here I come... Again.* The thought rang hollow, offering no comfort.

The campus was eerily quiet at this hour, the shadows long and deep in the deserted corridors. As he made his way to the parking garage, a lingering unease from earlier that day clung to him. The sound of strange footsteps that had followed him to Edward's office gnawed at the edges of his consciousness. He shook off the feeling, blaming it on the fatigue, but the shadows seemed more alive tonight, the flickering lights casting eerie shapes on the cold cement walls.

Reaching his SUV, Prasad unlocked it with a quick click of the button, the beep echoing loudly in the empty space. He hurried inside, the familiar smell of the vehicle providing a small measure of comfort. But just as he began to relax, he noticed a strange fog rising from the hood of the car.

Leaning forward, he squinted at the haze. *Is that steam?* he wondered, quickly checking the temperature gauge. Everything seemed normal. He shrugged, deciding to get it checked out tomorrow. As he pulled out of the parking garage and onto the freeway, the fog turned into thick smoke, pouring from under the hood. Panic surged through him as the smoke thickened, but when flames erupted from the engine, fear gripped him in a vice.

Prasad slammed on the brake, but the pedal wouldn't budge. The car's systems seemed to be failing one by one. His heart pounded in his chest as he frantically tried to lower the windows, but nothing responded. The vehicle began to drift left, and with every passing moment, the situation grew more desperate.

Coughing and gasping for air, Prasad struggled to think, to find a way out. His thoughts flashed to Asha and Ravi, the two people he loved most in the world. *This can't be it,* he thought, a mixture of terror and sadness overwhelming him. Just as he was beginning to accept the inevitability of his fate, a pounding on the window snapped him back to the present.

He turned, eyes wide with disbelief, to see a pickup truck keeping pace with his burning SUV. A man in the passenger seat was frantically shouting at him to roll down the window.

"I CAN'T!" Prasad yelled back, his voice laced with desperation.

The man didn't hesitate. Reaching under his seat, he grabbed a crowbar. "SHIELD YOUR FACE!" he yelled before smashing it against the window. The glass shattered with a deafening crash, sending shards flying into the night. The cold night air rushed in, providing a brief, life-saving respite from the smoke.

"CLIMB OUT THROUGH THE WINDOW!" the man shouted, extending his hand.

Prasad hesitated, fear paralyzing him. "I CAN'T DO IT!" he shouted, his voice cracking.

"DO YOU WANT TO DIE TONIGHT?!" the man roared, his hand outstretched.

Prasad's mind raced, images of his family flooding his thoughts. *Not yet*, he thought, steeling himself. With newfound resolve, he nodded, shifting his weight onto the driver's seat.

"ON THE COUNT OF THREE, PUSH OUT WITH YOUR LEGS!" the man instructed.

"READY?"

"YES!"

"ONE—TWO—THREE!"

Prasad pushed off with all his strength as the man pulled him into the truck. He felt his body being yanked through the window, the scorching heat clawing at his skin. In the next moment, he was inside the cab of the truck, the door slamming shut behind him.

"Put your seat belt on!" the driver ordered.

Prasad fumbled for the belt, his hands shaking, until he heard the reassuring click. The driver pressed the brake, slowing the truck as Prasad's SUV continued its fiery descent down the freeway. Suddenly, a massive explosion lit up the night sky, the blast reverberating through the truck as Prasad watched in horror. His SUV, engulfed in flames, was consumed by the inferno, leaving behind nothing but a smoking shell.

Prasad's breath came in ragged gasps, his mind reeling from the near-death experience. The only sound that filled the cab was the pounding of his heart and the echo of the explosion fading into the distance.

Chapter 29

EDWARD LEANED IN CLOSER his attention fully captured as Prasad recounted the harrowing events of the previous night. The vividness of Prasad's gestures and the energy in his voice brought the extraordinary tale to life, almost as if Edward could see the scenes playing out before him. "It sounds so unreal—like something ripped straight from a movie," Edward remarked, his eyes wide with disbelief. "You're lucky to be alive!"

"Don't I know it," Prasad replied, a touch of grim humor in his voice. "After he pulled me out, the car exploded into a fireball."

"Holy smokes," Edward muttered, shaking his head in astonishment. "And the guy who saved you—just a random stranger? A good Samaritan?"

"There were two of them," Prasad clarified, his enthusiasm rekindling as he spoke. "The driver was a woman—she kept right alongside my SUV the whole time, cool as a cucumber. They were like a superhero duo."

"From what you've described, it certainly sounds like it," Edward agreed, his tone a mix of awe and disbelief. "The guy who pulled you in must have been built like a tank."

"He was young, maybe twenty-five, and a firefighter. Strong as an ox," Prasad said, crossing his arms and leaning back slightly. "Reminded me of us when we were that age."

Edward scoffed playfully, "Right."

Prasad's tone grew more serious. "In all honesty, if I'd been in that car another twenty seconds, I wouldn't be here talking to you."

"Wow," Edward breathed, his voice laced with concern. "I'm just glad you made it out okay."

"Yeah, only a few bumps, bruises, and some scratches from the broken glass," Prasad said, shrugging it off.

"Just a few scratches?" Edward repeated, raising an eyebrow.

Prasad nodded. "But my coat didn't survive. It's a small price to pay."

"What caused the fire?" Edward asked, his curiosity piqued.

"The forensic firefighter at the scene said there was oil on the transmission pad and down the frame on the exhaust system," Prasad replied, his tone thoughtful as he recounted the details.

"Was the oil plug tight?" Edward asked, leaning forward.

"Yeah, but the oil filter was loose," Prasad answered, crossing his arms and settling into his chair.

"That's odd," Edward remarked, furrowing his brow. "When was the last time you had your car serviced?"

"A little over a month ago," Prasad said.

"That doesn't add up," Edward mused. "If it had been leaking since then, the engine should have caught fire much sooner."

"I know. That's why I don't buy it," Prasad said, his voice tinged with suspicion.

Edward fell silent, his mind reeling from the implications. "I'm just... shocked by all of this," he finally said, shaking his head as if trying to make sense of it.

"You're shocked? Imagine how I feel," Prasad replied, a hint of dry humor in his tone. "Do you have any theories about what might have caused it?"

Edward hesitated before asking, "Have you made any enemies lately?" His voice was tinged with sarcasm, but there was an undercurrent of concern.

Silence hung between them as Prasad's gaze drifted, his thoughts turning inward. Edward noticed the change and quickly added, "I was kidding, but... I might be on to something, huh?"

Prasad's expression darkened. "I'm afraid so. Yesterday, I had the unsettling feeling that I was being watched—maybe even followed."

"That's a bold statement," Edward replied, his voice now serious. "What makes you think that?"

Prasad explained, "While I was heading to your office, I heard something strange. I turned the volume on my hearing aid all the way up, and I could hear footsteps—deliberate, cautious, like someone trying not to be noticed."

"Are you sure?" Edward asked, leaning in, his expression intent.

"Absolutely," Prasad confirmed.

Edward let out a long breath. "Who did you piss off?" he asked, half-joking.

Without hesitation, Prasad replied, "Reverend Kay."

Edward's eyes widened in surprise. "I didn't expect a real answer! What happened?"

"She was furious about my proposal for the afterlife study," Prasad said, his voice tinged with lingering disbelief.

"And?" Edward pressed, his curiosity piqued.

"And after the IRB meeting, she stormed into my office and unleashed her anger," Prasad continued.

"No way," Edward said, his brows knitting together. "Reverend Kay? She always seemed so composed, harmless even."

"I strongly disagree," Prasad said firmly. "She said I was arrogant and went on a rant that I can't fully remember. I've never seen anyone that angry in my entire life."

"What did you say to her?" Edward asked, leaning closer.

Prasad hesitated. "I might have been a bit smug, made light of the situation."

"Jesus," Edward muttered, burying his face in his hands. "You don't do 'a bit smug,' Prasad. You're either a gentleman or an asshole—no middle ground."

"Me?" Prasad responded with mock innocence. "No way."

Edward's tone softened as he noticed Prasad's haunted expression. "You're really worried about this, aren't you?"

"I suppose I am," Prasad admitted, shrugging. "I was hoping you'd tell me I was being ridiculous, that there's no way Reverend Kay could be involved."

"She couldn't," Edward said, trying to offer reassurance. Prasad exhaled in relief.

"But," Edward added cautiously, "she could definitely authorize someone else to do something like that."

Prasad's eyes widened, his mouth falling open. "I know that's not what you wanted to hear, but I've never sugar-coated anything for you," Edward continued. "Now, what else did she say?"

"What?" Prasad asked, still reeling.

"What. Else. Did. She. Say?" Edward repeated, his tone firm.

Prasad rubbed his face, trying to recall. "She said something about God making no mistakes, then slammed her fist on my desk. I'm just glad it was the desk she hit, not me."

Edward recalled his interactions with Reverend Kay, always professional and composed. It was hard to imagine her being so aggressive. "Did you really think she was going to hit you?" Edward asked, skeptical.

"I did," Prasad admitted.

"Wow," Edward replied, shaking his head. "What did you get yourself into? I wouldn't want to be in your shoes."

He noticed Prasad's growing unease and asked, "Does she know I'm helping you?"

"No," Prasad replied quickly. "Absolutely not."

Edward let out a sigh of relief. "Good. Now, what else do you remember?"

"What does it matter?" Prasad asked, frustration creeping into his voice.

"It matters because I need to understand her mindset," Edward explained. "Was she just venting, or was she angry enough to, well, do something drastic?"

"I don't remember much else," Prasad admitted. "I know there was more, but I just can't recall."

Edward stood up, thinking aloud. "It was a traumatic experience, wasn't it?"

"Of course it was!" Prasad thundered. "I've never even sent a meal back at a restaurant, and here I thought she was going to hit me."

Edward nodded sympathetically. "I get it."

"I probably don't remember because I was distracted," Prasad said, rubbing his temples. "You would be too."

"I don't think so," Edward replied.

"What do you mean?" Prasad asked, confused.

"If I thought I was about to get punched in the face, I'd be hyper-aware. You would too," Edward said, pacing. "It's more likely you experienced memory loss due to psychological trauma."

"Memory loss?" Prasad repeated, scratching his head. "Is there anything I can do to get those memories back?"

Edward grinned mischievously. "How do you feel about hypnosis?"

Chapter 30

"HOW ON EARTH WOULD THAT HELP?" Prasad asked, shaking his head in disbelief. "Surely you know hypnosis isn't a reliable method for memory recovery."

"I'm aware," Edward replied, stepping closer with a calm determination. "But roll your eyes up for me."

"What?" Prasad's confusion was palpable.

"Roll your eyes up," Edward repeated, his voice steady. "I want to gauge your susceptibility to hypnosis."

"Alright," Prasad said, though skepticism flickered in his eyes as he complied.

Edward leaned in, studying Prasad's eyes intently. "This is known as the Hypnotic Induction Profile—or HIP test. It's a simple way to determine how susceptible someone is to hypnosis."

Prasad kept his eyes rolled up, still unsure of where this was leading. "Okay," he muttered, the doubt still clear in his voice.

Edward tilted his head, scrutinizing the visibility of Prasad's iris and cornea. "Your iris and cornea are barely visible," he noted, a hint of satisfaction in his tone. "I think it's worth a shot."

"This feels like a waste of time," Prasad retorted, still unconvinced. "Hypnosis doesn't exactly have a stellar track record for memory retrieval."

Edward crossed his arms, unfazed. "It can work with the posthypnotic amnesia technique, or PHA."

Prasad's brow furrowed in confusion. "PHA? Never heard of it."

Edward couldn't resist a smirk. "What's this? Does the great Prasad not know every little detail about psychology?"

Prasad rolled his eyes again, this time out of exasperation.

"Stop that," Edward chided lightly. "The HIP test is done." He began pacing the room, his tone becoming more serious. "The PHA technique can be particularly useful in cases of sudden memory loss caused by psychological trauma, like the one you experienced."

Prasad crossed his arms, still skeptical. "And you think I'm susceptible to hypnosis based on a little eye roll?"

Edward turned to face him, his expression serious. "Yes. The less of your iris and cornea I see when you roll your eyes, the more susceptible you are. Combine that with your tendency to daydream and get lost in thought, and it's clear you're highly hypnotizable."

Prasad glanced out the window, contemplating Edward's words. "Prasad?" Edward called out, noticing his friend's distant gaze.

Prasad didn't respond immediately.

"Prasad!" Edward raised his voice slightly, drawing him back.

"What?" Prasad replied, snapping out of his reverie.

Edward shook his head, half-amused, half-annoyed. "What's the earliest memory you can recall?"

Prasad's face tightened in concentration. "I remember my mother bathing me in the kitchen sink," he said slowly. "I must have been two, maybe three years old."

"See? You can recall memories earlier than most," Edward pointed out. "That suggests you're more susceptible to hypnosis."

Prasad shrugged, conceding slightly. "Alright, let's try it."

"Good," Edward said, gesturing for Prasad to sit. "Unless there's brain damage or disease, the memories should be retrievable if we can disassociate them from the trauma."

"Sounds easy enough," Prasad said, his voice dripping with sarcasm. "How exactly do you plan to do that?"

"By giving you permission to forget everything about your conversation with Reverend Kay until I give you a cue to remember," Edward explained.

"O—K," Prasad replied, his tone laced with uncertainty.

"Trust me," Edward said, switching off the light, the room falling into a softer darkness. "Just focus on my words and let everything else fade away."

Prasad closed his eyes, settling into his chair. "Get comfortable," Edward instructed, watching as Prasad propped his feet on the desk.

Edward's voice softened, taking on a soothing rhythm. "I'm going to start by priming your mind with a pattern of forgetting."

Prasad felt a smile tug at his lips. "I could get used to this."

"Shhh," Edward whispered. "Just listen and relax."

The room grew quiet, the only sound Edward's gentle voice.

"Isn't it interesting how memories fade over time?" Edward began, his tone measured and calming. "Remember that favorite toy you had as a child? You probably never went anywhere without it. Can you recall it now?"

Prasad's mind began to drift, his body sinking further into the chair as Edward's words washed over him. His eyelids grew heavier, resistance giving way to the hypnotic rhythm of Edward's voice.

"Over time, that toy got put away, maybe even lost," Edward continued. "And now, you can't even remember the name you gave it."

With each breath, Prasad felt himself slipping deeper into a state of relaxation. The room seemed to blur, the lines between reality and suggestion becoming indistinct.

"It's amazing how our minds remember to forget," Edward murmured. "You put your keys down one moment, and the next, you're tearing the house apart, searching for them."

He paused, allowing the words to sink in. "Or you walk into a room, determined to get something, only to forget what it was the moment you arrive."

Prasad imagined himself moving through his home, searching for something he couldn't name. The disorientation of the forgotten task seemed to pull him deeper into the hypnotic state.

"Forgetting is a powerful gift," Edward said, his voice almost a whisper. "It allows us to let go, to forgive, to move on."

Prasad's body relaxed further, his shoulders dropping as the tension melted away.

"No need to remember that argument with Reverend Kay," Edward suggested. "Why bother when you can simply... forget?"

The words echoed in Prasad's mind, the suggestion wrapping around his thoughts.

"Forget the smell of the room, the temperature, the words exchanged," Edward continued. "Forget the shouting, the look in her eyes, the way your heart raced. Forget the vein throbbing on your forehead... or was it hers? It doesn't matter now."

Prasad's breathing slowed, his mind obediently letting go of the memories.

"It's okay to forget," Edward assured him. "In fact, I want you to forget every... single... detail of that conversation with Reverend Kay..."

He paused, letting the suggestion take hold.

"But only until I say... *remember now.*"

Edward's gaze softened as he watched Prasad, who had fallen into a peaceful slumber in the chair. The lines etched on Prasad's face spoke of countless sleepless nights, and his graying hair looked as if it had been tussled by the relentless march of time. "What's happening to you?" Edward whispered, his concern evident. He stood and flicked the light switch on, casting a warm glow over the room.

Prasad's eyelids fluttered open, and a wave of disorientation washed over his features.

"Morning, sunshine," Edward quipped, a small smile playing on his lips. "Welcome back."

"Did it work?" Prasad asked, stretching his arms as if trying to shake off the remnants of sleep. "Did what work?"

"The hypnosis."

"You tell me," Edward replied, his tone teasing yet inquisitive.

Prasad tilted his head, thinking. "I remember I was supposed to forget something."

"And?"

"And I don't remember what I was supposed to forget," Prasad said, his brow furrowing as he tried to recall.

"*Remember now*," Edward commanded, his voice firm.

Prasad's eyes widened, memories flooding back. "Tell me about your conversation with Reverend Kay," Edward urged, eager to delve into the details.

"Uh—where should I begin?" Prasad's voice quickened, as if the dam holding back his thoughts had burst. "She was wearing a red pantsuit and these loud heels."

"Loud heels?" Edward echoed, intrigued.

Prasad nodded. "It was like she was marching with purpose, already seething with anger before she even entered my office. I could hear her coming from a mile away—I just didn't realize she was coming for me."

Edward leaned forward, his curiosity piqued. "And what did she say?"

"She accused me of disrespecting her, called me a child, and asked if I seriously thought she'd back such a ridiculous proposal," Prasad said, the words tumbling out. "And to top it off, she said I was all ego."

"Makes sense," Edward interjected without missing a beat.

Prasad shot him an incredulous look. "Now's not the time for that," he muttered.

"Right," Edward agreed, clearing his throat. "Please, continue."

Prasad sighed deeply. "I asked her if it was so foolish to believe that someone in her position would want to help people reach the next dimension. She accused me of insinuating that God made a mistake. And when I told her I'd call it more of a gap... well, let's just say she didn't take it well."

Edward's eyes widened in disbelief. "You didn't actually say that, did you?"

Prasad let out a heavy breath. "I'm afraid I did."

"You smug asshole," Edward said, shaking his head.

"Yeah, I may have pushed it a bit too far," Prasad admitted.

Edward dropped his head into his hands. "Is that all?" he asked, his voice muffled.

"She asked if I honestly believed I was the first to come up with this idea, and if I'd considered that maybe there's a reason no one's ever pursued it."

Edward frowned, trying to grasp her meaning. "What do you think she meant by that?"

"I don't know," Prasad replied, shrugging. "But whatever it was, I didn't like it, so I shot back that she was just concerned with self-preservation and job security."

"Hold on," Edward said, sitting up straighter. "What did you mean by that?"

"I was just trying to rile her up," Prasad confessed.

"But your comment must have come from somewhere," Edward pressed, crossing his arms.

Prasad shrugged again, as if dismissing the thought.

Edward waited, giving Prasad space to think. Finally, Prasad spoke again, his voice softer. "I guess I can see why a religious leader might have issues with my study."

"Then why were you so sure she'd support you?" Edward asked.

Prasad sighed. "Maybe she was right. Maybe it was my ego."

Edward exhaled heavily, rubbing his face with his hands. "Is that everything?" he asked, his tone weary.

Prasad shook his head. "No. She told me that if I thought she'd let me try to fix what I considered a mistake made by God, I was dead wrong. Then she turned around and said that God made just one mistake, and she was looking at him."

"Wow," Edward murmured, standing up. "That sounds like someone who might put a hit on your life."

"There's one more thing," Prasad said, his voice hesitant.

"What is it?"

"As she stormed out, she muttered something under her breath. She said, 'I'm done here, Bruno.' I don't think she meant for me to hear it, but I did."

Edward's gaze shifted to the hearing aid discreetly tucked behind Prasad's ear, almost invisible against his skin. "She clearly didn't know about your superhuman hearing."

Prasad tapped his hearing aid. "This little device has advanced speech enhancement technology. I hear everything."

Edward nodded, impressed. "So, what's this 'Bruno' about?"

"I have no idea," Prasad admitted. "I was hoping you might."

"Bruno... as in Mars?" Edward joked, a smirk tugging at his lips.

Prasad's eyes widened slightly. "Do you think it's related to astrology?"

Edward chuckled. "It's a pop culture reference. Forget I mentioned it."

Prasad considered this. "Maybe 'Bruno' is a cultural reference of some kind. Something I don't know about?"

"Like what?" Edward asked, puzzled.

"I don't know. Maybe it's a slang term for calling someone an idiot or a fool," Prasad suggested, his brow furrowing as he searched for an explanation. "In Hindi, we say 'dhongi,' in Spanish, they say 'tonto,' and in Filipino, they say 'bobo.' I thought maybe 'Bruno' might mean something similar."

Edward stared at him, still not fully following. "I'm not sure that makes sense, but I need to go," he said, standing up. "I'm meeting Emma to discuss the study—assuming you still want us to continue?"

"Yes, of course—keep going," Prasad urged. "I'll look into this 'Bruno' thing. Something tells me it's important."

"Alright," Edward said, heading toward the door. He paused, turning back to Prasad with a grin. "Oh—how rude of me—I almost forgot to say goodbye."

"Goodbye?" Prasad repeated, confused.

Edward smirked. "Bye, Felicia!" he called out as he exited, leaving Prasad shaking his head in bewilderment.

Chapter 31

A FAMILIAR COLD RUSH mixed with the musty, artificial floral scent enveloped Emma as she pushed open the heavy wooden door. The sharp contrast between the frigid temperature and the overpowering odor assaulted her senses. She had visited countless funeral homes over the years, more than she cared to remember, and each one shared this peculiar atmosphere—an unsettling chill combined with the persistent scent of flowers mingled with something less pleasant, a scent that clung to her memory long after she left.

Glancing at her phone, she noted the time—*4 PM*. Prime time for flower deliveries, when funeral homes were typically quieter, with fewer visitors milling about. In her experience, this was the hour when close family and friends of the deceased would often take a brief respite, stepping away for a quick shower or an early dinner before returning for the evening viewings.

Alone in the foyer, Emma pulled out her daily planner, a well-worn companion that held the key to her next steps. She flipped to the current date and found the name she was looking for—Michael Reed. He was one of the three names Edward had given her, along with strict instructions to maintain the integrity of the study by withholding any further information. Her task was simple, though the implications were anything but.

She surveyed the room, her eyes landing on a series of black letterboards with white plastic lettering outside each viewing room. Approaching the nearest one, her heart skipped a beat when she saw the name—Michael Reed. The letterboard stood solemnly outside the room, a silent sentinel marking the place where the deceased lay in state. Beneath it, a small wooden podium held a guest book and a pen adorned with a white feather, inviting visitors to leave their signatures as a mark of respect.

Although the room appeared empty, Emma reached for the pen, her hand hovering above the guest book. With practiced ease, she mimed signing her name, ensuring it looked as though she belonged there. She placed the pen down, her movements deliberate and slow, then cautiously stepped into the viewing room. Her gaze immediately locked onto the coffin at the front of the room, where an elderly man with thin white hair, wrinkled skin, and wire-framed glasses lay in eternal repose.

The stillness of the room pressed in around her, the quiet hum of the air conditioning the only sound. Emma took a deep breath, trying to steady her nerves. The weight of her task settled heavily on her shoulders as she approached the coffin, the reality of what she was doing sinking in. The sight of the man before her, so peaceful in death, contrasted starkly with the turmoil in her heart. She had come here with a purpose, but now, standing in the presence of the deceased, she felt a pang of uncertainty.

This wasn't just about the study anymore; it was about the questions that had haunted her for so long. Questions about life, death, and what might lie beyond. As she stood there, the room's chill seeped into her bones, and she found herself momentarily frozen, caught between the world of the living and the mysteries of the dead.

She had always found it strange when the deceased were buried with their glasses. What use were they now? Her thoughts flickered briefly to the practicality of it, before she pushed the notion aside. Scanning the room, she hoped to catch a glimpse of a spirit, something to validate her presence here. She knew that if a spirit lingered, it would likely be near its body, unwilling to part just yet from the vessel that had housed it in life.

But there was nothing. No cold chill, no flicker of movement—just an oppressive stillness.

Emma approached the coffin, her steps slow and measured. She closed her eyes and bowed her head, offering a silent prayer. *I know you don't know me, but rest in peace wherever you are,* she thought, her sincerity palpable. Suddenly, she felt something ice-cold brush against her arm, jolting her from her thoughts. Her breath caught in her throat as she spun around, only to find Edward standing beside her, holding a notebook.

"Sorry I'm late," Edward said, oblivious to the shock he had just given her.

She eyed the notebook's wire binding, the culprit that had grazed her arm, and let out a breath of relief. "Hope I didn't scare you," he added, his tone almost apologetic.

"You did, but that's okay," she replied, trying to steady her racing heart. "I'm not sure why I reacted like that."

"I don't blame you," Edward said, his gaze drifting to the coffin before them.

"There's nothing to be afraid of," Emma said, though her voice betrayed a slight waver. "My father always told me, 'Do not fear the dead—it's the living you should be concerned with.'"

"Wise words," Edward nodded, appreciating the sentiment.

"Anyway, there's nothing here. Let's move on," she said, eager to leave the oppressive stillness behind.

Edward glanced at his watch, a slight frown creasing his brow. "Have you been here long?" he asked.

"No, but I'm either going to see a spirit or I'm not—no sense in loitering."

"Okay, next one over then," he said with a shrug. "The name is Martha Johnson. I peeked into the viewing room on my way in. You were right about coming in now—it's completely empty."

They stepped out of the room and into the main hall, the silence almost suffocating. "Do you need to see the body of the deceased to see the spirit?" Edward asked, his curiosity piqued.

"They like to linger by their coffin, if that's what you mean," she replied. "It's the best seat in the house."

They entered the next viewing room with quiet footsteps, and Emma's gaze immediately fell on a tall silver urn standing atop a marble pedestal at the front of the room. Suddenly, Edward's earlier question made perfect sense.

"I don't need to see the body to see their spirit," she clarified.

Edward opened his notebook, jotting down Emma glanced over his shoulder, considering whether to share a memory of a young man she once saw—a spirit who had died in a gang fight, his body beaten beyond recognition. His family had been forced to choose between a closed casket or cremation due to the damage. They opted for cremation, the more affordable option. She decided against mentioning it, not wanting to dwell on the past.

Edward's pen hovered over the open page of his notebook, his thoughts swirling as he noted: *No dependency on the body. The body is not needed to witness the spirit.*

"How old was she?" Emma asked as they approached the urn. "Her name is Martha, right?"

"Does it matter?" Edward replied, barely looking up from his notes.

"No, I guess not," Emma muttered, rolling her eyes. She scanned the room, her gaze sweeping from corner to corner. "Nothing," she said, a hint of frustration creeping into her voice.

"Are you sure you don't want to sit for a while? We're the only ones here," Edward suggested, glancing at the rows of empty wooden pews that lined the room.

"No," she replied curtly, her tone leaving no room for debate.

"It just seems like you're making these judgment calls very quickly," he observed, his voice calm but probing.

"You've got your gifts. I have mine," she shot back, crossing her arms defensively. "Who's next?"

Edward sighed, sensing her impatience. "Jamie L. Miller, next room over."

"Male, female, non-binary?" she asked, her tone laced with sarcasm.

"Irrelevant," he replied as they exited the room.

As they stepped into the main hall, the mournful sound of a woman wailing echoed through the empty space, sending shivers down Emma's spine.

"There," Edward said, pointing to the viewing room with the letterboard that read *Jamie L. Miller*.

The wailing grew louder as they approached, a sound so raw and filled with despair that it made even Edward's heart ache. Emma paused at the podium outside the room, picking up the feathered pen.

"What are you doing?" Edward asked, puzzled.

"Shh!" she hissed, pretending to sign the guest book. "There are people inside—I'm acting like we belong here."

Edward nodded, catching on. "In that case, sign me in, too," he whispered, his voice tinged with a hint of amusement.

They entered the viewing room cautiously. Up front, a woman knelt before the coffin, her body wracked with sobs. Her long, blond hair was disheveled, cascading around her tear-streaked face as she clung to the coffin, as if hoping to bridge the gap between life and death for just one more moment. Beside her stood a man with dark hair, his cries quieter but no less heartbreaking.

Edward turned to Emma, noticing her furrowed brow and the way she crossed her arms, staring intently across the room. He followed her gaze but saw nothing. "What are you looking at?" he asked, concern creeping into his voice.

The room seemed to close in on her, the weight of grief pressing down on her chest. "Nothing," she said, her voice unsteady. "We should go," she whispered, turning to leave.

Edward followed her into the main hall. "Is something wrong?" he asked, concerned by her sudden need to leave.

"I didn't like how that guy was looking at me," she admitted, rubbing her arms as if to ward off the lingering chill.

"What guy?" Edward asked, confused. "The only guy I saw in there never took his eyes off the coffin."

"Can we just go now?" she said, her voice trembling slightly as she headed toward the exit.

"Emma, I really think you should give yourself a minute," Edward urged, but she continued walking, her steps quickening.

"Emma!" he called out in a hushed tone.

She finally turned to face him, her expression one of confusion and fear. "I saw him. A man, blond, early to mid-twenties."

"What? Where?"

"Up front, in the last viewing room," she said, her heart pounding. "He was near his parents—I'm assuming they were his parents."

Edward's eyes widened. "Holy moly," he muttered, his disbelief palpable. "Let's sit down for a minute," he suggested, leading her to a seating area near the foyer.

Edward sat down, his mind reeling.

"Well? Can you tell me now? Was I right?" Emma asked.

Edward rubbed his neck, trying to gather his thoughts. He opened his notebook, flipping to the relevant page. "Michael Reed, male, age 65, lung cancer. Martha Johnson, female, age 92, heart attack. Jamie L. Miller, male, age 23, motor vehicle accident."

Emma's eyes widened. "Jamie—that's him, right? That's the man I saw."

Edward nodded, confirming her suspicion.

"Does that line up with Prasad's theory? Do you know if he had a brain injury, an inactive TPO junction?"

"Yes," Edward replied, his voice distant.

"How can you be sure?" she pressed.

"The accident report said he hit a median and flew off his motorcycle."

Emma's breath caught. "Oh."

Edward hesitated, then continued, "He was speeding down the freeway at 90 miles per hour when it happened."

"Wow," she whispered, the full weight of the situation sinking in.

"There's more," Edward said, his tone grave.

Her brow furrowed in confusion. "What more could there possibly be?"

Edward took a deep breath. "He wasn't wearing a helmet."

Chapter 32

EDWARD'S EYES DARTED BETWEEN the road ahead and the photo clutched against the steering wheel, his mind a maelstrom of disbelief and burgeoning intrigue. The drive to his next destination wasn't long, but it afforded him just enough time to grapple with the bewildering events that had unfolded. He couldn't shake the astonishment that clung to him like a shadow—how could Emma have so accurately identified the sex, hair color, and approximate age of the deceased? The precision of her insights left him questioning the very foundation of the study he had once approached with unwavering skepticism.

His thoughts raced, each one tumbling over the next in a desperate attempt to make sense of the inexplicable. He bobbed his head from side to side, a nervous tic that had become a habit whenever he faced a particularly thorny problem. "Gender—50/50 odds. No way she could've been influenced by the name alone," he muttered under his breath, a practice honed from years of solitary contemplation. The traffic light ahead turned red, giving him a momentary reprieve to examine the photo more closely. A young man with blond hair stared back at him, his image frozen in time from the deceased's driving records. "Hair color—another 50/50 guess, based on the hair of the two relatives up front. Age range—she could've made an educated guess if she assumed they were the parents."

He had been scrupulous in his instructions to Emma, explicitly forbidding her from conducting any research on the deceased—no news clippings, no social media deep dives, nothing that could give her an advantage, however slight. And while he trusted that she had adhered to his directions, the scientist in him demanded irrefutable evidence. "Maybe it was just a lucky guess," he murmured, pulling into the parking lot of the funeral home. His eyes flicked to the rearview mirror, where Emma's car rolled in right behind him, solidifying her presence and the reality of the experiment. "One in three chance—more than 33%. Even a blind squirrel finds a nut now and then," he scoffed, though his voice betrayed a sliver of doubt as he cut the engine and stepped out of the car.

The cool evening air hit him like a slap, momentarily grounding him in the present. But as he walked towards the entrance, the photo still in hand, the weight of the unexplained clung to him like a second skin, each step forward a reluctant march into the unknown.

"Ready?" he asked as Emma approached the entrance.

"Ready," she replied, a hint of impatience in her voice. "Who's next on the list?"

"Not saying," he responded with a tight-lipped smile. Unlike the first funeral home, he had decided to keep the names of the deceased confidential this time.

As they approached the entrance, Emma let out an exasperated sigh. "You know, Dr. Clark—Edward—I figured you'd trust me more by now."

She paused, her expression softening. "Given our history and all," she added with a playful smile.

"Trust has nothing to do with science," he retorted, holding the door open for her.

"That's fair," she conceded, stepping inside.

The interior of the funeral home was a stark contrast to the simplicity of its exterior. Tall ceilings loomed overhead, and an elaborate tapestry adorned the walls, giving the space a grandiose, almost theatrical feel.

"It's a little over the top, don't you think?" Edward whispered as they took in the surroundings.

"I've seen worse," Emma replied, rubbing her arms against the persistent chill.

He scanned the hallway ahead, noting the symmetrical layout. "Interesting. The building is shaped like a cross."

"More like an upside-down cross," Emma countered, glancing back toward the entrance. "It's all about perspective."

She turned her attention to a flat-screen monitor mounted on the wall, displaying a digital layout of the building. "Looks like there are four viewing rooms down each hall. I've never been in a funeral home this big."

Edward joined her, studying the screen. "That's where we're going," he said, pointing to the last viewing room on the map.

They walked down the hallway, the silence amplifying their footsteps.

"What about that one?" Emma asked as they passed a viewing room.

"Not on the list," Edward replied without breaking stride.

They continued until they reached the designated room. "Here we are," he said, stopping at the threshold. A wave of sadness washed over him as his eyes landed on the light blue coffin at the front. Inside lay a boy, no older than nine or ten. Family photos surrounded the coffin, depicting happier times—a stark contrast to the sorrowful scene before them. The boy's parents and three younger siblings sat in the front pew, their faces etched with grief.

Emma peered over his shoulder. "There's nothing here. Let's go."

Edward's eyes widened. "That was even faster than before," he said, grabbing her wrist gently.

He had expected her to claim she saw the boy's spirit, considering his age and the likelihood that a traumatic accident—perhaps a fall—had caused a brain injury leading to his death.

"Yes, well, I know what I'm looking for," she replied, her tone curt. "Let's go, please."

Reluctantly, they retraced their steps down the hallway. Edward noticed Emma glancing into the next viewing room.

"Emma, I told you. It's not on the list," he reminded her.

"I'm putting it on the list," she shot back, her jaw clenched.

He sighed, resigning himself to her persistence. "Fine, we'll take a quick look."

As they reached the entrance of the viewing room, Edward paused, intrigued by the absence of a name or guest book on the podium outside. "No name, no guest book," he muttered under his breath, his curiosity piqued.

They stepped into the dimly lit room, the air thick with an almost oppressive stillness. It felt as though the walls themselves were holding their breath, waiting for something to happen. Edward's eyes were immediately drawn to a gold urn, partially hidden in a dark corner and surrounded by fresh white roses. The urn's placement struck him as odd, almost as if it were deliberately being kept out of sight.

"Why do you think the urn is in the corner and not in the center?" he asked, frowning. "And why is there nothing else in here?"

He continued scanning the room, his gaze sweeping over every detail, searching for answers to the growing number of questions in his mind. The eerie quietness of the room pressed down on them, making the atmosphere feel dense and heavy.

"Do you see anything?" he asked, his voice barely above a whisper, as if afraid to disturb the silence.

"I'm over here," Emma mouthed, waving her hand from the foyer. Edward rushed down the hall to meet her.

"Was I really talking to myself that entire time?" Edward asked, his expression a mix of disbelief and concern.

"I don't know," Emma replied. "The last thing I heard you say was 'no name, no guest book.'"

"I thought you were adding that viewing room to the list?" he asked, puzzled.

"I was," she said.

"So why did you take off?" he pressed, confusion deepening in his eyes.

"I'll explain later," she replied, her tone edged with agitation. "Just tell me which viewing rooms are on your list so I can do a quick walk-by."

"I'll walk with you," he offered.

"No!" she blurted out. "Please, it's just that I can move faster on my own—and I'll draw less attention if I'm alone," she added, her eyes clouded with distress.

"Emma, if this is making you uncomfortable, just say so—we can leave right now."

"Please," she insisted. "I just need a few minutes. I'll explain in the car."

He sighed, the tension easing slightly. "If you insist."

"I insist," she affirmed.

"We have two more on the list," he said, turning to the video screen. "They're down the same hall—these two here," he pointed.

She glanced at the screen, her gaze lingering on the restroom icon at the end of the hall. "Perfect," she said. "I'll meet you in the car in five minutes."

"OK, no rush," Edward said, stepping outside.

Though her tolerance for being in the funeral home—any funeral home—had long since waned, she pressed on, determined to finish what she had started. Her steps quickened, purposeful, as she moved toward the viewing rooms.

A woman crossed her path. "May I help you?" she asked.

Emma struggled to make out the woman's eyes behind the frames of her glasses. A quick glance at the gold pin on her lapel confirmed she was the funeral director. "Sorry to rush, but I need to use the ladies' room," Emma said, adding a slight knee shake for effect.

"Of course. It's just down the hall," the woman replied, pointing to a door at the far end.

"Thanks, and nice glasses."

Emma continued down the corridor, glancing into the viewing rooms as she passed. With a sudden jolt, she reached the restroom door, pushed it open, and moved swiftly to the sink.

She turned on the faucet, the urgency in her actions palpable as she washed her hands. After a quick rinse, she stepped back toward the door, pushing it open with a swift motion of her hips.

Chapter 33

EDWARD FLINCHED AT THE SUDDEN knock on the car window. He turned sharply, lowering the window with a quick press of the button. "That was fast," he remarked, still recovering from the surprise.

"Let me in," Emma replied, her chest rising and falling rapidly as she caught her breath.

Without hesitation, Edward unlocked the passenger door with another button press. As she climbed in, he couldn't help but notice the urgency in her movements. "Were you running?" he asked, watching her settle into the seat.

"Practically," she responded, shutting the door with a decisive click. "I pretended I needed to use the lady's room so I could get out of there faster." She paused, catching her breath. "Sorry if I was short with you earlier. I just didn't want to be in there any longer than I had to."

"I'm sorry," Edward said, his voice softened with understanding. "I assumed you were comfortable in funeral homes, given your experience."

"Far from it," she replied, shaking her head with a faint smile tinged with weariness. "Just because someone has experience with something doesn't mean they're comfortable with it."

He nodded slowly, the realization dawning on him. "You're right, of course. So, why are you doing this?"

The question hung in the air for a moment before Edward answered it himself. "Your father—right."

"Not completely," she said, surprising him.

"What do you mean?" Edward asked, his brow furrowing in confusion.

"I was planning to help you before I needed your help. Chances are, I would've offered my help even if you couldn't do anything for me."

"Don't tell Prasad that, though, OK?" she added with a sly grin.

Edward nodded, the corners of his mouth twitching into a smile. "But why help us if it makes you uncomfortable?" he pressed, genuinely curious.

"Because you helped me," she said, her eyes softening with gratitude. "Even if my issues hadn't been resolved, your actions showed that you cared. I wanted to repay you."

"Emma, you don't owe me anything," Edward said, raising his hands as if to deflect the weight of her words.

"I know," she replied without hesitation. "But I'm willing to deal with some temporary discomfort, just like you did for me. You know, what comes around goes around."

Touched by her sincerity, he smiled. "Thank you."

She returned the smile before shifting back into a more focused expression. "Alright, back to business. I saw nothing in the three viewing rooms on your list."

Edward's brows knitted together in surprise. It wasn't the response he'd expected. He had thought she might at least claim to have seen a spirit in one of the rooms, giving him grounds to challenge Prasad's hypothesis. "Are you sure?" he asked, still trying to process her answer.

"Yes," she confirmed. "But I saw something in that other viewing room—the one I insisted we check."

Edward tilted his head, perplexed. "But you didn't even step inside that room."

"I didn't need to," she replied matter-of-factly. "I saw them from the hallway."

"Them?" he echoed, taken aback.

"Yes, there were two of them," she explained. "A man and a woman. A bride and groom."

His curiosity piqued, Edward leaned in. "How do you know they were a bride and groom?"

"I didn't say they were married," she clarified. "I said it was a bride and groom. The woman was wearing a wedding dress. The man was in a tuxedo."

Edward raised his eyebrows in surprise. "Are you saying there were two people in that urn?"

"I'm saying I saw two spirits—a man and a woman—a bride and groom," she reiterated. "The woman was in a gorgeous wedding dress."

"What did it look like?" he asked, genuinely intrigued.

"It was a strapless fit-and-flare gown with a sweetheart neckline," she described, her eyes distant as if she were still picturing the scene.

Edward blinked in confusion. "What does that mean?"

She shot him an incredulous look. "A sweetheart neckline—the top of the dress resembles the top of a heart. The dress was fitted three-quarters of the way down, and then it flared out at the bottom."

"That's awfully specific," he noted, his mind racing. "There was no name or names assigned to that viewing room. I'll check today's obituaries." He pulled his phone from his pocket, tapping away on the screen with little expectation of finding anything.

"What did you find?" Emma asked, a hint of excitement in her voice.

"Local couple killed in golf cart accident on their wedding day," he read aloud, the bold headline sending a shiver down his spine. He turned to Emma, his face pale. "They died last week."

A gasp escaped her lips. "Oh my God," she whispered, her voice trembling.

Edward continued reading, "Jane Strideson and Michael Phillips, both twenty-eight, were killed as they were leaving their wedding reception after a car hit the golf cart they were riding in head-on."

Emma's hand flew to her mouth. "Oh my God."

"Strideson died at the scene. Phillips succumbed to his injuries at the hospital hours later," Edward recited, the words heavy with the weight of the tragedy. He could feel a tremor in his hands as he clutched his phone, trying to steady himself. "There's a picture," he added, his eyes glued to the screen. It was a photo of the couple on their wedding day, smiling and carefree in the back of a golf cart, a sign reading *Just Married* hanging behind them.

"Can I see it?" Emma asked, reaching out.

Wordlessly, he handed her the phone. She studied the image, her eyes widening with recognition. "That's the dress," she whispered, her voice filled with disbelief.

Edward leaned back in his seat, the leather creaking under his weight. "If they were just married, why weren't there any photos displayed in the viewing room? The room was completely empty," he mused, a puzzled frown creasing his forehead.

"Maybe they were just setting up. Maybe the viewing is tomorrow," Emma suggested, handing back his phone.

Edward began scrolling through his phone again. "What are you doing?" she asked.

"Looking for their obituary. I stopped searching when I found the news story. It should tell us when the services are scheduled."

His eyes scanned the screen, but after several moments of fruitless searching, he shook his head. "Nothing."

Emma exhaled in frustration.

Edward's gaze drifted to the sign over the door. "We're here; we might as well ask about the services inside," he decided, turning to her.

"Oh, okay," she agreed, reaching for the door handle.

"No, you wait here," he said gently, sensing the emotional toll this was taking on her. "I'll be right back." With that, he stepped out of the car and walked briskly toward the funeral home's entrance.

Inside, he looked around for someone who might be able to help. The building was quiet, almost too quiet, and for a moment, he thought he was alone.

"You look lost," a voice suddenly said, cutting through the silence.

Edward jumped and turned to see a woman with a gold pin on her lapel and oversized glasses that seemed to cling precariously to her face. "May I help you?" the funeral director asked, her tone polite yet distant.

He cleared his throat. "Yes, I'm wondering if the viewing for Jane Strideson and Michael Phillips is being held here?"

"Ah, yes, but you're early," she replied. "The viewing is scheduled for tomorrow evening."

"Oh, thank you," Edward said, feeling slightly foolish. "Silly me, coming all this way. I should have just waited for the obituary to be published."

The woman's expression tightened slightly, her gaze narrowing. "It would have done you no good, sir," she said.

"Why not?" Edward asked, a hint of confusion threading through his voice.

She lowered her chin, nudging her glasses up with a single finger, and fixed him with a look that suggested he should already know the answer. "Because there won't be an obituary," she scoffed.

Chapter 34

ARMONON PART IV

WHEN THE NUNS AT THE ORPHANAGE first laid eyes on Armonon, they assumed he'd be in and out in no time. He was a frail, diminutive child, smaller than most eight-year-olds, with wide, innocent eyes that seemed to plead silently for love. His story, a heartbreaking tale of loss and abandonment, seemed like the kind that would quickly tug at the heartstrings of prospective parents. But Armonon's refusal to speak and his determined unwillingness to embrace the role of an endearing orphan quickly made him an overlooked presence in the crowded orphanage. By the time he turned twelve, he had become a ghost, unnoticed and unwanted, left to navigate his existence in the shadows. When the day came that he was finally allowed to leave the orphanage for an hour each afternoon, he took to the streets with a hunger for freedom and a knack for disappearing into the background. He became a familiar, though unnoticed, figure at the nearby pizzeria. With a skill that belied his young age, Armonon deftly pickpocketed the unsuspecting patrons, using their stolen money to pay for his meals. He moved silently, his small frame making him nearly invisible as he slipped wallets from pockets with the precision of a seasoned thief.

"Hey, I saw you take that man's wallet," a voice said in Italian from behind him, followed by a firm tap on his shoulder.

Armonon froze, then slowly turned to face his accuser. The boy standing before him was unlike anyone Armonon had encountered. Dressed in sharp, well-tailored clothes, the boy looked like he belonged in a world far removed from the grimy streets Armonon knew so well. He was around thirteen, by Armonon's estimation, with an air of sophistication that seemed out of place in the pizzeria's casual setting. Despite the boy's polished appearance, his expression was one of curiosity rather than accusation.

"You move fast," the boy continued, his tone more impressed than hostile. "Where'd you learn to do that?"

Armonon merely shrugged, his dark eyes wary as he turned back to the line at the pizzeria, ignoring the boy who seemed far too interested in him.

Undeterred, the boy fell into step beside him. "I'm Tonio," he offered, his voice carrying a lilting accent that matched his Italian features.

Armonon was silent, his gaze fixed on the menu ahead as if he hadn't heard a word.

"Parli Italiano?" Tonio asked, his brow furrowing as he tried to make a connection.

Armonon remained silent.

"Parli francese? English? Sprichst du Deutsch?" Tonio pressed on, his tone growing more insistent as he rattled off a roll call of languages, each one sharper than the last.

At the sound of the last sentence, Armonon finally turned. He recognized the German, though most of what he once knew had long faded. Yet, for the first time in a while, he felt a flicker of something other than the cold detachment that had become his armor. He didn't trust easily, but there was something about Tonio—his boldness, the effortless confidence—that piqued his interest.

He wasn't sure what the boy wanted, but as they stood in line together, Tonio's strange mix of curiosity and charm intrigued him. He should have been wary, caught in the act and expecting consequences, yet the boy seemed more interested in befriending him than turning him in.

"Italiano," Armonon finally said, breaking his silence.

"Then why aren't you answering me?" Tonio asked, a flicker of annoyance crossing his face.

Armonon shrugged, his silence still his greatest shield, a defense he had learned to wield well.

"That's OK. Everyone around here talks too damn much anyway—that's what Pà says," Tonio remarked, as if trying to justify his growing interest in the quiet boy. "Anyway, I'm not getting back in line. I'm done eating—see you around."

And indeed, he did see Armonon again, same time, same place, as if it were a ritual they had silently agreed upon. Each day, Armonon treated Tonio to pizza and gelato. To Tonio, it was just a nice gesture from a new friend, but to Armonon, it was a calculated move, a way to keep Tonio from mentioning his pickpocketing to the pizzeria owner. Day after day, Armonon watched Tonio devour slice after slice, carefully avoiding any spill of tomato sauce on his fine clothing. By the looks of him, Tonio didn't need anyone to buy him anything, but he accepted the food without complaint, as if it were his due.

Armonon's attention was suddenly caught by a faint, unfamiliar scent that mingled with the usual aromas of basil and oregano. It was the unmistakable smell of expensive cologne, the kind that seemed out of place in the simple pizzeria.

"Pà, this is the kid I've been telling you about," Tonio said, turning toward the source of the scent. Standing beside him was a man, his presence commanding, his frame draped in a perfectly tailored black suit. The man's hair was slicked back, and he moved with a quiet authority that made everyone around him seem smaller, insignificant.

Armonon instinctively stood up straight, his body rigid as if he were a soldier at attention, trying to make himself presentable in the presence of someone clearly used to being in charge.

"I've chatted him up the best I could to feel him out. I can stand him, I really can," Tonio said, his voice carrying a mix of pride and urgency.

Armonon watched as Tonio's father sized him up, his dark, penetrating eyes moving over him with an intensity that made Armonon feel as though he were being assessed for purchase, evaluated like a commodity rather than a person.

"He don't say much, so I figured you'd like him," Tonio continued. "And he's real good. Show him, Armonon."

Without hesitation, Armonon moved toward the line of pizzeria patrons, ready to demonstrate the skill that had kept him fed for so long. But just as he was about to begin, a single word from Tonio's father froze him in his tracks.

"No."

The word hung in the air, and a heavy silence followed, thick with unspoken meanings and the weight of authority. Armonon stood there, his heart pounding in his chest, unsure of what to expect next. The man's eyes bore into him, and for a moment, Armonon felt as though every secret he had ever kept was laid bare before this stranger, who could see right through him.

"Why not, Pà? He's real good—give'im a chance."

"You already told me he's a good pickpocket. You think I think you's a liar?"

"No," Tonio replied, shaking his head. "So, that's it then? You gonna give him a job?"

"No," he scoffed, glancing at his watch. "It's 9 AM. I'll be back in a couple hours to grab a bite. If the kid has six million Lire for me when I get back, he's gotta job."

Tonio looked out of the pizzeria's front window at the Piazza di Trevi. "How's he supposed to do that, Pà? It's early—there's barely anyone here yet."

"He's gonna have to figure it out, then, ain't he?" he shrugged, walking away. "I'll be back in a couple hours—don't be late."

Tonio exhaled deeply and turned to Armonon. "Can't say I didn't try," he shrugged.

Armonon walked outside to the plaza as Tonio followed alongside him.

A harmonious blend of bubbling and splashing echoed through the air. The grand Trevi fountain, with its statue of Oceanus, the Titan God of the Earth, surrounded by mythical sea creatures and cascading waterfalls, stood just ahead—a sight to behold.

"A lot of dumb-dumbs think the god in the center there is Neptune," Tonio said, pointing at the majestic marble statue. "It's not, though. That's Oceanus."

Armonon's fixed his gaze on the statue.

"Pà calls the dumb-dumbs illiterates. Says he refuses to let me become one of them, so he teaches me a lot. Says I need to always be thinkin."

Armonon's gaze remained fixed on the fountain.

"What are you thinkin about? Why are you starin at the fountain?" Tonio asked. "You ain't thinkin about jumpin in and snatchin all the coins, are you?"

"No," Armonon replied.

"Good, cause it's a bad idea. It would take you all day, and no way you'd get away wit it," he said, his eyes scanning the plaza. "There's polizia all around just lookin for pickpockets."

Armonon turned his gaze to a sign that hung on a lamppost:

ATTENZIONE BORSEGGIATORI
BEWARE OF PICKPOCKETS

"Why are you staring at that sign?" Tonio asked. There was silence.

"Geez, sometimes I wish you'd talk more—just a little—you know?" he said, fixing his gaze on the sign. "What's going on in that head of yours? You thinkin or you's just distracted? I hope you's not distracted."

Armonon turned to him. "Why not?"

"Cause Pà always tells me you should never be distracted, never, never."

"Why not?"

"Well, ain't it obvious, kid?" Tonio asked, furrowing his brow.

"No," Armonon replied.

"Boy, oh boy, you's got a lot to learn," he said.

Armonon stared at him, unmoving.

"What?"

Armonon spoke slowly, emphasizing each word and syllable, "Why. Never. Be. Distracted?" he said.

"Because you can't spell distracted without *D-E-A-D*."

Chapter 35

ARMONON PART V

TONIO WATCHED IN AMAZEMENT as Armonon slipped through the crowded pier like a shadow—silent, unnoticed, and impossibly swift. His small frame wove effortlessly between the disembarking passengers. With a final, graceful leap, Armonon reached up and affixed the stolen sign from the plaza onto a lamppost, its bold letters immediately catching the attention of passing tourists.

"What's that sign for?" Tonio panted, struggling to keep pace as Armonon glided through the crowd with smooth, almost choreographed precision. But Armonon didn't answer, his eyes already locked on his next target—a tourist distracted by a guidebook in one hand and a precariously balanced cup of coffee in the other.

With a subtle bump and a quick, sincere apology in Italian, Armonon expertly slipped the woman's wallet from her purse.

"It's OK," she murmured, more concerned with the coffee spilling over her hand than the contents of her bag, oblivious to the skillful theft that had just occurred.

Tonio shook his head, smirking. "You think that wallet's gonna get you six million?"

Armonon glanced at a black plastic bag fluttering nearby. "Grab that," he said.

"Why?" Tonio asked, but he obediently scooped it up. Armonon snatched it from his hand, already moving toward the line of taxis, where drivers sized up the swarm of potential fares.

"Where you headed?" Tonio asked, frowning. "You never go anywhere."

"Civitavecchia," Armonon replied, handing the cab driver a thick wad of cash from the freshly stolen wallet.

"Why Civitavecchia?" Tonio pressed as he climbed into the taxi after him.

"You coming or not?" Armonon asked, already sliding into the back seat.

"Yeah, I'm coming," Tonio muttered, squeezing in beside him. "But how do you plan on getting six million? You really think you can pull it off?"

Armonon nodded, his expression serious and focused.

Tonio snorted. "Good luck, but it's impossible. Do the math. It's a thirty-minute drive to Civitavecchia. By the time we're back, you'll have barely an hour left to get the money."

"Plenty of time," Armonon replied with quiet confidence.

Tonio muttered to himself as the taxi sped away, "Why Civitavecchia? There's nothing there."

Armonon stayed silent, eyes forward.

As they drove along the coast, Tonio's curiosity grew. When they finally pulled into the bustling port of Civitavecchia, the reason became clear. A massive cruise ship loomed ahead, its towering presence dominating the skyline.

"Now *that's* a ship," Tonio breathed, his skepticism fading into awe. "I went on a cruise once. That thing must hold five thousand passengers, maybe more with the crew."

Armonon's gaze remained fixed on the passengers beginning to disembark. Moving with purpose, he navigated the thickening crowd with ease, while Tonio trailed behind, noticing how the tourists instinctively patted their pockets and bags after reading the sign Armonon had posted.

"They're practically advertising where their valuables are," Tonio whispered to himself, suddenly appreciating the brilliance of Armonon's scheme.

As the crowd thickened, Armonon's hands moved like lightning, relieving tourists of their cash without so much as a glance. Meanwhile, a plan was forming in Tonio's mind. He turned his attention to the line of waiting taxis.

"Hey, hold up a sec!" Tonio called to the driver at the front. "I'm waiting for someone coming off the pier."

The driver barely glanced at him. "Sorry, kid. First come, first serve. Time is money."

Tonio pulled a crumpled wad of bills from his pocket and waved it under the driver's nose. "I got plenty."

The driver eyed the money warily. "How's a kid like you carrying that kind of cash?"

Tonio shrugged. "Forget it. Not my business. Where to?"

"Piazza di Trevi," Tonio replied, sliding into the back seat. He spotted Armonon slipping through the crowd and waved him over. "HEY, ARMONON! OVER HERE!"

Armonon hurried to the taxi and climbed in, calm amidst the chaos. Tonio glanced at his empty pockets and sighed. "I told you, there's no way you'd get six million. No point rushing now."

Without a word, Armonon reached into his waistband and pulled out the black plastic bag, now bulging with cash. "U.S. dollars okay?"

Tonio's eyes widened as he dug through the bag. "U.S. dollars okay? Of course! Money's money, as Pà always says. Looks like you got currency from all over the world!" He pulled out a brown bill. "Hey, check this out. You know who this is?"

Armonon shook his head.

Tonio rolled his eyes. "Seriously? Never seen Gandhi before? You need to get out more."

Armonon ignored the jab, his gaze fixed on the city rushing by as the taxi sped toward Rome.

"Can we go now?" the driver asked, eager to leave the chaos behind.

"Yeah, step on it," Tonio said, checking his watch. "We've only got forty-five minutes, and we'll need every second with the streets packed like this."

Tonio noticed Armonon staring at him. "What? Why're you looking at me like that?"

Armonon stayed silent, his eyes steady.

Tonio huffed. "I know what you're thinking, and you're wrong. I didn't help you, okay? All I did was pay for the ride back. No way was I taking the train with the cattle... What am I, an animal?"

Armonon's mouth watered as he stared at the feast laid out before him. The aroma of freshly baked pizza—ripe tomatoes, fragrant basil, and a symphony of savory meats—filled the air, stronger than it ever had before. The pizza's thin, crispy crust was perfectly charred at the edges, crowned with bubbling, golden cheese that stretched with each bite. Wasting no time, Armonon lifted a slice, the gooey cheese pulling in strings between his fingers as he took a bite. "Yum," he mumbled through a mouthful, his words muffled by the taste of sheer indulgence.

Just then, Tonio's father entered the room, his imposing presence casting a long shadow over the table. Armonon barely had time to swallow before the tension shifted.

"Here," Armonon said, holding up the black plastic bag like a prized trophy. Tonio's excitement bubbled over. "There's way more than six million, Pà," he added, his voice shaking with eagerness. "I counted it—way more, especially with all the other valuables in there."

Tonio's father studied the bag with a faint smirk, the lines of his face hardened by years of command. He gave Armonon a rare pat on the head, his approval silent but palpable. "Good job, kid," he growled in his gravelly voice, his eyes glinting as he peeked inside the bulging bag. "How'd you pull it off?"

Tonio, unable to contain his excitement, jumped in, "Pà, you should've seen it! The way Armonon moved—I've never seen anything like it! It started when we were—"

"Enough," Tonio's father cut him off with a curt wave, taking a deep breath as if to still the room. His sharp eyes flickered with patience, but his lips pressed into a tight line. "You'll tell me the details another time."

Tonio deflated slightly, but his curiosity still burned. "So, what's Armonon's job gonna be, Pà? You making him a thief?"

His father's gaze shifted back to Armonon, sizing him up with the practiced scrutiny of a man who'd spent his life in the underworld. "No," he said, his tone dark and deliberate. "He's already a better thief than most of the guys under me."

There was a pause, heavy with unspoken meaning. His father leaned back, assessing Armonon with cold calculation. "He's smart, fast, and has sharp instincts. Reminds me of myself when I was his age."

He turned to Tonio, who watched the exchange with growing resentment. "And he listens. People who talk less, they hear more. That's exactly what we need."

Tonio's face flushed with frustration, his arms crossing defensively. "So if he's not gonna be a thief, what's his job going to be?"

The room seemed to hold its breath. Tonio's father allowed the silence to stretch, letting the tension simmer before finally answering, a smile creeping across his weathered face. "An assassin."

Tonio's jaw dropped. "You're kidding me!" he shouted, his disbelief palpable as his arms flew up in frustration. "Pà, that ain't fair! That's what I wanted to be, and you told me no!"

Tonio's father didn't flinch. His tone softened, though his authority remained unshaken. "Tonio, you're full-blooded Italian. You'll be a made man, like me. When a made man needs something done, we have associates to take care of the dirty work."

He glanced at Armonon. "That's his job. He's perfect for it."

Tonio's lips twitched with resentment, his arms crossing tighter across his chest. After a moment, he rolled his eyes. "Yeah, I trust him," he muttered, though the edge in his voice betrayed his jealousy. "Molto non giusto."

His father's gaze darkened, his voice like a knife. "What did you say?"

Tonio paled, his defiance melting instantly. "Niente," he mumbled. "I didn't say nothing."

"That's what I thought." His father turned his full attention back to Armonon. "So, what do you say, kid? You want the job?" he asked, extending is hand to him.

Armonon nodded, his face resolute, and shook his hand.

And with that, he was no longer just an orphan, no longer adrift. He had been chosen, pulled from obscurity and molded into something greater. He was about to be crafted into a weapon—a tool of precise lethality. His training would take place far from here, in the ancient, hidden strongholds shared between the Mafia and the Church, known only to the most trusted.

This alliance, steeped in secrecy, was a contradiction. The Mafia's roots ran deep in Catholicism, yet their actions—murder, extortion, violence—stood in stark contrast to the Church's teachings. Publicly, the Church condemned the Mafia, yet behind closed doors, they exchanged favors, a strange dance of faith and corruption that had lasted for generations.

No longer under the care of the nuns who had once raised him, Armonon's new life would be one of brutal, disciplined training. He would learn the art of killing—the patience, the silence, the cold precision needed to carry out assassinations without a trace. He would master the deadly arts of hand-to-hand combat, weapons training, and psychological warfare. But the greatest lesson of all would be patience—to strike at the perfect moment, to become a ghost that no one ever saw coming.

Tonio's father looked at Armonon with quiet pride, his grin widening.

"What is it, Pà? Why you looking at him like that?" Tonio asked, unable to mask his jealousy any longer.

With a wide, toothy grin, Tonio's father answered, "Because they'll never see him coming."

Chapter 36

"ARE YOU CERTAIN THERE ISN'T another explanation?" Prasad asked, his voice tinged with disbelief as he leaned forward, trying to wrap his mind around the information. The events that had unfolded with Emma at the funeral homes seemed impossible, like something out of a supernatural thriller rather than a scientific study. It wasn't that he didn't want to believe it—he had spent years pursuing the impossible—but hearing Edward, a man known for his skepticism, speak so matter-of-factly about it was unsettling.

Edward met Prasad's gaze with a calm yet resolute expression, his usual air of clinical detachment replaced with something more serious. "I've gone over the data, Prasad. I've double-checked, triple-checked. This is real."

He paused.

"We still have a lot of work to do, but based on the data we've gathered so far and Emma's input, it seems your hypothesis is correct—the TPO junction just might be the key to the afterlife."

Prasad's mind reeled. This was beyond anything he had expected. He sat back in his chair, his mouth slightly agape, words escaping him as he tried to absorb the gravity of what Edward was saying.

"I don't understand," Edward said, observing Prasad's stunned reaction. "Why do you look so surprised? I thought you'd be dancing on your desk when I gave you the news."

Prasad shrugged, still trying to wrap his mind around it. "I suppose I wasn't prepared for you to start drawing conclusions so soon—especially you, of all people, and on something like this. It just seems—"

"Too good to be true?" Edward interrupted, raising an eyebrow.

"Exactly," Prasad admitted, finally finding his voice.

"Well, you know I'd love nothing more than to poop on your hypothesis, but so far, it's holding up," Edward said, a hint of a smile tugging at his lips.

"'Poop'?" Prasad echoed, smiling despite himself.

"I have a kid—what can I say?" Edward shrugged, the moment of levity grounding them both.

Prasad appreciated Edward's candor. It was a refreshing change from the usual echo chamber he found himself in, surrounded by colleagues who rarely challenged his ideas. This moment reminded him why he valued Edward's input so much. Prasad's eyes drifted to the poster on his wall:

> *When two people always agree, one of them is unnecessary.* - William Wrigley Jr

Edward continued, his tone more serious now. "You should have seen her, Prasad. Emma spotted those spirits faster than I could spot my daughter at school pickup."

Prasad crossed his arms, leaning back as he tried to make sense of it all. "I've never heard you sound so convinced about something like this, Edward. Why now?"

Edward exhaled, the weight of his words evident. "You know I've never seen a spirit in my life—until now, I didn't even believe they existed outside of a body."

Prasad nodded, understanding the gravity of that admission.

"But I've given this a lot of thought," Edward continued. "Even if we assume Emma guessed correctly at the first funeral home, there's no explaining what she told me she saw at the second."

Prasad leaned in, his curiosity piqued. "What did she say she saw?"

"A bride and groom that were cremated together," Edward replied, placing a newspaper on Prasad's desk. "There was no identifiable information on them in the building."

Prasad picked up the newspaper, his brow furrowing as he studied the front page. "What am I supposed to be looking at?" he asked.

"That's the couple she saw," Edward said, pointing to an image. "She identified the bride down to the sweetheart neckline on her dress—the same dress she was wearing when she died."

Prasad's confusion deepened. "What's a sweetheart neckline?"

"It's when the neckline—" Edward began, but then shook his head. "Never mind, it's not important."

Prasad set the newspaper down, his skepticism resurfacing. "How can you be sure she didn't hear about this in the news? It made the front page, after all."

"Even if we assume she did, there was nothing in the funeral home that indicated the couple was supposed to be there," Edward explained. "They had just started setting up."

Prasad's mind raced, searching for a rational explanation. "Where did she see them?" he asked.

"In a viewing room—but the only things in that room were a single urn and a floral arrangement. Nothing else."

Prasad's skepticism turned to suspicion. "Why would she lie about something like this, anyway?" Edward asked, his frustration evident. "You already agreed to perform the procedure, and she agreed to help with the study—she has nothing to gain from lying to us."

"It's not about what she has to gain, it's about what she has to lose," Prasad replied. "I haven't performed the surgery yet. If I were her, I'd want to make myself indispensable—at least until the procedure is done."

"She wouldn't do that," Edward said, shaking his head firmly. "You, maybe—but not Emma."

Prasad stood, needing to clear his head. "Listen, just give me a moment—I need to think."

"By all means," Edward replied, stepping back to give Prasad space.

Prasad paced the length of his office, his mind working overtime to find a flaw in Edward's reasoning. "She could have learned about the service through the obituary," Prasad suggested.

"There is no obituary," Edward countered. "The funeral director told me the families chose not to publish one because of all the media attention."

Prasad's skepticism wavered, but he pressed on. "Are you certain?"

"Yes, and there are twenty funeral homes in the Chicago area—she couldn't have known which one I was planning to take her to," Edward said, his conviction unshakeable.

Prasad's resolve began to falter. "Well, she could have called ahead, then."

"She could have, but it wouldn't have done her any good."

"Why not?"

Edward picked up the receiver of the desk phone. "Come here," he said, handing it to Prasad.

"Who are you calling?" Prasad asked, taking the receiver.

"Parkside Funeral Home—that's where the couple's viewing is being held," Edward replied, pulling up their number on his phone.

Prasad sat behind his desk, the receiver pressed to his ear as Edward dialed. "What am I supposed to say?" he asked, anxiety creeping in.

"Ask what time the viewing for Jane Strideson and Michael Phillips begins," Edward instructed.

"Hello, and thank you for calling Parkside Funeral Home," a woman's voice answered.

"Yes, hello!" Prasad stammered, caught off guard. He cleared his throat. "Can you please tell me what time the services for Mrs. Jane Strideson and Mr. Michael Phillips begin this evening?"

"I'm sorry, but there are no viewings scheduled for anyone by that name this evening," she replied.

Prasad's eyes widened in disbelief. "Are you certain?" he asked, his gaze darting to Edward. "Perhaps I've got the date wrong."

"No, sir," she answered. "No one by either of those names has been here, nor are they scheduled to be."

"Oh," Prasad mumbled, his mind racing. "Thank you."

He hung up the phone, his hands trembling slightly. "What did they tell you?" Edward asked, his voice calm but insistent.

"They said there are no services scheduled there for anyone by that name," Prasad replied, his voice barely above a whisper.

"They told me the same thing," Edward said, nodding. "It makes sense—the last thing the families want is a bunch of strangers showing up because of all the press."

Prasad's mind reeled. He placed his hands on his head, trying to make sense of it all. "Holy shit," he muttered, the reality of what Edward was saying finally sinking in. "She couldn't have known."

Chapter 37

EDWARD FOUND HIMSELF IN AN FAMILIAR ROLE—the skeptic now turned believer, trying to persuade Prasad of Emma's abilities. For most of his career, Edward had been the one challenging claims of paranormal activity, always demanding proof, always the hardest to convince. But now, as he sat across from Prasad, he realized something was different. Prasad seemed distant, harder to read, as if there was something more going on beneath the surface. Edward leaned back in his chair, studying him, trying to gauge what might be swirling in that brilliant mind.

What is going on in that genius mind of yours? he thought, almost saying it out loud. Instead, he muttered, "Now there's something I would never say out loud."

Prasad looked up, catching Edward off guard. "I find that hard to believe," Prasad said.

"What?" Edward asked, momentarily thrown off.

"That there's something you would never say out loud."

"You're teetering on invasion of privacy," Edward scoffed, shaking his head. "So, are you any closer to figuring out what Reverend Kay might have meant with that whole Bruno reference?"

Prasad's expression darkened. "Oh God, I'd rather we continue discussing ghosts."

"Yes, well, it sounds like it's not the dead you need to be concerned with right now."

"You're not wrong, my friend," Prasad replied. He slid a manila folder across his desk toward Edward.

"What's this?" Edward asked, picking up the folder.

"My research," Prasad said simply.

Edward opened the file, his eyes scanning the document inside. The contents were unexpected.

"Read it," Prasad urged.

Edward began, "*Hypatia of Alexandria—Hypatia, a renowned mathematician, astronomer, and philosopher in ancient Alexandria, was brutally murdered in 415 AD. Her death was a result of political and religious tensions, as her ideas and teachings were seen as a threat by some factions.*"

He looked up at Prasad, who nodded for him to continue.

"*Galileo Galilei—Galileo, an Italian astronomer and physicist, faced persecution by the Catholic Church for his support of the heliocentric model and his promotion of the idea that the Earth revolves around the Sun. While he was not murdered, he was put on trial, convicted of heresy, and placed under house arrest for the remainder of his life.*"

Edward's brow furrowed as he continued reading. "*Socrates—Socrates, a classical Greek philosopher, was sentenced to death by drinking poison in 399 BC. His execution was a result of his teachings challenging traditional beliefs and authority in Athens.*"

He paused, looking at Prasad with concern. "I'm seeing a pattern here."

"There's one more," Prasad said, raising a finger. "This one's the kicker."

Edward turned back to the document. "*Giordano Bruno.*" The name made his heart skip a beat. He read on, "*Bruno, an Italian philosopher and mathematician in the 16th century, was burned at the stake in 1600 for his unorthodox ideas, including his support for the Copernican heliocentric model of the universe and his pantheistic beliefs.*"

He stopped at the word *pantheistic—from the Greek words pan, meaning all, and theos, meaning god.* Edward's puzzled expression deepened. He looked up at Prasad, searching for answers. "Pantheistic—meaning all gods. The Global Assembly of Religious Leaders is made up of religious leaders with various beliefs. What are the chances that's a coincidence?"

Prasad shook his head slowly. "It's not. The Bruno reference was a breadcrumb."

Edward nodded, realizing the gravity of the situation. *Reverend Kay wouldn't have said it if it didn't carry meaning.* She didn't mean it as a term of endearment—that much was clear.

"Reverend Kay implied I'm not the first to come up with this idea," Prasad continued, his voice growing more intense. "I have to assume my predecessors were also silenced by a powerful multi-billion-dollar religious industry that sees my research as a threat."

"You're being silenced by the Church?" Edward asked, his voice laced with disbelief.

"No," Prasad replied, his tone grim. "Silenced by all the Churches."

Edward stood up, pacing the room as the weight of the situation settled on him. He thought about Reverend Kay's role in the IRB, her uncharacteristic behavior, her position in the Global Assembly of Religious Leaders, Prasad's study on the afterlife, the stalking, the fire—everything seemed to connect. "Maybe she was trying to warn you?"

"Warn, threaten—it's all the same," Prasad said, his voice thick with tension. "I'm in danger, and Reverend Kay has something to do with it."

Edward felt a chill run down his spine. The idea of Reverend Kay being involved in something so sinister was almost too much to believe. "I can't imagine Reverend Kay would risk getting her suit dirty to get under your hood," Edward said, attempting to lighten the mood with a poor pun.

Prasad shot him a look that spoke volumes about what he thought of the joke.

"Sorry, bad choice of words," Edward admitted, lowering his head. "I just mean, if she had anything to do with the fire, she wouldn't be the one to do the dirty work."

"I get it," Prasad replied, his voice distant, his mind clearly elsewhere.

Edward's thoughts turned to Prasad's family. "It's a good thing Asha and Ravi are away."

"Yes... Good thing," Prasad replied, his voice hollow, as if he was trying to detach from the world around him.

"Listen," Edward said, his tone firm. "You need to resolve this before your family returns, or they might not have you to come home to." He crossed his arms, staring at Prasad with unwavering determination. "So how do you intend to resolve this?"

Prasad stared into the distance, the weight of the situation evident in his expression. "I have no idea," he admitted quietly. "But I have a feeling I don't have much time to figure it out."

Chapter 38

JOSEPHINE GRIPPED HER HUSBAND'S HAND, her heart racing with determination as the dimly lit ambulance sped toward their home. Her eyes, glassy with unshed tears, fixated on Emmanuel's still form, lying motionless on the stretcher. She reached out with trembling fingers to gently caress his thinning hair, her touch as tender as the love that had bound them for decades. "We're almost home," she whispered, her voice trembling with a fragile mix of hope and fear that caught in her throat.

For days, Emmanuel had been locked away in the silent prison of his coma, yet Josephine's voice never ceased, a steady stream of words flowing between them as if her constant chatter could bridge the vast, aching distance that now separated them. She spoke of the small, mundane details of her day—the errands she ran, the meals she prepared—painting a picture of the life they had shared for so long. She kept him informed on the latest news in politics and sports, knowing how much he had always relished a good debate.

Emmanuel had always been the talker, filling their home with the warmth of his voice and the comfort of his laughter. Now, in this heartbreaking role reversal, Josephine found a bittersweet solace in finally having the floor to herself. But there was no joy in it, only a poignant ache that threatened to consume her. Perhaps she was clinging to a denial she wasn't ready to relinquish, refusing to confront the shadow of the inevitable that loomed over them. But as long as he was here, even in this silent, unresponsive state, she refused to squander a single second.

The ambulance screeched to a halt, the sudden jolt breaking the tense silence. The doors swung open, flooding the space with the bright afternoon sun. Josephine shielded her eyes, momentarily overwhelmed by the harsh light.

"Watch your step," the paramedic said, extending a hand to her.

"Thank you," Josephine replied, gripping his hand as she carefully stepped out of the ambulance. She took a deep breath, bracing herself for whatever the day might bring.

Emma was waiting outside, her face etched with concern. "Is there anything I can help with, Mom?" she asked.

"Yes, angel," Josephine said, her voice steady. "Let the paramedics in and show them to your father's room."

"Got it," Emma replied, quickly pulling out her keys and jogging to the front door.

Josephine watched as the paramedics carefully maneuvered the stretcher out of the ambulance and onto the street. "That's my daughter," she said, pointing to Emma at the door. "She'll show you to his room."

The paramedic nodded in acknowledgment.

"Mrs. Perales?" an unfamiliar voice called out.

Josephine turned to see a woman with dark hair, dressed in neatly pressed yellow scrubs, extending her hand. "Hello, I'm Nurse Evelyn. It's a pleasure to meet you."

"Hello," Josephine replied, shaking the nurse's hand. "The doctor mentioned you'd be checking in." She glanced at her wristwatch. "Will you be here long?"

"I'll be hooking Mr. Perales up to an IV and setting up some equipment," Nurse Evelyn explained.

As the nurse spoke, Josephine's attention was drawn to a cleaning van parked down the street, its presence seeming oddly out of place in their familiar neighborhood. Her thoughts briefly wandered to a neighbor's comment about her daughter, Joy, starting a cleaning business with her husband. *Joy knows better than to park on the street*, Josephine thought.

"Mrs. Perales?" the nurse prompted, drawing Josephine's attention back.

"Yes, of course. Thank you," Josephine said. "I'll show you in." They headed toward the house together.

"He's all set," the paramedic said, rolling out the empty stretcher.

"Thank you," Josephine replied, stepping inside with the nurse. She turned to Nurse Evelyn. "His room is straight ahead—the door's open."

"Are you doing OK, Mom?" Emma asked, her eyes full of concern.

"I'm fine," Josephine replied, exhaling deeply. "There's just a lot happening."

"Are you sure you want to go through with this?" Emma asked gently.

Josephine had spent countless hours in prayer and contemplation. Despite Dr. Vedurmudi's study being based on an unproven hypothesis, she trusted Emma's judgment. She knew Emma wouldn't subject her father to something so drastic unless she truly believed it was worth the risk. And given Emmanuel's prognosis, what did they have to lose? "What do we have to lose?" Josephine echoed aloud.

"Do you think it's what Dad would want?"

Josephine shot Emma an incredulous glare, her expression saying more than words ever could. "I know, I know," Emma conceded. "You wouldn't be doing this if you weren't sure it's what he would want."

A knock on the door interrupted their conversation.

"That must be them," Emma said, moving to open the door. "Hi, come in, gentlemen," she said as she welcomed the doctors inside.

Josephine stepped forward, her gaze shifting between the two men. "You must be Dr. Vedurmudi," she said, addressing Prasad.

Prasad's eyes widened with mock surprise. "Who, me?" he said, pressing his index finger to his chest in a playful manner.

There was a moment of silence.

"Oh, I'm so sorry!" Josephine exclaimed, her face flushing. "I shouldn't have assumed—"

"I'm kidding!" Prasad interrupted, extending his hand with a grin. "It's a pleasure to meet you. I hope you don't mind my sense of humor. The room felt a bit tense—I thought I'd try to lighten the mood."

Josephine hesitated for a moment before reaching out to shake his hand. But instead of a simple handshake, she pulled Prasad into a tight embrace. "Thank you, doctor," she whispered, her voice thick with emotion.

Prasad, taken aback, managed to reply, "You're welcome—happy to help," as she released him.

He glanced at Emma. "You should thank your daughter—she can be quite convincing."

"I know it," Josephine said, her voice soft with gratitude.

"Hello, I'm Dr. Edward Clark," the second man said, stepping forward and offering his hand.

Josephine gripped his hand firmly and pulled him into an embrace as well. "Thank you, thank you," she said. "May God bless you."

Edward, slightly winded from the tight hug, smiled. "You're welcome. I'm just here to help."

Josephine looked up at him with tearful eyes. "Emma told me how much you helped her," she said, her voice trembling slightly as she turned to include Prasad in her gaze. "I'm just so grateful for both of you."

"And we're grateful for Emma," Prasad replied. "I understand she has quite a gift."

"She's always been very intelligent," Josephine said, pride evident in her voice.

"Yes, that too," Prasad replied with a knowing smile.

Josephine furrowed her brows slightly, wondering what he meant by that, but before she could dwell on it, Nurse Evelyn emerged from Emmanuel's room.

"All done here," the nurse said. "He's resting comfortably."

"Thank you," Josephine replied.

"I'll be back tomorrow to check on him and administer his meds," the nurse said, heading for the door. "See you in the morning."

"Bye!" Emma called after her, closing the door. She turned to Edward and Prasad, her voice tinged with excitement. "OK, what's next?"

Before they could respond, Prasad turned to Josephine with a gentle expression. "Before we do anything, are you sure you want to go through with this? We can still back out."

Josephine didn't hesitate. "I'm sure," she said firmly. "I know there's no guarantee it will work, but my husband would want us to try."

"OK, then," Prasad said, his tone resolute. "Try we shall," he added, turning to Edward.

A mischievous glint appeared in Edward's eyes as he turned to Emma. "*There is no try—*"

Emma silenced him with a sharp look. "DON'T even think about it," she warned.

Chapter 39

EDWARD METICULOUSLY WASHED HIS HANDS, standing at the brink of a monumental decision, his thoughts racing between potential outcomes, both triumphant and disastrous. The soap foamed between his fingers, but his mind was elsewhere, fixated on the gravity of what lay ahead. *Am I really going through with this?* The question echoed in his thoughts, the weight of his choice bearing down on him.

"I don't think they can get any cleaner," Prasad's voice broke through the fog of uncertainty, waving off the steam that filled the small, sterile space with a towelette in hand.

Edward, still lost in thought, placed the towelette over the faucet, creating a barrier between his freshly scrubbed hands and any lingering contaminants. He turned to Prasad, his brow furrowed. "What's your confidence level that this will work?" he asked, his voice edged with the anxiety he couldn't quite hide.

"There's no way to know," Prasad replied with a shrug, the nonchalance in his tone a sharp contrast to the seriousness of their situation. "There's no precedence for this."

"Then why try?" Edward pressed, searching Prasad's eyes for something—anything—that would reassure him.

"Because that man has nothing to lose, and neither do I," Prasad answered, his words laced with a quiet resolve.

Nothing to lose? Edward's mind reeled. He remembered Prasad talking about the financial pressures that came with a new mortgage, his son Ravi's private school tuition, and the looming costs of college. "Did you and Asha come across an inheritance you didn't tell me about?" Edward asked, drying his hands with a fresh towelette, his tone half-joking, half-concerned.

"No," Prasad scoffed, a bitter smile tugging at the corner of his mouth. "Wouldn't that be nice?"

"That tells me you need your job as much as I do," Edward said, the tension in his voice rising. "So, why risk your career over this?"

"We've been over this, haven't we?" Prasad snapped, frustration seeping into his voice.

Edward exhaled deeply, realizing he wasn't looking for answers but inadvertently trying to plant seeds of doubt to soothe his own fears. "I'm sorry," he muttered.

Prasad softened slightly. "Listen, I've reached a point in my life where I want to do something that really matters."

"You're a neurosurgeon and professor at a renowned university—that matters," Edward countered, his gaze intense, searching for a crack in Prasad's resolve.

"This is different—I have a renewed sense of purpose," Prasad said, his voice firm, the conviction in his words undeniable.

Edward nodded slowly. "Okay," he said, the resignation in his tone evident. "I get it. I can respect that."

"Thank you," Prasad responded, a rare sincerity in his eyes. "And what about you? Before you answer, let me remind you that consent forms are signed, and emergency protocols and infection control measures are in place."

He paused, his gaze steady on Edward.

"And if all that goes to shit, you were never here."

Edward knew working outside the lines was a dangerous game, one he didn't play lightly. The memory of the last time he'd bent the rules flashed in his mind—an unorthodox decision that ended in success but at the cost of sleepless nights. "Give me a minute," Edward said, his voice barely above a whisper. He crossed his arms, his mind racing as he weighed the risks, the potential fallout, the ethics of what they were about to do. Finally, he stepped into the living room, where Emma and her mother waited.

"Emma, Mrs. Perales, may I have a word with you?" Edward asked, his tone professional, masking the turmoil churning inside him.

"Yes?" they replied in unison, their eyes wide with anticipation.

"I want to be explicit about my role here," Edward began, the words measured and careful. "I have the utmost confidence in Dr. Vedurmudi's ability, but I believe a procedure of this nature is best performed in a hospital setting."

Emma's brows shot up in surprise. "Oh, right, I understand," she said, quickly catching on to the subtext. "You're here to offer final advice to Dr. Vedurmudi on the matter, and that's all."

Josephine leaned in, her confusion evident. "I don't under—"

"We understand," Emma interrupted, placing a reassuring hand on her mother's arm. "Thank you for clarifying, Dr. Clark."

Prasad, sensing the tension in the room, stepped forward with a nod. "Now that we've gotten the formalities out of the way, shall we get started?"

"The room is ready for you," Emma said, her voice a mix of hope and fear. "Everything is laid out just as you instructed. My mom even shaved the back of his head for you."

"Wonderful, thank you," Prasad replied, glancing around the pink walls of the room.

"This used to be my room," Emma said, her voice tinged with nostalgia.

Prasad's gaze lingered on the walls, noticing the absence of windows. "No windows?"

"Yes, well, my dad was protective of me when I was growing up," Emma replied, the weight of her words hanging in the air.

Edward had noticed too, but given his history with Emma as a patient, he understood why. "Are we ready to get started?" Edward asked, eager to steer the conversation back on track.

"Yes," Prasad nodded. "Emma, please lock the door behind you."

Emma furrowed her brow. "But—"

"Darling, I assure you—you do not want to be in here to see this," Prasad interrupted gently.

"Let's go, angel," Josephine said, her voice soft yet firm.

As they left, closing the door behind them, Prasad leaned over Emmanuel's freshly shaved head. "They did a good job," he remarked, his voice all business now. "Now help me flip him on his stomach."

Edward moved to Prasad's side, a flicker of unease passing over his face as he recalled the last time he had to move an unconscious patient. The memory sent a shiver down his spine.

"What's the matter?" Prasad asked, noticing Edward's hesitation.

"Nothing," Edward lied, shaking off the memory. They positioned themselves, hands under Emmanuel's body, ready for the delicate maneuver.

"On the count of three," Prasad instructed. Edward nodded, bracing himself. "One, two, THREE!" With coordinated strength, they carefully turned Emmanuel onto his stomach.

"Okay, now what?" Edward asked, his voice tense.

"Start by sterilizing the back of his head," Prasad said, prepping the anesthesia. "I've got the antiseptic solution ready for you."

Edward's movements were precise, almost mechanical, as he cloaked the dresser with surgical drapes, creating a sterile field. He applied the antiseptic solution to Emmanuel's scalp, scrubbing with meticulous care, ensuring every inch was sanitized.

"Don't forget the sterile drapes," Prasad reminded him.

"Getting there," Edward replied, tearing open the package with deliberate care, the crinkling plastic breaking the silence that had settled in the room.

Prasad, satisfied with the preparations, turned his attention to the monitoring equipment. "Heart rate, blood pressure, oxygen levels, and breathing all look good," he said, more to himself than to Edward. "Now, for the fun to begin." He marked the spot on Emmanuel's scalp where he would drill.

"You are a sick, sick man," Edward muttered, crossing his arms.

"Drill, please," Prasad said, extending his hand.

Edward passed the cranial drill to him and stepped back as the device buzzed to life, sending a fine mist of bone dust into the air. The scent—powdery, with a faint, musty earthiness—permeated the room.

"Lead, please," Prasad requested. Edward handed him the coated wire, watching as Prasad carefully threaded it through the hole in the skull.

"Now I'll create a subcutaneous tunnel for the extension," Prasad explained. "Blunt dissector, please."

"I know what it is," Edward snapped, passing the thin, angled instrument to Prasad, who began to tunnel through the tissue with practiced precision. The sight made Edward's stomach churn.

"Nope, can't do it," Edward said, turning away, his face pale.

"I haven't even used the tunneling forceps yet," Prasad scoffed. "I'll get them myself."

With his back to the procedure, Edward folded his arms, trying to block out the unsettling sounds behind him. "Would you like me to describe what I'm doing? Paint you a picture?" Prasad teased.

"No need," Edward replied, his voice strained. "You're digging the tunnel for the wire—I got it."

"Very good," Prasad quipped. "I'm glad Emma explained it to you."

Edward rolled his eyes, his discomfort palpable. A tense silence fell over the room as Prasad focused on threading the extension through the tunnel. Edward stayed quiet, knowing that distraction could be disastrous.

"You can turn around—the worst is over," Prasad finally said.

"What's next?" Edward asked, cautiously turning back.

"I'll make a pocket on his chest for the neurostimulator," Prasad replied, holding out his hand. "Scalpel, please."

"Nope," Edward said, shaking his head again.

"Fine, I'll get it myself," Prasad muttered, clearly annoyed. He picked up the scalpel and resumed his work.

A sharp, metallic clink broke the silence—Edward recognized it as the sound of the scalpel being put down.

Edward reached for a small device resembling a pacemaker. "Here's the neurostimulator," he said, handing it to Prasad.

"Well, look who decided to join us!" Prasad exclaimed, taking the device. "You're just in time to watch me connect the extension."

Edward watched as Prasad connected the wires to the device. There was a soft click.

"Voilà!" Prasad declared, satisfaction in his voice. "Now, I'll suture the incisions. When I'm done, you can apply the sterile dressing."

"Aye-aye, captain," Edward replied, the tension easing slightly as he fell back into a familiar rhythm.

"Captain, huh? I could get used to that," Prasad joked.

"No need," Edward shot back. "Regretted it the moment I said it."

Prasad glanced at the clock. "Going on four hours... Time flies when you're having fun," he said with a wry smile.

"Don't let Emma hear you say that," Edward warned with a smirk.

"Why not?" Prasad asked, genuinely confused.

"Never mind," Edward replied, the ongoing inside joke between him and Emma making him chuckle to himself.

"What on earth is going on between you two?" Prasad asked, half-joking, half-concerned.

He paused.

"You know what? Perhaps it's best I don't know."

Chapter 40

THE RHYTHMIC CREAKING OF the aged wood floor echoed through the room as Emma paced, her steps betraying the turmoil churning within her. She paused momentarily, rolling her neck to release the tension that had built up, the cracking sound like a small explosion in the oppressive silence. She could feel her mother's eyes on her, heavy with concern.

"What?" Emma snapped, her voice sharper than intended.

"I wish you'd stop doing that," her mother replied, her tone gentle but firm.

"Doing what?" Emma shot back, though she knew exactly what her mother meant. Almost defiantly, she extended her fingers and cracked each knuckle, the popping sounds reverberating through the small room.

Her mother shook her head, a frown of disapproval deepening the lines on her face. "It's bad for you."

"That's a myth," Emma retorted, resuming her pacing, though her steps were more measured now.

"Can you please sit down, angel? You're making me nervous."

Emma sighed and sank onto the couch beside her mother, resting her head on her shoulder, seeking the familiar comfort of her mother's touch. For a moment, she allowed herself to be still, to breathe.

But something was off. She could sense it in the way her mother's body remained tense, in the way she stared at the floor as if trying to solve a puzzle with no solution. The air between them crackled with unspoken words, thick with a tension that made Emma's chest tighten.

"Is there something you're not telling me?" Emma finally asked, lifting her head to search her mother's face, hoping for reassurance but fearing the worst. "Is there anything you want to talk about?"

Her mother looked up, her eyes searching Emma's face for something. "What did the doctor mean when he said they were grateful for you and your gift?" she asked, her voice tinged with curiosity and something deeper—fear, perhaps. "What *gift*?"

Emma had known this question was coming. She just hadn't expected it so soon. She took a deep breath, steeling herself for the conversation she had dreaded. "Emma?" Her mother's tone was more insistent now, the sternness catching Emma off guard.

She never calls me that.

"They're just grateful because I'm helping them with the study—it's no big deal," Emma said, trying to sound casual, but her voice betrayed her.

"And your gift?" her mother pressed, leaning in slightly as if the physical proximity would bring her closer to the truth.

Emma crossed her arms, exhaling loudly. "I told them I have the gift of discerning spirits."

Her mother's eyes widened in shock. "Emma. Marie. Perales. You did not."

Crap, my full name.

The use of her full name sent a chill down Emma's spine, recalling memories of childhood scoldings that always followed such formalities. She instinctively stood and took a step back. "What's the big deal?" she asked, her voice defensive.

"Well, by itself, I suppose it's not a big deal," her mother began, her voice tight with restrained emotion. "Unless you're using it to help with their study."

Emma's gaze flicked to the front door, her mind racing for an escape from this confrontation.

"Emma Maria Perales—you must be kidding me!" her mother's voice rose, tinged with a mix of fear and anger.

Crap... Spanish. This is bad.

"Mom! Shh!" Emma hissed, glancing anxiously toward the room where the others were, trying to contain the situation.

"I'm sorry—it's just, after all you've been through?" Her mother's voice wavered, a pained expression crossing her face. "After everything, you're putting yourself back into this?"

"Mom, I had to," Emma insisted, trying to keep her voice steady. "I mean, I was already considering it because of how Dr. Clark helped me with my nightmares."

"Emma Marie—"

Here we go again.

"You owe no one anything," her mother said, her voice firm, leaving no room for argument.

"I know, but I wanted to help," Emma replied, her voice softening. "Then Dad had the stroke, and I told them I'd help in exchange for them helping Dad."

Her mother buried her face in her hands, the weight of Emma's words settling heavily between them.

"You're an adult—I get it," she said, raising her head, her voice quieter now, filled with a mother's worry. "But I'm still your mother, and I worry. That doesn't just stop when you turn eighteen."

Emma felt a pang of guilt at the sight of her mother's distress. She sat back down, gently rubbing circles on her mother's back. "I know," she whispered.

A subtle click broke the tension, and they both turned as Prasad emerged from the room.

They rushed toward him, their hearts in their throats. "How is he?" Emma asked, her voice trembling.

"He's doing as well as could be expected," Prasad replied, his tone professional but not unkind. "Edward is finishing up with the sterile dressing now. When he's done, I'll program the device that will deliver the electrical signal to the targeted area in his brain."

"He's ready!" Edward's voice called from the other room, a note of urgency in his tone.

"Can we be there for this?" Emma's mother asked, her voice tinged with hope.

"Yes, of course," Prasad nodded, leading them back into the room.

Prasad retrieved a small electronic tablet from his bag. "This is the programming device," he explained, showing them the screen. "It allows me to adjust the stimulation settings—voltage, frequency, pulse width, and electrode configuration." He powered on the device, his fingers moving deftly across the screen.

"Typically, I'd get feedback from the patient when adjusting these settings, but in this case, we don't have that luxury," he added, his gaze flicking to Emmanuel's still form on the bed.

Emma and her mother watched intently as Prasad initiated the programming. The air in the room was thick with anticipation, the only sound the rhythmic beeping of the heart monitor.

"Electrical stimulation has commenced," Prasad announced, his eyes switching between the tablet and Emmanuel.

Emma's eyes never left her father. "Should something be happening?" she asked, her voice barely above a whisper.

"Ordinarily, we might see muscle contractions or tremors, depending on the area of the brain being targeted. But in this case, we're working with a region related to visual perception and spatial awareness, so it's unlikely we'll see a physical response," Prasad explained. "I'm increasing the voltage."

The room seemed to hold its breath as they all waited, the tension almost unbearable.

Prasad finally exhaled, a sound of both relief and resignation. "Okay—I'm done here," he said, stepping back.

"Did it work?" Emma's mother asked, her voice trembling with hope and fear.

"It's hard to say," Prasad admitted. "The procedure went as planned, but it's the first of its kind. There's just no way to know if it yielded the intended benefits until—"

"Until he passes," Emma finished, her voice flat.

"Right," Prasad confirmed, a frown tugging at his lips.

Suddenly, a chill swept through the room, a cold that seemed to pierce Emma's very bones. She shivered, wrapping her arms around herself. "Did the heat just shut off?" she asked, her voice shaky.

"I don't think so," her mother replied, her brow furrowed. "Why?"

"That's strange. I just felt so cold all of a—" Emma's words trailed off as her eyes widened in shock, her gaze fixed on something that seemed to defy reality. A mix of fear and astonishment danced across her face as she struggled to comprehend the impossible sight before her.

Chapter 41

JOSEPHINE'S GAZE FELL UPON EMMA. Her daughter's eyes were wide, her mouth slightly open, as if she had been mid-sentence but suddenly lost her train of thought. "Angel, what's the matter?" Josephine asked, her brow furrowing as worry deepened the lines on her face.

"Dad?" Emma whispered, her voice distant, her eyes locked on a seemingly empty corner of the room. Josephine followed her daughter's gaze, but saw nothing out of the ordinary. "Angel, what's happening?" she asked, her voice trembling with rising anxiety.

Edward, standing nearby, quickly scanned the monitoring equipment, his instincts kicking in as the sense of urgency spiked. "Prasad!" he called out, his voice sharp with alarm.

Prasad, immediately sensing the seriousness in Edward's tone, spun around to face Josephine and Emma. "I need you two out—NOW," he ordered, his voice firm and unyielding.

Josephine's heart pounded in her chest as she hurried to guide Emma out of the room, closing the door behind them. She turned to her daughter, who stood motionless, her eyes still fixed on the door as if she could see right through it.

"What is it, angel?" Josephine asked, her voice soft but strained. "What's wrong?"

Emma remained silent for a moment, then whispered, "He's gone."

Josephine's heart skipped a beat. "What?"

"He's gone," Emma repeated, her voice eerily calm, almost devoid of emotion. "It worked."

"Are you sure?" Josephine's voice wavered, teetering between hope and despair.

Emma nodded, her expression blank. "I saw him. He saw me. He was looking right at me."

The door to the bedroom opened, and Prasad stepped out, his face a mask of solemnity. "His heart stopped," he announced flatly.

Without hesitation, Josephine pushed past him and rushed into the bedroom, Emma following closely behind.

Inside, Emmanuel lay utterly still, his chest no longer rising and falling with the rhythm of breath. The room seemed to hold its breath with him.

"There's no activity," Edward said, his voice tight as he pointed to the EEG monitor. The screen displayed a flat, gray image—no flicker of life, no brain activity. "No activity whatsoever."

"But the procedure worked," Emma insisted, her voice rising with a desperate certainty.

"It doesn't appear so, darling," Prasad said, shaking his head, his eyes clouded with disappointment. "I'm so sorry."

"No—I'm telling you, it worked!" Emma's voice was urgent, insistent, as she pointed to the EEG monitor. Suddenly, bursts of bright yellow, red, and green flashed across the screen, lighting up the room with a strange, hopeful energy.

Prasad's eyes widened in disbelief. "It worked," he murmured, astonishment creeping into his voice. "The TPO junction is active!"

"I saw him," Emma said quietly. "And then he was gone."

Prasad stood, speechless, his mind grappling with the impossible.

Josephine watched the scene unfold, aware of the gravity of the moment but unsure how to process it.

She placed a hand over her heart, feeling the weight of the situation press down on her like a physical burden. She had known this moment was inevitable, but that knowledge did nothing to lessen the shock. He was the love of her life—not a perfect man, but a good one, with flaws and virtues that made him uniquely hers. Her heart had always been a steady presence in her chest, its rhythm a constant reassurance. But now, it felt as if it were folding in on itself, collapsing under the weight of her grief—breaking from the inside out.

Emma turned to her, eyes filled with shared sorrow, and pulled her into a tight embrace. It was a gesture of comfort, though the solace they sought seemed to elude them both, slipping away like sand through their fingers. Together they stood, bound by a love and a pain that words could never fully capture, clinging to each other as they faced the unbearable.

Josephine's arms hung limp at her sides, her gaze unfocused, her thoughts swirling in a chaotic mix of hope, fear, and disbelief.

Emma stepped back, her voice steady as she spoke. "Mom, it's going to be OK," she said. "I'm here—we'll get through this."

A sudden chill swept through the room, sending a shiver down Emma's spine. "Did the heat just shut off?" she asked, glancing around.

"I don't think so," her mother replied, her voice distant. "Why?"

"I just felt so cold all of a sudden," Emma began, but her words faltered, her eyes widening in shock as something unseen yet deeply felt washed over her.

"BRING HIM BACK!" Josephine suddenly screamed, her voice cracking with raw emotion.

Emma's body jerked in response to her mother's outburst, her eyes wide with fear and confusion.

Prasad and Edward turned to her, their expressions mirroring Emma's shock and confusion. "Do as she says!" Emma shouted, her voice rising in urgency. "BRING HIM BACK!"

The room exploded into frantic motion. Edward, his hands trembling, leaned over Emmanuel's lifeless body and began chest compressions, his palms pressing rhythmically against his chest. The sound of each compression echoed through the room, a desperate beat against the silence of death.

Minutes dragged on, each one feeling like an eternity, as Edward fought to revive Emmanuel's stopped heart. Sweat beaded on his forehead, his breath coming in ragged gasps as he pushed himself to the limit.

"Nothing is happening!" Edward's voice was strained, frustration and despair lacing his words as he continued the relentless compressions.

"Keep trying!" Josephine commanded, her voice shaking with the intensity of her emotions. She watched, her heart in her throat, as Edward struggled, the room thick with the tension of life hanging by a thread.

"Prasad, I need you to take over," Edward gasped, stepping back as Prasad moved in to continue the compressions, his face set with grim determination.

Josephine, unable to stay back any longer, moved to the bed, gripping Emmanuel's hand tightly. "Mom! What are you doing?" Emma cried, fear lacing her voice. "Give him room!"

But Josephine was beyond hearing. She bowed her head, closed her eyes, and began to pray, her voice trembling with both desperation and faith. "Dear God, I come before you humbly asking that your presence be in this room with us, no matter the outcome. Lord, I know your power knows no bounds and ask that you heal your son and servant, my husband, Emmanuel." Her voice cracked with emotion. "And if it's his time, Lord, I know you will embrace him with open arms, and I am so grateful for that."

She felt a hand on her shoulder and opened her eyes to see Emma beside her, head bowed in silent prayer.

"We need to let him go," Emma whispered, her voice thick with emotion. "He's in a better place... where he was meant to be."

A tear slipped down Josephine's cheek as she nodded, her heart heavy. "OK," she whispered, her voice breaking.

Suddenly, Prasad's voice rang out, cutting through the silence. "We have a heartbeat!" he shouted, his voice filled with disbelief and triumph.

The heart monitor beeped, the sound like a lifeline thrown into the dark abyss.

Josephine let out a sob of relief, raising her hands to the heavens. "Hallelujah!" she cried, her voice cracking with joy as she looked upward, tears streaming down her face.

She reached for Emma's hand, but her daughter stood frozen, her eyes wide as they locked onto her father's face. "Angel, what's wrong?" Josephine asked, her joy dimming with concern.

Emma stared at her father's face, her expression a mix of disbelief and something deeper, something unspoken. "Is this a dream?" she whispered, her voice trembling as she struggled to comprehend what she was seeing.

"It's not a dream," Emma murmured, her voice barely above a whisper. "His eyes are open."

In the confines of the cleaning van, the air was thick with the scent of determination and meticulousness, mingling with the faint aroma of industrial cleaning supplies. The streets of Chicago, cloaked in the darkness of the late hour, provided the perfect shroud for Armonon's lethal operation. His eyes drifted to the creased photo of his target, a dark-haired man with a proud smile, dressed in a white lab coat—the symbol of his success. The photo, now worn from handling, lay face down on the dashboard. He picked it up, studied it one last time, and with a swift motion, tore it in half. "First time is luck," he murmured, discarding the pieces without a second thought.

His eyes glowed with an unnatural, eerie green hue as he peered through his night vision binoculars, every movement inside the house becoming a vivid, ghostly image in his mind. The hours he had spent in broad daylight, stalking the house and memorizing its layout, had honed his focus to a razor's edge. Each square foot, every potential obstacle, and all possible escape routes were etched into his memory with precision.

Time slipped by, the minutes ticking away in silence as Armonon's gaze remained locked on the house, his senses attuned to any sign of vulnerability. Growing impatient, he finally decided to close the distance. Slipping out of the van, he moved toward the house like a wraith, his steps soundless on the pavement. The recon had revealed that the undressed window above the kitchen sink provided the clearest view into the heart of the home. He approached it, a dark silhouette blending seamlessly with the shadows.

Peering inside, his gaze turned cold and calculating as he scanned the room. The two women inside caught his attention first—one with graying hair and lines etched deep into her aging face, the other younger, her long dark hair cascading over her shoulders, her complexion fair and unblemished. Their presence barely registered as a concern, merely obstacles to be accounted for.

The door inside the home swung open.

A surge of adrenaline shot through his veins as his target emerged into view. A predatory smile crept across Armonon's face, his lips curling in sinister satisfaction. Slowly, he reached into his jacket and drew his gun, the weight of the cold metal comforting in his hand. The weapon caught the dim light, casting a fleeting glint on the window's surface. With a steady hand and unyielding resolve, he took aim, his finger resting lightly on the trigger.

But the target moved again, retreating back into the room, the women unknowingly blocking the clear shot Armonon had waited for. His patience, already worn thin, was further tested. He lowered the gun, frustration simmering beneath his calm exterior. "No windows," he muttered, recalling the layout of the house with acute accuracy. The realization that his opportunity was slipping away ignited a low growl in his throat.

With a steely gaze, his mind raced through his options. The night was still young, but his tolerance for delay was not. He knew the risk of being spotted increased with each passing second. Yet, he also knew that a botched job was not an option. He would wait for the perfect moment, or he would create it.

"Second time is chance," he whispered to himself, his voice laced with a chilling calm. Armonon's eyes flicked back to the house, his resolve hardening.

Chapter 42

"NEVER IN MY WILDEST DREAMS did I expect this," Prasad said, his voice barely above a whisper as he stared in wide-eyed amazement at the EEG monitor. The screen, once eerily silent, now pulsed with vibrant activity, displaying a flurry of electrical signals across Emmanuel's brain.

"I DID!" Josephine shouted, her voice ringing with jubilant conviction. "WOOO! PRAISE THE LORD!" She threw her arms wide and began to sway from side to side, her face beaming with uncontainable joy.

Edward, still fixated on the monitor, furrowed his brow. "There's so much activity across the board—it isn't isolated to the area you treated," he said, his voice laced with confusion. "How did this happen?"

Prasad, still processing the surreal turn of events, nodded slowly. "It appears the DBS jump-started activity in the entire brain."

"Jump-started?" Emma echoed, her face a mask of puzzlement.

"Yes—jump-started," Prasad repeated, turning to her. "Think of the brain as a complex engine with countless interconnected parts. If one component malfunctions, it can cause the entire system to fail. We may have just reverse-engineered what Neelima experienced."

"This is incredible," Edward said, awe creeping into his voice as he continued to watch the monitor.

Suddenly, Emmanuel's fingers twitched, and he whispered, "Tengo sed."

Emma's heart skipped a beat. "I'll get you some water," she said, her voice trembling slightly as she hurried toward the kitchen.

Josephine grasped Emmanuel's hand, pressing it to her lips in a tender kiss. "How do you feel?" she asked, her voice thick with emotion.

"Tired," he replied, his voice faint but steady.

"I can deal with tired," she said, her lips curling into a soft smile.

"Here, Mom," Emma said, returning with a glass of water. Josephine carefully held the glass to Emmanuel's lips, allowing him to take a sip.

"Thank you," he whispered, his eyes fluttering open, revealing a glimmer of life that hadn't been there moments before.

"Dad, do you remember anything?" Emma asked, her voice filled with cautious hope.

Emmanuel nodded slowly. "Yes, I remember. I saw you and your mother in the living room. I knew my body was in the bedroom, but I could see you looking directly at me." He paused, collecting his thoughts. "I heard Edward call for Prasad, and I saw them examining me here in the bedroom."

Prasad's eyes widened in disbelief, his gaze darting to Edward. "He knows our names," he said, his voice tinged with astonishment. "He couldn't have known our names." Despite the numerous accounts he had read of patients describing unexplainable experiences after clinical death, this was the first time he had encountered it firsthand.

Emmanuel's gaze locked onto Prasad, his expression serious. "I believe you are being hunted," he said, his voice carrying an ominous weight.

Prasad's eyebrows shot up in surprise, his heart skipping a beat. "Pardon me?" he asked, his voice shaky with disbelief.

"There was a man outside," Emmanuel continued, his voice steady despite the alarming revelation. "He had a picture of you. I saw him looking into the house through the kitchen window. He said, 'first time is luck.'"

"First time is luck?" Emma repeated, her brow furrowing in confusion. She turned to Prasad. "Does that mean anything to you?"

Prasad exhaled deeply, the weight of Emmanuel's words settling heavily on his shoulders. "Unfortunately, yes," he replied, his voice barely above a whisper.

"Who could possibly be after you?" Emma asked, her voice tinged with growing fear. "And why?"

"Reverend Kay—it has to be," Prasad answered, shaking his head as if trying to rid himself of the thought.

"A woman?" Emma said, her confusion deepening. "But my dad just said it was a man he saw outside."

Edward interjected, "Reverend Kay is part of a powerful organization—the Global Assembly of Religious Leaders. They could have sent him."

"Why would they do that?" Josephine asked, her face etched with confusion.

"Reverend Kay is also a member of the university's Internal Review Board," Prasad explained. "When I presented my proposal for the afterlife study, she vehemently disapproved."

Emma's eyes widened in disbelief. "And you think that's enough for her to send a hitman after you? Because of a disagreement?"

Prasad shook his head, the gravity of the situation weighing heavily on him. "It's not just that," he said, his voice tinged with regret. "She stormed into my office after the IRB meeting, and I... I felt threatened."

"Apparently, she isn't keen on the idea of using brain science to affect the afterlife," Edward added. "She claimed Prasad was trying to play God."

Emmanuel, still weak but eager to share his perspective, cleared his throat and whispered, "May I offer my professional opinion?"

Prasad turned to him, his expression eager and respectful. "Yes, of course," he replied.

"You are speaking of affecting the afterlife, correct?" Emmanuel asked.

Prasad nodded. "So to speak."

"If that is the case, your claim will undoubtedly weaken the fabric of Reverend Kay's existence... and mine as well," Emmanuel said, his voice carrying a weight of understanding.

Prasad furrowed his brow. "How so?" he asked, genuinely curious.

"Religious leaders have spent their entire lives, built entire careers gaining power using their expertise on the afterlife, teaching how one must live to avoid the fiery gates of hell," Emmanuel explained.

Edward nodded slowly, realization dawning on him. "It's bad for business," he said, his voice laced with understanding.

"That's the least of it," Emmanuel continued, his voice growing stronger. "The real issue is the misconception that disembodied spirits can remain on earth."

Emma's brow furrowed in confusion. "But that's the premise of the whole study," she said, her voice tinged with uncertainty.

Emmanuel shook his head. "Bad premise," he replied, his voice firm. "Spirits are not meant to linger on earth. They are meant to move on. That's the natural order."

Prasad's mind raced as he processed Emmanuel's words. Everything he had been working toward suddenly felt shaky, the foundation of his research questioned by someone who had just experienced the very thing he was studying. He knew he was standing at a crossroads, one that could redefine not only his career but his entire understanding of life and death.

Chapter 43

"I'VE SEEN THEM" Emma declared, her voice trembling as she locked eyes with her father. The conviction in her words was unshakable, as though her entire life depended on the truth she had always believed in. "You know I have."

Her father inhaled deeply, his face a mask of sorrow. "Mija, there is no such thing as ghosts."

The words hit Emma like a physical blow. Her eyes widened in disbelief, her mouth falling open as though she had forgotten how to speak. How could he say this? The man who had always stood by her, believed her, defended her when her mother dismissed her claims, was now denying everything. "Dad—how could you?" she whispered, her voice cracking under the weight of betrayal. "After everything I've been through?"

Edward, who had been quietly observing, finally spoke up, his voice tinged with disbelief. "You lied to us?"

"No, of course not!" Emma blurted, her tone a mix of desperation and incredulity.

She turned back to her father, her eyes pleading. "Dad, I saw them—you know I did. I still see them. I just went with Edward to a couple of funeral homes this week, and I saw them."

Her father's expression remained firm, but there was a flicker of something—regret, perhaps?—in his eyes. "Why would you do that?" he asked, his tone laced with disappointment.

"To prove Prasad's theory. And I saw them—I proved his theory," she insisted, her voice growing louder as if volume alone could force him to believe her.

Her father shook his head slowly. "The only thing you proved is that demons are cunning and keenly aware of our weaknesses and desires."

Emma's heart sank. "I don't understand... Dad, please help me understand," she begged, gripping his hand as if it were a lifeline.

He took a deep breath, as if preparing himself to shatter her world. "There are no such things as ghosts, only demons that are very capable of appearing as the dead, as well as taking on any number of deceptive disguises for the purposes of evil."

Emma's eyes searched her father's face, hoping to find some trace of the man who had always believed her. But his expression was resolute, and her hopes began to crumble. "You didn't tell me when I was younger because you didn't want to scare me," she said, more a statement than a question, as realization dawned on her.

"And I thought there was a chance you would grow out of it," he added softly.

An unsettling silence enveloped the room, thick with the weight of unspoken fears and shattered beliefs. "I'm sorry, mija. I was wrong."

Emma's grip on her father's hand tightened as she tried to process this new reality. "That's why I always felt oppressed when I was around them. That's why I always ran the other way."

Her father nodded solemnly. "Because you felt the evil, even if you didn't know it was there."

"The gift of discerning spirits," Emma whispered, her voice tinged with awe as the pieces began to fall into place. "I get it now... It's not about seeing ghosts—it's about distinguishing spirits—good from evil." She turned to Prasad, her eyes blazing with intensity. "We shouldn't even be talking about this."

Prasad, taken aback by her sudden change in demeanor, crossed his arms. "Explain."

Emma began pacing the room, her movements sharp and rapid as she tried to articulate her thoughts. "Let's say someone is thinking about their afterlife—we all do it at some point—and they think there's a good chance they're destined for hell. Or maybe they're not even sure—maybe they think it could go either way for them. If they buy into your theory, what's to stop them from putting a bullet in their head?"

Prasad frowned, struggling to keep up with her line of reasoning. "I suppose..." he began, but Emma cut him off.

"Which means what?" she demanded.

"I don't know," Prasad admitted, his frustration growing.

"It means the poor soul that takes their own life goes to hell while the demon that corrupted them stays in this dimension for eternity," Emma's voice was almost a growl, her fear morphing into anger.

"Absolutely," her father interjected, his voice filled with the certainty of years of experience. "And that is the larger, far more sinister issue at hand."

"An infestation of the worst kind," Emma muttered, her mind racing.

Prasad, still reeling from the rapid shift in the conversation, shook his head in confusion. "An infestation? With all due respect, darling, don't you think you're being a bit dramatic?"

"Not even close," her father countered, his voice stern. "Saint Angela Merici once said, 'Consider that the devil doesn't sleep but seeks our ruin in a thousand ways.' And the traditional prayer to Saint Michael asks for God's protection from 'Satan and all the evil spirits who prowl about the world seeking the ruin of souls.' There is no such thing as a random occurrence of bad luck. Demons manipulate everything."

Prasad stared at him, trying to wrap his mind around the implications. "How do you know all this?" he asked, his voice barely above a whisper.

"He's not only been a pastor for more than three decades," Emma said, her voice strong and clear, "but he's also performed countless exorcisms and has a Ph.D. in theology. Trust me when I say he knows a thing or two about evil."

Chapter 44

PRASAD'S MIND RACED as he tried to process the gravity of Emmanuel's words. They had ventured into uncharted territory with the afterlife study, driven by curiosity and a desire to understand what lay beyond the veil of death. But now, the stakes seemed far higher than he had ever imagined. The idea that he could be responsible for unleashing an infestation of evil into the world felt like an absurd notion. Yet, as he stared at Emmanuel, who spoke with such conviction, the absurdity began to waver.

Prasad met Emmanuel's gaze, his voice steady but laced with uncertainty. "When you said demons are capable of deceptive disguises, even appearing as the dead, were you suggesting the ghosts—the demons—Emma saw *wanted* to be seen?"

Emmanuel took a deep breath, his expression grave. "Let me ask you something... Did Emma telling you what she saw serve as some kind of validation? Encourage you to continue with the study?"

"Absolutely," Prasad admitted without hesitation.

"In that case, not only am I saying they wanted to be seen, but I'm also saying evil is following you—studying you—watching your every move."

A chill ran down Prasad's spine as the weight of Emmanuel's words settled over him. "You're saying I'm a pawn?" he asked, his voice tinged with disbelief.

"Yes," Emmanuel replied, his tone unwavering.

Prasad scoffed, trying to shake off the unease creeping into his thoughts. "And what gives you that idea?"

Emmanuel's eyes narrowed, his voice calm yet firm. "If you don't mind me asking, have you been depressed lately? Possibly ill?"

Prasad hesitated, the question catching him off guard. "No," he replied, though his voice lacked conviction. "How is that relevant anyway?"

Emmanuel leaned forward, his gaze intense. "I'm asking the question to determine if there is a pattern. You see, just as scientists and doctors use patterns to explain natural phenomena, the same is true for theologians and the spirit world."

Prasad's skepticism began to wane as he listened. "And what type of pattern would support your theory that evil is following me?"

"There are five stages to demonic activity," Emmanuel stated matter-of-factly.

Prasad's eyes widened in surprise at the speed and certainty of Emmanuel's response. "The first stage is encroachment, also known as permission or invitation," Emmanuel continued. "Demons most often target the young and vulnerable."

"I'm not young. Are you suggesting I'm vulnerable?" Prasad asked, trying to mask the unease creeping into his voice.

"I'm no mind reader—I can't answer that," Emmanuel replied calmly. "But for reference, someone going through a very tough period in life, like losing a loved one or battling addiction, for example, may be vulnerable."

Prasad shifted uncomfortably, crossing and uncrossing his arms as if trying to find a stance that didn't feel defensive. "OK," he said, his tone cautious.

"The second stage is infestation... Evil begins surrounding you, watching you." Emmanuel's gaze flickered to Emma, who nodded in understanding.

"It's why I saw what I did—it was all part of their plan," Emma said, shaking her head as if trying to shake off the memories.

"The third stage is oppression... Evil invades one's thoughts," Emmanuel continued, his voice taking on a darker tone. "And the fourth stage, although uncommon, is possession... Evil invades one's body."

Prasad's heart pounded in his chest as he asked the inevitable question. "And the last stage?"

Emmanuel's eyes met his, filled with a somber truth that sent a shiver down Prasad's spine. "If not dealt with appropriately?"

"Yes," Prasad replied, his voice barely above a whisper.

"Death."

The word hung in the air like a death knell, the finality of it striking Prasad to his core. The idea that the study he had championed, the research he had poured his heart and soul into, could lead to something so dark, so irreversible, shook him in a way he had never experienced.

"But there has to be a way to stop it, right?" Emma asked, her voice trembling with fear and desperation.

Emmanuel nodded slowly. "There is, but it's not something that can be taken lightly. You must be prepared to confront this evil directly and with the right knowledge and support. It's a battle, and like any battle, it requires strategy, faith, and unwavering resolve."

Prasad stood in silence, the weight of the decision before him pressing down like a ton of bricks. The path forward was shrouded in darkness, but one thing was clear: they couldn't afford to make the wrong move.

Chapter 45

FLASHING RED AND BLUE LIGHTS cut through the darkness, illuminating the night as paramedics carefully loaded Emmanuel onto the stretcher and into the waiting ambulance. "His vitals are stable, but he should be monitored overnight, just to be safe," Prasad said, his voice calm yet firm as he extended his hand to Josephine, guiding her gently toward the open ambulance doors. His touch was steady, filled with compassion, as she gripped his hand and stepped up into the vehicle.

"I understand. Thank you for everything," Josephine murmured, her voice soft with gratitude.

"I'll catch up with you soon, Mom," Emma said from outside, glancing at her phone. "It's late—I'm going to stay here tonight."

"Okay, angel," Josephine replied, offering a tired but reassuring smile. "I'll see you in the morning."

The paramedic closed the ambulance doors with a firm click. "You know where to find them," he said as he walked away, his tone laced with the weariness of a long night.

Emma nodded. "Yes, thank you."

As the ambulance pulled away, its siren a distant wail, a man in a blue police uniform approached Emma, tapping her lightly on the shoulder. "Excuse me, ma'am," he said, his voice tinged with professional concern.

"Yes, officer?" Emma replied, turning to face him.

"May I have a word with you?" he asked, gesturing toward his patrol car parked nearby.

"Certainly," she said, her tone composed.

Prasad hesitated, unsure if he should follow, but ultimately decided to stay where he was, watching as Emma walked away with the officer. His curiosity got the better of him, and with a quick tap on his smartwatch, he discreetly tuned in to their conversation.

"We've circled the property three times," the officer said, his voice steady but lacking reassurance. "I don't doubt that you saw something, but whoever it was is long gone."

"Are you sure?" Emma's voice was laced with concern, her brow furrowed.

"We searched everywhere," he continued. "He probably took off when he saw the flashing lights. It happens all the time."

Prasad shook his head, frustration gnawing at him. The officer's words were meant to be comforting, but they only deepened his unease.

"There's nothing more we can do here," the officer added, his tone final. "We'll be heading out now."

"I understand. Thank you for your time," Emma replied, her voice polite but tinged with disappointment.

As Emma walked back toward Prasad, Edward stepped forward, his expression mirroring the worry in his eyes. "Did they find anything?" he asked.

"No," Emma said, shaking her head. "Nothing."

"Have a good night!" the officer called out before shutting the patrol car door and driving off into the night.

Prasad stood silently, watching the taillights disappear, an unsettling feeling gnawing at the edges of his thoughts. *Am I just being paranoid?* he wondered, trying to shake the persistent doubt. Perhaps Emmanuel had hallucinated the entire thing. He shook his head, as if to rid himself of the conflicting thoughts swirling in his mind.

Emma turned to him, her face etched with concern. "What are you going to do?"

"What can I do?" Prasad replied with a helpless shrug. "It's not like I can file a police report based on what your father claims to have seen while he was unconscious."

A heavy silence settled between them.

"I suppose you're right," Emma finally said, her voice tinged with frustration. "I just wish there was something I could do."

"It's okay," Prasad said, offering a small, weary smile. "I'm sorry for burdening you with all of this."

"Hey," Emma said, reaching out to take his hand, her grip firm and reassuring. "You are not a burden—you're a blessing," she said, her eyes soft with empathy, holding an unspoken promise of support.

"You're too kind," Prasad replied, his voice warm with gratitude. "Thank you, darling."

"What if you stayed here tonight?" Emma suggested, glancing around. "The officer said the coast is clear."

"I don't think that's a good idea," Edward interjected, his voice cautious. "He could still be around, and if he is, he's probably watching."

"He's right," Prasad agreed, the unease in his voice returning. "No sense in putting either of us in danger. I'll call for a ride."

"Why don't I drive you?" Edward offered.

"No, I couldn't live with myself if I put you at risk too," Prasad replied. "You should get home to your family. It's been a long day."

Just then, Prasad's head snapped around, his eyes widening as a familiar sense of dread washed over him, making his heart pound against his chest. He froze mid-step, his breath caught in his throat.

"What's wrong?" Emma asked, her eyes wide with alarm.

"We should go inside," Prasad whispered, the hairs on the back of his neck standing on end as the feeling of being watched intensified.

Edward furrowed his brow, confusion and concern etched across his face. "What's going on?"

"Step back," a deep, menacing voice growled from the shadows.

"He's holding a gun," Prasad whispered, his body stiffening as he felt the cold metal press against his back.

Edward and Emma instinctively took a step back, their eyes locked on Prasad, who stood frozen with fear.

"Come with me," the assailant ordered speaking broken English and a thick Italian accent, his face partially obscured by the faint glow of the streetlights, casting eerie shadows across his features.

"What do you want with him?" Emma demanded, her voice trembling with a mix of anger and fear.

"Not your concern," the man snapped, tightening his grip on Prasad's arm. "Phones on the ground."

Emma and Edward exchanged a fearful glance before slowly placing their phones on the ground.

Without warning, the assailant raised his gun and fired two shots at the devices, the sound of the gunfire echoing through the quiet night. Emma and Edward flinched, shielding their faces from the blast.

"DON'T!" Emma shouted, taking a step forward in defiance.

"Don't move," the assailant warned, his gun now trained on her. Emma hesitated, her foot hovering in mid-air, but Edward quickly pulled her back.

"Listen to him!" Prasad urged, his voice trembling, but his eyes held a gentle strength as they met Emma's. "It's okay—I'll be okay, my darling," he said, offering her a reassuring smile, even as fear gripped his heart.

Chapter 46

THEY STOOD STILL AND LOOKED ON as the assailant led Prasad down the street, each of his steps imbued with a chilling, deliberate menace. Edward had never imagined he would find himself in a situation like this, and now, faced with the terrifying reality, he felt paralyzed by uncertainty. The scenario posed too many challenges, and his usually sharp intellect scrambled for a solution. The assailant had a weapon. Any attempt to intervene would likely result in both Prasad's death and his own. He couldn't call for help—his phone lay shattered on the ground. And the command not to move echoed in his mind, a binding constraint that left him with only one option: a desperate, foolhardy act of heroism.

He thought of his wife and young daughter. *They need me.* As much he wanted to jump in and help, he couldn't bring himself to risk it. A sudden tug on his grip snapped him out of his thoughts. He turned to Emma, his voice urgent and low. "What are you doing? He said not to move."

"He's got his back to us," Emma replied, her voice steady, almost too calm. "Besides, it's dark—he can't see us from all the way down there."

Edward watched in disbelief as Emma pressed and held the side button on her watch, then swiped across the display. "My friend was just abducted at gunpoint. Please send police to 374 Nash Street right away," she whispered into the device, her voice firm.

His eyes darted to the obliterated phones on the ground. "How did you—how were you able to make a call?" he stammered.

"I have Wifi calling enabled. I'm connected to the Wifi in my parents' house," she said, her words clipped as she began moving purposefully toward her car.

"Where are you going?" he asked, incredulously.

"I'm not going to stand around and wait for the police to arrive," she shot back. "It could be too late."

"But you don't even know where he's taking him," Edward protested, reaching out to stop her.

A muffled thud echoed through the night, amplifying the tension in the air.

"Did you hear that? It was the sound of a car door closing," Emma said, her tone tinged with urgency. "They must be in that van parked down the street."

"How could you possibly know that?" Edward demanded, his voice rising with disbelief. "They can't see us, which means we can't see them."

"The van's been there since this morning—it's the only car parked on the street," Emma explained, her pace quickening. "No one in this neighborhood ever parks on the street—it's not safe."

Edward grabbed her arm, stopping her in her tracks. "You're not seriously going after them, are you?"

Emma's eyes blazed with determination as she stared at him, her breath quickening with each second that passed. His grip faltered, and he let go.

"You're really not going over there, are you?" he asked again, his voice wavering. But she ignored him, focused entirely on her mission. He watched, stunned, as she reached into her pocket, pulled out her keys, and began fiddling with the key control.

"What are you doing?" he asked, panic rising in his chest.

"I'm using the manual key to open the car door," she explained, her voice calm, methodical. "If I use the remote, the alarm will beep, and it could draw attention."

She unlocked the door and leaned into the car, emerging with a gun in her hand.

Oh my God, she's really going through with this, he thought, his heart pounding. "This is a suicide mission!" he hissed in a loud whisper. "I don't know what your thinking but you'll get yourself killed!"

Emma fixed him with a piercing gaze, her head tilting slightly as if studying him. "You really don't know what I'm thinking?" she asked, her voice a mixture of frustration and disbelief.

Edward stared back, bewildered, trying to grasp the meaning behind her words. "I don't understand," he admitted, shaking his head. "How can you be so bold about this?"

Her expression softened slightly, though the intensity in her eyes remained. She tilted her head to the other side, as if considering him anew. "You really don't know?" she whispered, almost to herself. She began walking toward the van, her footsteps fast and resolute.

"No," he replied, a note of desperation creeping into his voice as he walked behind her. "I guess I don't."

Emma paused, her gaze fixed straight ahead as if lost in the painful memory. "Just imagine," she murmured, her voice thick with regret, "if I'd acted faster that night with Brianna."

Edward's mind raced back to the story Emma had confided in him, replaying the details of that terrible night. An unwelcome guest had shown up at Brianna's house, and Emma, recovering from surgery, had hidden in the pantry, following Brianna's desperate orders. Weak and heavily medicated, Emma realized they were in danger and tried to call the police, but there was no signal. Everything had unraveled so quickly, spiraling out of control before she could act.

"The past, despite its wrenching pain, cannot be unlived," Emma said, her voice steady despite the weight of her words. "But if faced with courage, need not be lived again."

Edward's eyes flickered in recognition, and his voice was barely a whisper as he said, "Maya Angelou."

Emma nodded slightly, her resolve clear. "Yes," she confirmed, her tone carrying the weight of that truth. "I can't change the past, but I can change the future. That's why I'm going over there. You don't have to come with me," she added, her tone firm yet gentle. "You have a family to protect."

Edward's heart clenched in panic as he realized her reckless resolve might cost her life. "Emma, no—please!" he shouted, lunging toward her, his voice raw with desperation. "I'm begging you! Think of your mother!"

Chapter 47

ARMONON'S EYES GLINTED WITH cold determination as he led Prasad to the van, his grip unyielding, his steps methodical and deliberate. "Keep walking," he commanded, his voice a low growl that brooked no defiance.

"What do you want from me?" Prasad's voice quivered, betraying the fear that coursed through him.

"Quiet," Armonon snapped, pressing the cold barrel of his gun against Prasad's side, guiding him toward the passenger side of the van. With a swift, almost mechanical motion, he yanked the door open. "Get in," he ordered, his grip tightening on the handle with unnatural force. A low, ominous ripping sound followed as the handle buckled under the pressure, the metal warping in his hand.

Prasad hesitated only a moment before climbing into the van, his movements stiff with fear.

"Don't move," Armonon warned, slamming the door shut with a force that made the entire vehicle shudder. He stood for a moment, staring coldly through the window, his gaze as icy as the night air around them.

Inside, Prasad sat rigid, his eyes darting around the dimly lit van. The enclosed space amplified the pounding of his heart, each beat echoing in his ears. Armonon moved around the vehicle, his footsteps slow and deliberate, the weight of his presence filling the night. He opened the driver's side door and slithered into the seat, the gun never wavering from its aim at Prasad.

For a fleeting moment, he considered ending it right then and there. The mission had dragged on far too long, the weight of it pressing down on him like a vice. His finger twitched against the trigger, the itch of impatience crawling up his spine like a shadowy hand urging him to finish the job. One pull. That's all it would take. The target would crumple to the floor, nothing more than a lifeless heap in seconds. He could dump the body, grab the motorcycle stashed in the back of the van, and vanish before anyone even knew he was there.

But something stopped him—a hesitation that had never once plagued him before. His mind replayed the conversation he'd overheard through the thin walls of the windowless room. It had sunk its claws into him in a way nothing ever had. It wasn't just idle curiosity. It was something darker, more primal, a gnawing need that throbbed in his chest. His fists clenched involuntarily as memories of his mother flickered like broken film reels in his mind—the way she'd suffered, the cruel twist of fate that had stolen her from him after that head injury. She was gone, and he'd never had answers.

His pulse quickened, his breath shallow as he stared at the man kneeling in front of him. *He knows something. He has to.* Somehow, in the pit of his soul, he knew this man held the key to the truth he'd been chasing for so long. It wasn't a matter of salvation for himself—he'd made his deal with the devil the moment he shook Tonio's father's hand all those years ago. Every drop of blood spilled since had cemented his place in hell.

But if there was one thing left to cling to, it was the hope that his mother had found her way to heaven, away from the torment that now gnawed at him like a rabid beast.

This man... he wasn't just a target anymore. He was the key to unlocking the past.

"Is it true?" Armonon asked, his voice steady, betraying none of the turmoil that churned beneath the surface. The Glock 38 in his hand hovered in the air between them, half-raised, as though suspended by the gravity of the question.

"Is what true?" Prasad replied, his brow furrowed, confusion mixing with fear that dripped from every word. His pulse quickened, each beat an echo of his rising panic.

"Brain injury affecting the afterlife." Armonon's voice was cold, mechanical, the calm before the storm. His eyes never wavered, locked on Prasad, calculating, dissecting.

Prasad blinked, as though momentarily disarmed by the weight of the inquiry. "Oh... yes, but not just any brain injury," he stammered, the words barely forming as he struggled to get the words out.

"Explain," Armonon demanded, his voice cutting through the tension like a scalpel, his expression a mask of unyielding focus.

Prasad swallowed hard, and coughed to clear his throat, as if every word were a struggle. "The TPO junction—the area where the temporo, parieto, and occipital lobes meet—it acts like a navigation system for the transition to the next dimension." His voice trembled. "A kind of... compass."

"A compass?" Armonon's tone was edged with skepticism, though his gaze never left Prasad's face.

"So to speak," Prasad echoed, shrinking under the weight of the man's unwavering stare.

"You're certain?" Armonon's eyes narrowed, the intensity in his gaze pressing down on Prasad like a physical force.

"I have... a limited sample size," Prasad admitted, his nerves unraveling under the pressure. "These things are hard to test, you know, considering—" His words faltered.

"Would you bet your life?" Armonon interrupted, his voice dropping to a deadly whisper as he raised the gun fully, the barrel now aimed squarely at Prasad's chest. The question hung in the air, cold and final.

Prasad's breath caught in his throat. His eyes, wide with terror, fixated on the cold, unfeeling barrel of the gun. "I... I... I—" His voice cracked, his body trembling as the words stuck.

"Yes. Or. No," Armonon demanded, his finger resting ever so lightly on the trigger.

In a barely audible whisper, the word slipped from Prasad's lips, "No."

Armonon's face remained impassive. "Changes nothing," he said flatly, devoid of any emotion. He cocked the gun with a smooth, deliberate motion, the metallic click cutting through the air like a guillotine blade. The sound was a death sentence, final and cold.

"Third time is skill."

Chapter 48

HE FELT THE WORLD CLOSING IN around him. The seconds stretched out, each heartbeat pounding in his ears like a ticking bomb, each one louder than the last. The weight of inevitability pressing down, thick and suffocating, as the words of his assailant echoed relentlessly through his mind—*third time is skill*.

Prasad had gotten lucky before—surviving the car fire ordeal by a miracle, a twist of fate that felt unreal even now. And maybe, just maybe, he had been momentarily shielded by the strange, protective aura of Emma's windowless bedroom.

But now?

Prasad's breaths came in shallow, ragged bursts, his lungs burning with the rising panic that threatened to consume him. His body screamed for action—to move, to fight, to *do* something—but the sheer force of dread kept him pinned, frozen by the terrifying realization that this time, it was different. There was no room for luck, no space for miracles. No one was coming to save him.

The cold, unwavering barrel of the gun aimed directly at his chest offered only one certainty: there would be no escape this time. No more chances.

His eyes darted frantically around the van, searching for something—a distraction, a weapon, a way out. But all he saw was his own fear reflected back in the cold, lifeless eyes of his captor—a man who exuded the practiced calm of someone who had done this countless times before. *Of course*, Prasad thought bitterly, *he made sure the van was cleared of anything that could be used against him*. The realization tightened like a noose around his throat. *It's over*, his mind screamed, his thoughts racing toward one final, desperate prayer.

The cold steel of the gun pressed against his temple, the only certainty in a sea of the unknown. His eyes widened at the deafening cock of the gun, the sound amplified tenfold by his hearing aid, each metallic note drilling into his skull. The barrel of the gun seemed impossibly close, as though it were an extension of the dread coursing through his veins. Time seemed to slow, every heartbeat pounding in his ears like a countdown to the inevitable. In a desperate bid for peace, Prasad closed his eyes, forcing himself to steady his racing thoughts. His mind drifted to Asha and Ravi, their faces flickering in his memory like a fading photograph. For a fleeting moment, warmth coursed through him, cutting through the cold terror that gripped his body. "I pray I see you again, sweet Asha... Ravi," he muttered, his voice barely audible, trembling beneath the weight of his fear.

Then, cutting through the suffocating silence, came a whisper: *"Farfalla dorata."*

The words were delicate, barely more than a breath, but Prasad's heightened hearing aid picked them up like a whisper in the dark. His mind latched onto them, recognizing the language instantly—*Italian. Farfalla, like the bow-tie pasta*, he thought absently, a fleeting distraction from the terror that gripped him. Slowly, cautiously, he opened his eyes, shifting his gaze toward his captor without making a sound. The man leaned forward, momentarily distracted, his focus fixed on something beyond Prasad.

There, perched on the windshield, was a butterfly—its wings shimmering, metallic gold. The delicate, lace-like wings fluttered gently, catching the faint light, making it seem almost unreal, as though crafted from precious metal. It glowed with an otherworldly radiance, an eerie contrast to the suffocating tension that filled the van.

For a heartbeat, everything stilled.

Suddenly, like a lifeline pulling him back from the edge, Emma's voice—firm yet distant—echoed in his mind: *Get creative if you must, because doing nothing is not an option!*

The urgency in her words jolted him back to reality. His pulse pounded in his ears, but he forced himself to reign in his spiraling thoughts, his mind sharpening as he calculated his next move. *I have to do something*, Prasad thought, panic surging through his veins like fire as he frantically scanned the cramped, dimly lit van. The space was suffocating, filled with clutter—brooms with splintered handles, worn-out mops with dirty, sagging heads, and vacuums that had seen better days, all beyond reach.

Useless, all of it.

Think, Prasad, think!, his mind screamed.

His eyes darted, feverishly searching for something—*anything*—that might turn the tide in his favor.

Then he saw it.

His heart skipped a beat.

A paint bucket, secured to the base of his seat with fraying nylon rope, caught Prasad's eye. It was crammed with an assortment of cleaning supplies, haphazardly tossed inside. Most were unremarkable, but one item stood out—a clear plastic dish soap bottle, filled to the brim with a transparent liquid. The original label had been peeled away and replaced with a hastily scribbled, handwritten tag. In the dim light, the words barely came into focus, but when they did, a surge of adrenaline shot through him: s*odium hypochlorite.*

His heart pounded in his chest. *This could work.* His pulse thundered in his ears as he leaned sideways, inch by inch, careful not to alert his captor. His fingers brushed the cold plastic of the bottle, and he gripped it with trembling hands as he tried to push out thoughts of what could go wrong. The bottle felt heavier than he'd expected, the liquid sloshing ominously inside. *Come on, come on,* he urged himself to work up the courage to pop open the bottle. He knew the risk—the loud pop of the cap could give him away. But he had no other choice. Feeling the weight of his life teeter on the edge of this single moment, he drew a deep, steadying breath. His hand trembled as it gripped the dish soap bottle, the slick plastic surface cool against his clammy fingers. His thumb found the small indent on the cap, pressing into it with just enough force to feel the tension of resistance. Each turn felt like an eternity, the ridged edges biting into his skin, reminding him how fragile the line was between life and death.

Finally, with a sharp *pop*, the cap gave way. The sound exploded in the small, suffocating space of the van, ricocheting off the metal walls like a gunshot. Every nerve in Prasad's body jolted as the man's head whipped around, his eyes locking onto Prasad like a predator spotting its prey. The suspicion in the man's gaze darkened, turning into something far more dangerous.

There's no time. Every millisecond counted, every heartbeat bringing Prasad closer to the point of no return. His muscles tightened, coiling like a spring about to snap. His breath caught in his throat, and with a single, desperate motion, he squeezed the bottle with all his strength.

A jet of liquid shot from the nozzle with startling force, splashing directly into the man's eyes. A primal roar of agony ripped through the van as the burning chemical seared his skin, the man's hands flying to his face in a futile attempt to wipe away the pain. He staggered back, his body thrashing, blinded by the caustic substance.

Prasad's heart thundered in his chest. The acrid scent of chemicals filled the air, sharp and choking. Panic surged through him, but the sight of his attacker writhing in agony was all the encouragement he needed. There was no time for fear—only survival. The sharp fumes clawed at Prasad's throat, his lungs screaming for fresh air as his eyes watered uncontrollably. He gasped, coughing violently as panic surged through his veins. His heart pounded erratically as he reached for the door handle, his fingers scrabbling desperately for release. But it remained stubbornly jammed—the handle was broken.

He flicked his gaze back to his assailant. The man thrashed wildly, one hand blindly clawing at his face while the other fumbled for the gun, the barrel wavering dangerously in Prasad's direction. Time slowed, every detail etched into Prasad's mind—the metallic glint of the weapon, the man's finger trembling on the trigger, the overwhelming certainty that this would be his last breath.

Terror gripped him, tightening his throat as a ragged whisper slipped past his lips, a prayer offered to the darkness. "Oh, dear God," he breathed, staring into the abyss, feeling its pull like a distant tide ready to swallow him whole.

But Emma's words still echoed sharply in his mind—*Doing nothing is not an option.*

With no other choice and nothing to lose, Prasad lunged toward the gun, his hands slick with bleach. His fingers, trembling and wet, slipped against the metal, unable to find purchase. The assailant reacted instinctively, squeezing the trigger.

The gun erupted.

Pain ripped through Prasad's body like a lightning bolt, searing his nerves. His scream pierced the van's suffocating air, raw and desperate, as a wave of agony crashed over him, blurring the line between life and death.

Chapter 49

A THUNDEROUS ERUPTION TORE through the stillness of the night, sending a shockwave of panic rippling through the air. Edward felt a jolt of pure terror surge through his veins.

"It's too late," he murmured, his voice barely above a whisper, his mouth hanging open in disbelief, his spirit crushed by despair. But before he could fully process the thought, Emma was already sprinting down the street, drawn toward the sound of gunfire like a moth to a flame.

"Emma, wait!" he called out, his voice laced with urgency. Unable to let her face the danger alone, he willed his legs to move, racing after her.

"Hold on," Emma commanded sharply as they neared the van. Her eyes narrowed, zeroing in on the vehicle. "Something's happening... Inside the van—it's moving."

Edward stared at the van, his heart hammering in his chest. The frame of the vehicle quivered ever so slightly, as if it were alive, pulsing with a strange, eerie energy. A flicker of hope ignited within him. "He must be alive... The old man's fighting back!" Edward exclaimed, the words tumbling out in a rush, clinging to the possibility.

"Can you see anything?" Emma asked, rising onto her tiptoes, her voice tight with tension as she strained to get a better view.

"No," Edward replied, squinting at the van's dark windows, straining to make out any movement.

They edged closer, the tension between them taut like a wire ready to snap.

"I see them," Edward finally said, his spirit rekindling with determination. "They're on the driver's side."

"OK, let's go around to the passenger's side," Emma instructed, holding her gun close to her body, every muscle in her frame coiled like a spring, ready to act. "Open the door, and I'll shoot."

"No, *you* open the door," Edward countered, his voice tinged with desperation. "Give me the gun—*I'll* shoot."

"I'm not giving you my gun," Emma snapped, glaring at him with fierce incredulity. "You said you've never used a gun before."

"Well, no, but—"

"No? So, because you're a man, you think my gun is better off in your hands?" she challenged, her eyes boring into him, daring him to justify himself.

"No," he muttered, his confidence evaporating under her stare.

"Or is it because you still see me as the person I was a year ago—just a shell of the person I am now?"

They moved cautiously toward the van door, the air thick with unspoken tension.

"A lot can change in a year," she said, her voice steady as she raised the gun, her determination unshakable. "Is that not yet clear to you?"

"It's crystal clear. I'm sorry. It's just—"

"It's fine," she interrupted. "Now shut up and open the damn door."

Edward reached for the door, only to find it unyielding. "I can't get in... He broke the handle," he whispered, frustration clawing at him. "Can you shoot through the window?"

Emma's eyes darted back and forth between the chaotic struggle inside the van. Edward sensed the weight of the decision pressing down on her. "No," she replied, her voice strained with tension. "If I shoot through the window, I could hit Prasad."

Edward's gaze followed hers, taking in the frantic scene of bodies locked in a desperate fight for control of the gun. His mind raced, grasping for a solution in the tangle of limbs and the blur of motion, but every option seemed fraught with risk. The complexity of the situation gnawed at him, the stakes higher than he'd ever imagined.

He turned to Emma, swallowing hard, the gravity of the moment reflected in his eyes. His usual confidence wavered, replaced by a raw vulnerability he rarely allowed himself to show. With a deep breath, he let go of the last shred of his pride. "Tell me what to do," he said, his voice steady but laced with a plea for guidance.

Good, now we're getting somewhere, Emma thought, her pulse quickening. "Let's try the rear door," she urged, her movements swift as she circled to the back of the van.

Edward followed closely, grabbing the door handle and giving it a hard yank. It didn't move. "It's locked," he muttered, frustration cutting through his voice as he jiggled the handle again, fruitlessly.

"Step back," Emma ordered, her voice steady, already raising her gun. There was no time for subtlety now.

Edward immediately retreated, pressing his fingers into his ears as he stepped aside. The night air seemed to hold its breath for a moment—then the gunshot rang out, echoing like a crack of thunder. The sound sliced through the quiet, followed by the sharp metallic clang of the lock shattering under the force of the bullet.

Edward flinched, instinctively pulling back before he cautiously approached the van again. Placing his fingers into the jagged hole left by the shot, he gripped the remains of the lock and tugged the door open.

"Ouch," he hissed, shaking his hand out as if burned.

Emma shot him an incredulous glare, her eyes wide with disbelief.

"What?" Edward said defensively, rubbing his hand. "It's hot!"

As the door swung open, a thick, pungent wave of chlorine bleach slammed into them like a wall. The stench was suffocating.

"Oh my God!" Emma gasped, choking on the acrid air as she instinctively covered her nose, her eyes watering. She staggered back for a moment before steeling herself, holding her breath as she stepped cautiously into the van. The atmosphere inside was even worse—thick with fumes that stung her throat and made her vision blur.

Through the haze of chaos, her eyes locked onto Prasad. He was grappling desperately with his assailant, both men entangled in a brutal struggle for control of a gun. The sight of the attacker made her stomach lurch. His face was grotesque—a horrifying canvas of inflamed, raw skin, peeling in red patches. His eyes were swollen completely shut, leaking tears that streaked down his cheeks. Blind and panicked, he lashed out wildly, his movements erratic, driven by sheer desperation and instinct for survival.

Emma's heart pounded in her chest as she tried to assess the chaotic scene, her instincts screaming that she had only seconds—if that—to act. Her eyes darted around the cramped, dimly lit space, desperately searching for a way to intervene. A motorcycle, chained to the van's walls, blocked her path, its bulky frame making it impossible to line up a clear shot.

She cursed under her breath, her pulse racing as the confined space closed in around her. Prasad's strained grunts and the wild thrashing of the assailant only heightened the urgency. She needed to move—*now*—but every possible angle was cut off. Her mind raced, searching for an opening, any opening.

Prasad let out a guttural grunt of pain as the assailant's fist connected with his jaw, sending him reeling. Gritting his teeth, Prasad turned his gaze toward

Emma, his eyes wild with desperation. "*Shoot him!*" he shouted, his voice strained.

"I can't get a clear shot!" Emma cried, her voice taut with frustration as the fight escalated, the two men thrashing violently in the cramped space of the van. Her eyes darted to Edward, desperation flickering in her gaze.

"*Any ideas, genius!?*" she snapped, her tone dripping with sarcasm and mounting frustration.

"Yes," he replied, his gaze focused on the driver's side where the struggle was most intense.

"I'm all ears," she replied.

"Can you shoot out the driver's side window from there?"

Emma's mind whirled with possibilities as she assessed the situation. Her eyes locked onto the window, noting the clear line of sight. "Absolutely," she said, determination hardening her voice.

"I'll go around and try to get you that clear shot. Wait for my signal," Edward instructed, stepping out of the van. Before he left, he turned back to her, his eyes serious. "Listen, when I reach the window, I'll knock hard. That's your cue. After you hear the knock, count to three to give me time to get out of the way and take cover, then shoot out the window. Got it?"

"Got it," Emma nodded, her grip tightening on the gun as she prepared to execute the plan. The air inside the van was thick with tension, the stench of bleach burning her lungs, but she kept her focus locked on the window, ready to act.

Chapter 50

EDWARD INSTICTIVELY DUCKED as the driver's side window exploded in a storm of shattered glass and splintering fragments. "She didn't wait for my signal," he muttered, a mix of frustration and urgency coloring his voice.

Rising quickly, he moved toward the driver's side door, making sure to stay out of the assailant's sight. With careful, calculated movements, he climbed onto the step bar of the van.

Prasad's eyes widened in surprise as they caught sight of him.

Edward reached through the broken window, grabbing hold of the seat belt. He carefully reeled it out, grip by grip, until it was fully extended. Holding his breath, he wrapped one end of the belt around his wrist, securing it tightly, while gripping the other end firmly in his hand.

This better work...

He leaned further into the van, trying to loop the belt around the assailant's neck. But the man was just out of reach.

Edward locked eyes with Prasad, then held up the belt, signaling for him to push the assailant closer.

Prasad's face tightened with a mix of strain and determination. With a groan, he braced himself against the passenger seat and pushed the assailant toward the window, his feet slipping through a paint can as he used all his strength to close the distance. Edward stretched on his tiptoes, the belt hovering inches from the man's neck.

"Just a little more," Edward whispered, his eyes never leaving the assailant. Then, with a sudden burst of effort, Prasad shoved the man even closer, and

Edward seized the moment. "There!" In a swift motion, he pulled the seat belt over the assailant's face and tightened it around his neck, yanking back with all his strength as he dropped to the ground.

"*NOW, EMMA, NOW!*" Edward shouted.

Emma threaded her arm through the hanging, tangled chains encasing the motorcycle in the van, her movements deliberate and measured. Time seemed to stretch as her focus zeroed in, her eyes locking onto her target. The weight of the gun in her hand felt both alien and oddly reassuring. The tension in the air was palpable, and when she cocked the gun, the sound was sharp and final, slicing through the chaos.

This was no dream. *I've never shot anyone before, let alone killed*, she thought, doubt seeping into her mind like a slow poison. Her gaze flickered between her target and Edward, who was far too close for comfort. The chaos of overthinking clouded her judgment, making her aim waver.

"*NOW, EMMA, NOW!*" Edward shouted, his voice strained, the belt digging into his hand, turning his knuckles a painful shade of purple. "You can do it! You know you can!"

Her eyes darted to Prasad, who was on his knees, gasping for breath, his strength utterly drained. The sight of him, so vulnerable, made the weight of the gun in her hand feel as if it had doubled, the enormity of what she was about to do pressing down on her like a physical force.

Emma took a deep, grounding breath, willing herself to push past the fear threatening to paralyze her. As she tightened her grip, the gun transformed from a burden into an anchor, something solid and unyielding that she could cling to in the storm of chaos. She forced her doubts aside, allowing the training she had drilled into herself to take control. Her aim steadied, the trembling in her hands ceased, and her focus sharpened into a laser-like precision.

With a final surge of determination, she squeezed the trigger, the action definitive and resolute. The shot rang out, cutting through the chaos with brutal clarity.

The blast reverberated through the van, a deafening crack that seemed to freeze time, the sound resonating with a bone-shaking intensity. Prasad instinctively shielded his face, recoiling from the force as the air seemed to thicken, every molecule vibrating with the aftershock.

Silence settled over the van, thick and oppressive. Emma's breath caught in her throat as she surveyed the scene. Prasad lay on the floor, covered in blood, while Edward was nowhere in sight. Panic flared as her eyes finally landed on the assailant, motionless and lifeless. She raised a trembling hand to her mouth, her voice barely a whisper as the reality of what she'd done set in.

"*Oh my God.*"

Chapter 51

EDWARD GOT ON HIS FEET, unwinding the belt from his wrist, wincing as he shook out his hand and stretched his fingers. The vivid trail of bruises across his pale skin throbbed with pain. "That's definitely going to leave a mark," he muttered, glancing at the discoloration. "Is everyone okay?" he asked, peering through the broken window.

"I'm okay," Prasad rasped, his voice hoarse and shaky. He grimaced, holding up his hearing aid between his thumb and index finger, the tiny device smeared with blood. "I may have busted an eardrum from that first blast," he added, his bloodshot eyes blinking away the sting as his clothes, speckled with droplets of crimson, clung to his trembling body.

His breath came in ragged gasps, the weight of the moment pressing down on him like a heavy blanket, but somehow, through the chaos, he was still standing.

Edward turned to Emma, who stood frozen, her face pale and her wide eyes fixed on something through the windshield.

He followed her gaze but saw nothing. "She must be in shock," he said softly.

Prasad turned his attention to her. "Emma, darling, are you alright?" he asked, his voice laced with concern.

She nodded slowly, still staring ahead. "Do you see something out there?" Edward asked, his tone cautious. "Is there someone else coming?"

Emma shifted her gaze between the two men, her expression blank. "No," she replied in a flat tone.

"You're in shock," Prasad said gently. "That's natural after something like this."

"I'm fine," she insisted, finally meeting his eyes. "Are you two okay?"

"Yeah," Prasad grunted as he struggled to stand, his body stiff from the ordeal.

"Me too," Edward confirmed. His eyes swept across the van, landing on the utility shelf. "Grab some towels from the shelf to your right. Let's cover him up."

Emma nodded and reached for the shelf, grabbing a microfiber cleaning towel before tossing it to Edward.

Prasad unfolded the towel with trembling hands and draped it carefully over the remains of the assailant's mangled head, his movements slow and deliberate, the weight of the grim task settling in.

The overpowering smell of bleach still lingered in the van, burning Edward's nostrils. It was clear now—Prasad had managed to get hold of some bleach and use it against his attacker. Edward scanned the cramped interior, searching for the empty bleach container, surprised that the assailant had failed to anticipate something so basic could be used against him.

"Where's the bleach container?" Edward asked, his voice tense.

"There isn't one," Prasad replied, holding up the clear bottle of dish soap, the hand-written label glaring back at them: *100% BLEACH.*

Edward's eyes widened in disbelief as the memory of the man's thick Italian accent and broken English resurfaced. He shook his head, the pieces clicking into place. *He could barely speak English*, he thought. "He couldn't read it," he muttered, the absurdity of it sinking in.

Red and blue lights flashed once again across the dark neighborhood, casting an eerie glow over the quiet streets. Prasad waved off a concerned paramedic. "Thank you, I'm fine," he insisted, his voice firm despite the exhaustion evident in his posture.

"Are you sure you're going to be okay?" Emma asked, her eyes scanning him for any sign of weakness.

"Yes," Prasad replied. "I just need a hot bath and some rest."

He stepped back, his gaze lingering on Emma. Amid the chaos and devastation of the night, she stood tall, seemingly unshaken—not like someone who had been in shock just minutes earlier. There had to be more to it. His curiosity gnawed at him. "You saw something out the window, didn't you?"

Emma's eyes darted away, her body stiffening as though trying to avoid the question. *I knew it*, Prasad thought. "What did you see out there?"

"What do you mean?" she replied, her tone guarded.

"In the van, after you opened fire. You were staring out the window," he pressed. "What did you see?"

"It's not important," she said, shaking her head. She turned away, but the tension in her shoulders was unmistakable. Then, almost as if something inside her snapped, she spun back around to face him.

"I won't hold my tongue. You need to put an end to the study. Whoever sent this man after you is bound to send someone else."

Edward approached them, sensing the tension. "Is everything alright?" he asked, glancing between the two.

"We're fine," Prasad replied, trying to sound reassuring. "Emma, I'm doing this on my terms—now please, tell me what you saw."

"Nothing," she insisted, looking away again.

"Darling, you clearly saw something. Why are you holding back?" Prasad asked, his voice tinged with frustration.

Emma let out a long, heavy sigh. "Because I don't want to tell you anything that might encourage you to continue with the study," she snapped, throwing her hands up in exasperation. "Okay?!"

Prasad turned to Emma, his expression a mix of pleading and determination. "Darling, I, I—"

"You heard what my father said—it will be catastrophic if this gets out!" she shouted, cutting him off.

"Well, yes, but think of all the good that could come from this," Prasad countered, his voice calm but insistent.

"Think about all the bad that could come from this," she retorted, her tone firm and unyielding. "I have witnessed, experienced even, evil in this dimension firsthand... and now, so have you. And you want to risk bringing more of that into this world?"

Prasad crossed his arms, his stance becoming more defensive, his gaze dropping to the ground as if searching for answers in the dirt.

"Just think of what you're doing—unleashing a foothold for evil to terrorize this dimension!" Emma exclaimed, her voice rising with urgency. "There's enough evil in it as it is."

Prasad finally looked up, turning to Edward. "Edward, what is your opinion on the matter?" he asked, his voice heavy with the weight of the decision before him.

Edward sighed, the pressure of the moment evident in his expression. "It's a tough call. As scientists, we thrive on learning, uncovering, and sharing our discoveries with the world," he said slowly, choosing his words carefully. "So I could argue that this is a fascinating finding we should share with the masses."

He paused, his thoughts clearly weighing on him.

"But information is a tricky thing—and a wise old man once told me, for what it's worth, that we must exercise our personal judgment to determine if the benefits of sharing knowledge, whatever that may be, outweigh the potential consequences."

The gravity of Edward's words hung in the air, pressing down on Prasad like a heavy burden. He lowered his head, the full impact of the truth sinking in. Finally, he lifted his gaze, fixing Edward with an intense stare. Inhaling deeply, he muttered with a hint of irony, "*Old man*, huh?"

Chapter 52

THE STERILE TANG OF ANTISEPTIC lingered in the air, mingling with the soft hum of the overhead lights. Despite the chaos of the previous night, Edward had dragged himself to the office, his ingrained sense of duty overpowering the fatigue that clung to him like a second skin. Prestige aside, he still had a mortgage to pay and a family depending on him.

"How's your father doing?" Edward asked, his voice edged with concern.

Emma offered a calm nod. "He's doing well," she said. "They're keeping him for observation for a few days, but so far, things look good."

Her expression was resolute, a quiet strength shining through despite the gravity of the situation. No matter how rattled she might have been, she remained unbroken—steady in the face of uncertainty.

Edward subtly flexed his wrist, wincing as a dull ache reminded him of its presence. A small price to pay, considering what could have been. But his mind wasn't on his own discomfort. He was far more concerned with how Emma and Prasad were holding up after the whirlwind they'd endured. Seated across from him, Emma appeared tired but composed, her eyes shadowed with the weight of recent events. "And you? How are you holding up?"

She forced a small smile, though it faltered before reaching her eyes. "Never better."

"Well, I appreciate you both coming," Prasad said from behind his desk. "I know we had a hell of a night."

"Why are you even here?" Edward asked incredulously. "You should be at home resting."

"Well, it's like they say, no rest for the weary," Prasad replied, managing a small smile.

Edward leaned over Prasad's desk, bringing himself closer to Prasad's face. He studied him carefully, searching for any signs of distress, but there were none—no dark circles, no bags under his eyes, not even a hint of fatigue. "It's incredible," Edward remarked, his voice tinged with disbelief. "I don't see any bruising at all." He leaned in further, his gaze narrowing as if expecting to find some overlooked mark. After everything, he appeared completely untouched.

"Asha left some concealer behind—nothing a little makeup couldn't fix," Prasad said, rubbing his jaw lightly with a half-smile. "Still, to think... I might not be here if it weren't for a butterfly and the two of you."

The night before, Prasad had spoken to Edward about the butterfly that had mysteriously distracted his assailant. He'd described it with such awe, as if it were something otherworldly. The vivid memory had driven Edward to research the insect, curious about its origins. Now, he placed a color printout on the desk. "Is this what you saw?" he asked, pointing at the image.

Prasad reached for the printout, bringing it closer to his face, his brow furrowing in concentration. "That's it," he confirmed, his voice quiet with wonder. "Is there anything special about it?"

Edward nodded, his expression thoughtful. "It's called the golden butterfly, native to the Mediterranean region."

Prasad's eyes widened, a mix of disbelief and curiosity washing over him. "That's a long way from home."

"The Greek word for butterfly, *psyche*, also means soul," Emma interjected, her voice cutting through the moment. "In ancient Greece, butterflies symbolized the human spirit."

Both Edward and Prasad turned toward Emma, momentarily caught off guard by the depth of her knowledge. Emma raised an eyebrow, noticing their surprise.

"What?" she asked with a casual shrug. "I was involved in Greek life in college... I know things. I could probably still recite the Greek alphabet backward if I tried."

"No!" Prasad and Edward exclaimed in unison.

"That won't be necessary," Prasad added quickly, a smile tugging at his lips.

"Suit yourselves, but if you ask me," Emma continued, undeterred, "that butterfly sounds more like your guardian angel." She paused, her expression softening as she shifted from playful to sincere. "My father says we all have one."

Oh boy, Edward thought, his stomach tightening at the prospect of yet another dive into the supernatural. He shifted uncomfortably, turning his gaze toward Emma, his mind swirling with unspoken questions about her actions the night before. Despite his efforts to focus on the present, the events of that evening gnawed at him. He exhaled slowly, gathering his resolve.

"Can I ask you something?" he said, his voice quieter than usual, but edged with the weight of the thoughts that had been tugging at him since the previous night.

"Sure," Emma replied, meeting his gaze.

"What were you thinking?" he asked. "You headed straight for your car to get your gun the first chance you got while I was still trying to unfreeze."

"It all happened so fast," she shrugged. "I remember you telling me to think of my mother—and I thought, *if he only knew...*"

She paused, her expression softening.

"I was thinking of my mother the whole time."

"What about?" Prasad asked, his brow furrowed in curiosity.

"I was thinking about what she would do if she were in the same situation," Emma replied. "She wouldn't just stand around doing nothing, that's for sure."

"Your bravery—your decisiveness, it was incredible," Edward said, still amazed by her calm under pressure.

"No big deal," she said, brushing off the praise. "I'm hard-wired to stand up for myself and the people I care about."

Edward's eyes narrowed slightly at her choice of words. "Hard-wired?" It was a term he had used often during her treatment.

She nodded.

It can't be a coincidence, he thought. "You never stopped dream training, did you?"

"No," she replied, her tone matter-of-fact.

"You've continued dream training this entire time?" Prasad asked, clearly impressed.

"The entire time," she nodded.

"Holy shit," Edward said, shaking his head in disbelief. "Your bravery, your confidence, your quick thinking..."

"I've been conditioning myself this whole time," Emma said. "Even after the nightmares stopped."

"But why?" Edward asked, genuinely curious.

"Why not work on my mental strength while sleeping?" she shrugged.

Edward leaned back in his seat, considering her response. "I guess you're right," he conceded.

"What about you?" Emma asked, turning the tables on him.

"What about me?" Edward replied, confused.

"What gave you the idea of using the seatbelt to subdue the bad guy?" she asked. "That was amazing!"

Edward crossed his arms and leaned back, clearly uncomfortable with the attention.

"Yes, how did you think of it?" Prasad asked, leaning in with interest. "Seems a bit... out of character."

Edward's cheeks flushed with embarrassment, betraying his discomfort.

"Oh, now we have to know!" Prasad said loudly, rubbing his palms together in anticipation.

"Fine," Edward said, finally giving in. "I was inspired by a social media video my wife sent me."

"You learned that on social media?" Emma asked, her eyebrows raised in surprise.

"I said I was inspired," Edward clarified. "The video was of a police officer demonstrating a self-defense move in her car. In the video, a guy is hiding in the back seat. The officer gets in the driver's side, and the guy in the back puts a rope around her neck from behind."

Emma and Prasad listened, intrigued by the story.

"So the officer pulls her seatbelt through the rope around her neck and pulls on it while reclining on her seat to escape," Edward explained.

"I don't understand," Emma said, tilting her head. "What's so embarrassing about that?"

"That's not the end of the video," Edward replied, his voice dropping. "At the end, a man attempts to recreate the move. The clip ends with Sarah McLachlan's *In the Arms of an Angel* playing, and the man being memorialized at his funeral."

"Wow," Emma said, her eyes wide. "That took a dark turn."

Chapter 53

REVEREND KAY LEANED INTO THE DOOR, straining to catch fragments of the conversation from the muffled voices seeping through the cracks. *Was there a change to our meeting time?* she thought, glancing at her gold bangle wristwatch. Her breath caught in her throat as the door swung open from the inside.

"Dr. Reverend Kay!" Prasad announced with forced enthusiasm. "I thought I heard you. Please, come in!"

She paused at the threshold, her hesitation palpable.

Edward turned to greet her. "Hello, Dr. Reverend Kay—this is Emma, a former patient of mine."

Emma turned to her with a warm smile and waved.

Seems harmless enough, she thought, stepping inside cautiously.

"That's a gorgeous pantsuit," Emma said, her tone sincere.

"Thank you," Reverend Kay replied, her eyes narrowing slightly as she turned to Prasad. "Did I not get the reschedule notice?" she asked, her voice laced with irritation.

"No, we're still on," he replied smoothly.

"Then why are they here?" she asked, addressing Prasad as if the others were invisible.

"Oh, Emma just dropped by to say hello while she was on campus," Prasad explained. "She's also a former patient of mine. We were just catching up."

Reverend Kay's eyes flickered with suspicion as she studied Prasad, her gaze sharp and assessing. The thought crossed her mind that he had brought the others in to stand as witnesses, perhaps to deflect her anger or shield himself from the inevitable confrontation. But she wasn't easily fooled.

"We'll meet another time, then," she said coolly, her tone laced with restrained judgment as she turned to leave, her movements deliberate and dismissive.

"Please, stay!" Prasad exclaimed, a note of urgency in his voice. "This won't take long. I just wanted to thank you... in person."

His words caught her off guard. For a brief moment, she was sure she hadn't heard him correctly. She hesitated, her steps faltering as she turned back to face him, her brow furrowed.

"Thank me?" she asked, her voice laced with genuine confusion. "Thank me for what?"

"For your professional opinion at the IRB meeting the other day."

"Oh?" she responded, tilting her head slightly, her curiosity piqued.

"Yes," Prasad continued, his tone measured and deliberate. "After further consideration and consultation with Dr. Clark, I want you to know that I fully support your decision." He paused, clearing his throat. "The board's decision."

She narrowed her eyes, nodding slowly as she absorbed his unexpected words, her gaze sharp, scanning his face for any hint of deception. Her mind raced, trying to discern whether his sudden change of heart was genuine or merely calculated.

He pressed on, "And I apologize if I disrespected you..." He paused and took a deep breath. "...for the way I disrespected you and your opinion."

Her gaze bore into him, skepticism etched in her expression.

"The way I spoke to you... It was no way to speak to a lady. Especially not a reverend. I am truly sorry."

After decades of working within the church, a male-dominated patriarchy, she had developed a keen sense for recognizing bullshit when she saw it. Some might even say she had a nose for it. And while it was clear he seemed to be laying it on thick, there was something disarmingly sincere about his tone. Still, she wasn't about to let her guard down so easily.

"Why the change of heart?" she asked, her voice cautious, laced with just enough curiosity to mask her suspicion.

"I may have had something to do with that," Edward interjected, raising his hand slightly.

Reverend Kay turned to him, eyebrows arched. "Oh?"

"Yes," Edward replied, meeting her gaze. "Dr. Vedurmudi came to me with the board's decision, and I have to admit, I was quite relieved."

"Relieved?" she echoed, her chin dipping as she scrutinized him.

Edward nodded. "I mean, the study could have been fascinating... but only if there were any real way to prove it."

She nodded slowly, her sharp expression softening just a fraction. "I agree."

"If we had a spirit detector, maybe," Prasad chimed in with a laugh, trying to lighten the mood.

"Wouldn't that be something?" Edward added, smiling faintly.

Reverend Kay, however, was far from amused. She turned her piercing gaze toward Prasad. "So, I take it you are no longer pursuing the—what did you call it—*afterlife study*?"

"Absolutely not," Prasad replied quickly, his tone unwavering. "Dr. Clark and I are wrapping up the NDE study and moving on to our next respective assignments."

She shifted her gaze toward Emma, who returned the look with a naive smile—an unspoken signal that she was merely a spectator, unaware of the deeper undercurrents in the conversation. Her petite frame, coupled with her silence, only reinforced the impression. *Clearly no threat*, Reverend Kay thought, dismissing her with a subtle flicker of disinterest.

Reverend Kay had heard enough. Prasad might be cavalier enough to continue the study without IRB approval, dismissing the protocols entirely, but not Edward. He was a by-the-book professor, with a young family and a promising career. She knew he wouldn't dare cross that line. And that, at least, gave her some measure of reassurance.

"Well," Reverend Kay said, clearing her throat, her voice calm but authoritative. "Thank you for the apology."

"You are more than welcome," Prasad replied, his smile polite and measured.

"Will that be all?" she asked, her eyes scanning the room once more.

"That's all," Prasad confirmed.

She moved toward the door, her posture rigid. "OK then, I'll let you get back to your... reunion."

Chapter 54

WITH A FINAL LINGERING GLANCE, Reverend Kay left the room, her presence still palpable even after the door clicked shut. The tension she left behind buzzed in the air, thick and electric. Edward held his breath until the sharp clacking of her heels faded into silence.

"What was that all about?" Edward asked, finally exhaling in an audible sigh of relief.

"What did I tell you?" Prasad replied with a smirk. "Loud heels."

Edward shook his head, irritation seeping through his voice. "Enough with the jokes!"

"Okay, okay..." Prasad raised his hands in mock surrender, but his tone shifted, turning more serious. "Let me explain," he said, his voice steady, yet carrying a weight beneath it. "I wanted you both here when I told her I'm not proceeding with the study."

"Why?" Emma asked, her tone curious but cautious.

"For two reasons—I wanted to show you both that I am serious about not moving forward with the study," he said. "Reverend Kay has known me for many years. She might think whatever she wants about me, but she knows I am no liar."

"And the other reason?" Emma pressed.

"In the event my apology isn't enough, and they send someone after me, I wanted to make it clear that you two have nothing to do with this."

"Thank you for doing that," Emma said quietly, her voice softened by a mix of gratitude and concern.

Prasad bowed his head, a gesture that didn't go unnoticed by either of them.

Edward, sensing that Prasad had more to say, asked, "What is it?"

Prasad inhaled deeply, as if preparing to unburden a heavy load. "Prasad, you're among friends," Emma added gently. "What are you not telling us?"

He raised his head slowly, the weight of what he was about to reveal evident in his eyes. "I'm afraid I've misled you." The words hung in the air, causing a ripple of unease.

Edward felt a knot tighten in his stomach. Just minutes earlier, Prasad had asserted he was no liar. "How have you misled us?" Edward asked, his voice tinged with apprehension.

Prasad moved behind his desk and sat down, his movements deliberate and measured.

He let out a deep, audible sigh. "My motivation for moving forward with the study—it's not what I led you to believe."

"You lied about being related to Neelima?" Edward interrupted, his impatience getting the better of him. He needed to know the truth, now.

"No, of course not," Prasad replied, his voice firm. "What I told you about that is true. But it wasn't the only thing that set me on this path—this quest for knowledge."

He paused, as if the next words were difficult to say.

"I suppose it doesn't matter," he shrugged, his resignation evident. "It changes nothing—you two were right about ending it. It was the right thing to do."

"Tell us about your true motivation for this quest for knowledge, then," Emma urged, her tone gentle but insistent.

Prasad leaned in, his voice low. "Darling, you risked your life for me, so let me ask you... What would motivate someone to go on a fool's errand? To do something they would never do otherwise?"

"Money? Fame, maybe?" Emma guessed, furrowing her brow.

"Is that why you risked your life for me?" Prasad asked, his gaze fixed on her. "To go down in history as a hero?"

"Of course not," Emma replied, shaking her head.

"Love," Edward interjected quietly.

Prasad turned to him, caught off guard. "Pardon me?"

"You asked what would motivate someone to go on a fool's errand. To make them do something they likely would never do otherwise—it's love," Edward explained, his voice steady.

"Elaborate," Emma urged, turning to Edward.

Edward took a deep breath, his eyes reflecting the weight of his thoughts. "Look, I'll be the first to admit that I could never do what you did, Emma—not in a million years."

He paused, memories flooding his mind. He saw his wife's smile on their wedding day, his daughter's first steps, the small moments that made life precious. His eyes welled up with tears as he continued, "But if my wife and daughter were on the line—I would do anything at any cost for them."

Prasad nodded, his expression softening. "We are very much the same, you and I," he said, then turned to Emma. "As are we, my darling."

Emma's brow furrowed in confusion. "What does this have to do with you misleading us?" she asked.

Prasad exhaled, the sound heavy with emotion. "They passed away."

"Who passed away?" Emma asked, her voice barely above a whisper.

"Asha and Ravi."

"WHAT?!" Edward exclaimed, standing up so abruptly that his chair nearly tipped over. "Oh, my God!" he cried out, beginning to pace the room, his mind reeling with disbelief.

The tension in the room became almost unbearable.

"I'm so sorry," Edward said, his voice choked with emotion.

Emma stood as well, her face a mask of confusion and concern. "I don't understand," she said. "What are you doing wasting time talking to us here? You should be on a plane to India!" she exclaimed.

Prasad crossed his arms, looking away. "They passed away ten months ago."

Edward's shock deepened. He desperately tried to understand why Prasad was just now revealing such tragic news. He had seen Asha and Ravi on campus not long ago, or so he thought. The memories of their laughter, their warmth, filled his mind, making the revelation even harder to comprehend.

"I'm sorry I withheld it from you," Prasad said quietly.

"Why didn't you tell me?" Edward asked, feeling blindsided by the revelation, his emotions a swirling mix of shock, disbelief, and betrayal. He thought he knew Prasad's life inside and out, but now it seemed there was an entire chapter he had never been privy to.

"I know why," Emma said, her voice firm. "He didn't want to re-experience what he went through—to think about what they must have gone through. He didn't want to question every single decision that led up to that moment each time some well-meaning person asked how he was doing."

Prasad exhaled audibly. "You are exactly right, my darling."

"I can relate," she said softly. "And you didn't mislead us—how you choose to grieve is none of our business."

Speak for yourself, Edward thought, shaking his head. His mind raced as he tried to process the enormity of what Prasad had been hiding. How had he missed this? He realized he had been so caught up in Prasad's connection to Neelima and the study that he hadn't seen the pain his friend had been hiding. The realization stung, filling him with guilt for not being more perceptive, for not truly seeing his friend.

His eyes locked on Prasad's gold pendant. "It was Asha's, wasn't it?" he asked quietly, the pieces of the puzzle finally clicking into place.

Prasad held up the pendent, its gold gleaming softly under the light. "This is Lakshmi, a Hindu goddess," he said, his voice thick with emotion. "Asha wore this necklace all the time."

"What happened to them?" Emma asked gently, her voice barely above a whisper. "If you don't mind my asking."

"They were driving through the Chümoukedima district, visiting Asha's family in eastern Nagaland," Prasad began, his eyes distant as he recounted the tragedy. "A boulder rolled down the mountain and crushed three vehicles, including the one carrying Asha and Ravi."

He paused, his breath catching as his eyes welled up with tears. "They died instantly."

Prasad's mind raced, still struggling to process the magnitude of the loss. He tried not to imagine the horrific scene—a massive boulder crashing down a mountainside, mercilessly obliterating everything in its path. The image was almost too unbearable to contemplate.

"They succumbed to the type of brain injury that you thought might keep you from reuniting with them," Edward said, his voice strained.

"Yes," Prasad replied, his tone hollow.

"When my wife and son passed," he continued, his voice faltering, "I found peace in knowing that our time apart was only temporary—I was convinced I would see them again in the afterlife."

"And then you thought you discovered the TPO junction's role in guiding the spirit to the afterlife," Edward said, piecing together the tragic puzzle.

Prasad nodded. "I thought of Asha and Ravi, and the idea that I would never see them again—and the grief rushed in as though I lost them all over again."

He paused, his pain visible in the lines of his face. "Except this time, I found no peace—only pain."

Chapter 55

EDWARD'S GAZE FELL TO THE FLOOR, his chin sinking into his chest as the weight of Prasad's words pressed down on him. He had sensed all along that Prasad was carrying a burden, something deeper than he had let on. Now, it all made sense. "The afterlife study—it gave you purpose beyond your pain," Emma said softly, understanding dawning in her eyes.

Prasad nodded. "I realized, if I could prove that the TPO junction was the key to the afterlife, it would mean Asha and Ravi are still in this dimension, and it would only be a matter of me finding them, and..."

He stopped, his face contorting with a mix of embarrassment and despair. His eyes held a haunting glimmer that sent a shiver down Edward's spine.

"And taking your life so that you could reunite with them in this dimension," Edward finished, his voice heavy with the realization.

Prasad nodded again, his voice barely a whisper. "The study, the possibility that I could see them again, be with them again... It was the only thing that got me out of bed in the morning—I saw death as merely an end to my pain and an opportunity to reunite with my family."

The room fell silent, the weight of his confession hanging in the air. Prasad looked at them, his emotions swirling in his chest, and took a deep, steadying breath.

"They say death is contagious, but seeing how much you two cared, how you risked your lives for me—made me realize it doesn't have to be," he said, his voice quivering with vulnerability.

Emma stood and walked around the desk, placing a comforting hand on his back. "It's OK," she said, rubbing gentle circles on his back. "You've been through so much."

Prasad turned to her, his eyes filled with remorse. "I'm so sorry. I'm no better than the man that was sent after me—likely worse. I realize now how selfish I was being. You made me see that I need to find something else to fight for—I'm just not sure what it is yet."

"I'm so sorry for your loss, Prasad," Emma said, her voice thick with compassion. "But it pains me that you would compare yourself to that *evil* man."

Evil man? Edward looked up at Emma, his eyes flickering with realization as it dawned on him what Emma must have seen when he walked up to Prasad pressing her for answers the night before. "You saw him, didn't you?" he asked. "You saw his spirit."

She dropped her head and nodded, clearly disturbed by the ordeal. "He was a demon."

The room fell quiet.

"I kept it from you two because I didn't want Prasad to continue to believe that the TPO junction had anything to do with me seeing what I saw."

"Wow," Edward said. He turned to Prasad. "She's right, you're *nothing* like him."

Emma nodded, her expression resolute. "You could have used your knowledge, position, and power to pursue your interest and caused harm to countless others—but you didn't."

Edward watched the exchange, a deep sense of admiration for Emma swelling in his chest. She had grown so much, becoming the strong, confident woman he always knew she could be. A smile tugged at the corners of his mouth as he recalled her last visit with him as a patient, and a mischievous thought crossed his mind:

Should I dare?

Chapter 56

"YOU ARE TOO KIND, darling," Prasad said. "I understand why you didn't say what you saw—that demon—and I agree... Knowledge, position, and power have the potential to do immense good... Or tremendous evil."

"I couldn't agree more," Edward added, turning to Emma with a rascally glint in his eye. "It's like they say... With great power—"

"Don't!" Emma interrupted sharply.

What's this about? Prasad wondered, frowning as he glanced between the two, puzzled by the sudden tension.

But Edward pressed on, undeterred. "Comes..."

This must be that inside joke Edward mentioned, Prasad thought, feeling increasingly left out. I want in on this. He leaned forward, his forehead creasing as he tried to decipher what was happening.

"Stop," Emma said, clearly unamused. "I need to check on my dad." She began to rise from her seat.

"Great..." Edward continued, barely able to suppress his grin.

"Not doing this. See you later!" Emma declared, heading for the door.

Prasad's curiosity spiked. He leaned in even closer, desperate to crack the code before she slipped through the door. Time was running out—she was almost gone. His mind raced as the phrase danced on the edge of his consciousness. *With great power... comes... great...* Come on, Prasad, think!

His fists clenched, knuckles white with tension as fragments of past conversations flitted through his mind. Emma had stopped Edward once when he said,

"There is no—" and Edward warned not to let Emma hear him say, "Time flies when you're having fun."

The realization hit him like a bolt of lightning...

They're all clichés.

His eyes widened in sudden clarity, and with a burst of energy, he shot up from his seat, his chair crashing to the floor behind him. "RESPONSIBILITY!" he shouted, the word echoing through the room as if it held the key to everything.

Emma froze mid-step, her hand hovering over the doorknob. Slowly, she turned around, her eyes narrowing at Prasad as she tried to suppress a smile. Edward, on the other hand, couldn't hold back his laughter any longer. He doubled over, clutching his stomach, as the sound of his amusement filled the room.

Prasad stood there, his chest heaving from the adrenaline of his sudden outburst, his face a mixture of triumph and embarrassment. The intensity of the moment faded, replaced by a shared sense of camaraderie that hung in the air.

Emma shook her head, finally letting a grin break through her stern expression. "You just had to go there, didn't you?" she said, her voice tinged with playful exasperation.

Edward wiped a tear from his eye, still chuckling. "Welcome to the club, old man."

KEEP READING...

AN EXCERPT FROM THE AUTHOR'S UPCOMING NOVEL

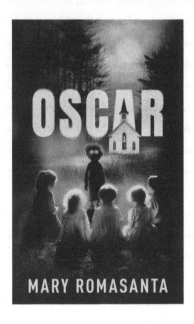

THE IMPACT OF THE WHITE PORCELAIN vase shattering against the wall coincided precisely with the deafening clap of thunder that reverberated through the building. Dr. Everhart, dressed casually in khaki pants and a gray cardigan, leaned back in his chair, crossing his legs as the relentless sound of pouring rain broke the unsettling silence in the room. Outwardly, he appeared completely unfazed by what had just occurred—the vintage, trophy-style vase with its elegant gold-leaf pedestal, a cherished family heirloom passed down from his great-grandmother, had levitated from his desk and hurled itself across the room, shattering into countless pieces. He didn't so much as flinch. Inwardly, it was anybody's guess what thoughts were running through his mind.

Clearing his throat, he asked, "Is that some kind of, I don't know, party trick?" His tone was light, but his eyes were sharp as they focused on his subject, Brianna Brown, a first-time patient. "I must say... I'm impressed."

All eyes in the room turned to Brianna in unison.

"It wasn't me," she replied coolly, tucking a strand of her dark, curly hair behind her ear. Despite being barely sixteen, she remained fully composed, her posture and demeanor strong and unyielding. She crossed her arms and legs, her gaze sharp and intense as she locked onto an object across the room—a puppet perched atop the desk. Her father had placed it there in a seated position, its black marble eyes facing the group as though it were an active participant in the session. "It was Oscar," she said sternly, her tone dripping with disdain.

The puppet remained still, its bright red, wispy hair swaying gently in the draft that swept through the room. Its black, beady eyes seemed to stare everywhere and nowhere all at once, a sinister presence that seemed to shift the very air around them.

"Enough!" Brianna's father suddenly exclaimed, his voice cutting through the tension like a knife. He slammed his fist on the desk with commanding authority. It was a tone he used sparingly, one that, when coupled with his piercing gaze, left no room for negotiation.

Brianna bit her lip and dropped her head, her defiance crumbling in the face of her father's stern command. Until now, the only sign of vulnerability she had shown was the slight bouncing of her knee, a subtle tell of her underlying anxiety. She had maintained an aura of perfection—poised and composed, not just on the surface but seemingly in every aspect of her life. But in this moment, her prim appearance, her years of steadfast obedience, her status as a model student, and her regular attendance at Sunday school—all these things seemed to vanish, replaced by the uncertainty and fear that now clouded her expression.

Brianna's mother, her face etched with worry, directed her tearful gaze toward Dr. Everhart and Reverend Rogers, who were seated side by side. "Haven't you seen enough?" she asked, her voice trembling as she sniffled and wiped her tears with a tissue.

The two men exchanged glances, their responses coming simultaneously:
"Yes."
"No."
They exchanged glances again, a silent tension brewing between them.

"Dr. Everhart, with all due respect, I believe it's clear what we are dealing with here," Reverend Rogers said, his voice firm, his attire—black slacks, a striped tie, and a white-collar shirt—exuding the solemnity of his office.

"Is it? If that's the case, why come to me?" Dr. Everhart retorted, standing from his seat and walking across his office to the water cooler. His casual demeanor clashed with the gravity of the situation, a stark contrast to the reverend's urgency.

The reverend scoffed, a trace of frustration in his voice as he shrugged. "A formality, I suppose."

Dr. Everhart scoffed in return and rolled his eyes skyward. "I don't sign off on formalities," he said, pouring a cup of water. He turned to Brianna and handed her the cup. "Here you go," he said, his eyes void of judgment.

"Surely you don't believe the puppet is behind this," the reverend said.

Dr. Everhart returned to his seat, leaned back, and fixed his gaze on the puppet. There was no denying that the thing was unsettling, enough to send a shiver down his spine. Of course, that in itself wasn't a point of argument. There's a reason, after all, that pupaphobia—fear of puppets—is so common, just below the fear of clowns. Perhaps it's the eerie suggestion of life where there should be none, a hollow vessel animated by unseen forces, that makes even the toughest of characters uneasy. He stared at it for a moment, contemplating the bizarre nature of the situation, before shifting his gaze to Brianna. Her posture was upright, her eye contact steady—certainly not the body language of someone exhibiting signs of fear or trepidation.

"I don't know yet," he finally said, his tone measured and noncommittal.

The reverend released an exasperated sigh, frustration etched into every line of his face. They had been in the same room for just over an hour—hardly enough time for Dr. Everhart to reach a formal conclusion—but the reverend's patience was clearly wearing thin. "What about my observations?" the reverend asked, his voice tinged with impatience. "Are you taking them into consideration?"

Dr. Everhart flipped through the pages of Brianna's file, his fingers tracing the words scrawled by Reverend Rogers in hurried, anxious handwriting. The reverend had noted several concerning observations:

Depression, dark thoughts—likely brought on by demonic oppression.

Physical resistance, fighting when stepping foot in a place of worship.

When physically restrained and forced to sit in the church:

Wailing, panicked breathing.

Convulsions, jerking, and stiffening.

Drooling.

Unresponsiveness.

"Into consideration—yes," Dr. Everhart replied, his eyes still on the file, his voice cool and detached. "Into account? Not even close."

He didn't bother to look up to acknowledge the reverend, the sharpness of his words hanging in the air like a challenge. The reverend's face flushed with indignation, but he held his tongue, recognizing the futility of pushing further just yet. The tension in the room was palpable, the divide between the rational and the spiritual widening with every passing second.

TURN THE PAGE FOR MORE FROM THIS AUTHOR...

PRAISE FOR AVICI SAGGA

FIVE STARS.
—Reader Views

DARK AND ADDICTIVE.
—The Prairies Book Review

SENSATIONAL LITERATURE.
—Ultimate World Books

THRILLING, SHOCKING, AND MEMORABLE.
—The Red-Headed Book Lover

Twenty-nine-year-old Emma is an intelligent, strong-willed, and ambitious PR exec, has always relied solely on herself. But when her recurring nightmares start taking a toll on her health, she turns to renowned University of Chicago psychiatrist and oneirologist, Dr. Edward Clark for help.

Dr. Clark learns that Emma's nightmares all revolve around her past love interests, a theme not uncommon among his patients. But, as they delve deeper, they discover a disturbing truth—Emma is losing touch with reality. The traumas from her nightmares are bleeding into her waking life, leaving her trapped in a waking nightmare.

In a race against time, Emma and Dr. Clark uncover the dark secrets buried deep within her psyche. As they unearth violence, control, and manipulation from her past, they realize that her diagnosis is more horrifying than they ever imagined. They must fight for Emma's life or risk succumbing to the relentless grip of unspeakable evil.

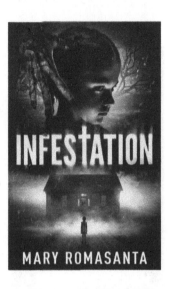

Infestation by Mary Romasanta is a chilling tale where the cost of salvation could very well be the soul itself.

Struggling to keep the doors of his church open, Pastor Emmanuel Perales moves his young family into an abandoned house across from a cemetery just outside of Chicago, where darkness unfurls its tendrils through the splintered frame of the home. Amidst the decay, ancient whispers breed within the walls, and six-year-old Emma's innocent eyes see a world veiled to others. Her gift, a rare discernment of spirits, reveals a spectral horde as vast as the cemetery itself. Her warnings fall on disbelieving ears until each unsettling encounter with the unseen erodes their reality, pushing them to the brink of madness.

When the distinction between the living and the oppressed is no longer discernible, the family's hope to save their church becomes a desperate battle to save their souls from a home hell-bent on their destruction. With the last hour ticking mercilessly close, they must uncover the secrets rooted in the house's dark core before they find themselves permanently entwined in its insidious branches.

Acknowledgements

The publication of *The Eternal Secret* in 2024 holds a special place in my heart, marking not just the completion of this novel but also my transition from a two-decade career in information technology to fully embracing my passion for writing. The butterfly, a central theme in this book, symbolizes transformation—an apt reflection of my own journey.

While the following list may not be exhaustive, it includes many who have been instrumental in my technological career and continue to offer their unwavering support. I extend my heartfelt thanks to: Joe Benavidez, Marisa Brewster, Dale Robinson, Steven Garcia, Terri Beth Goodrich, James Hutchinson, Lesley Judkins, Robert Judkins, Melissa Rose Kancov, David Kerstine, Prasad Kodibagkar, Tracy Maldonado, Tony Macias, Tiana Reeves, and Rao Vedurmudi.

These individuals have profoundly shaped my path as a technologist and played a significant role in who I am today. For that, I am *eternally* grateful.

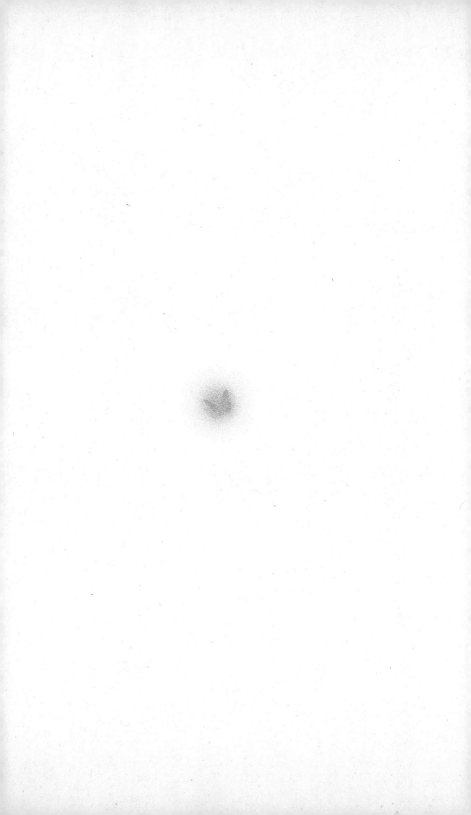

Milton Keynes UK
Ingram Content Group UK Ltd.
UKHW021344021124
450572UK00014B/82/J